ROBERT MITCHELL EVANS

VULCAN'S FORGE

This is a **FLAME TREE PRESS** book

Text copyright © 2020 Robert Mitchell Evans

FLAME TREE PRESS
6 Melbray Mews, London, SW6 3NS, UK
flametreepress.com

Distribution and warehouse:
Baker & Taylor Publisher Services (BTPS)
30 Amberwood Parkway, Ashland, OH 44805
btpubservices.com

Thanks to the Flame Tree Press team, including:
Taylor Bentley, Frances Bodiam, Federica Ciaravella, Don D'Auria,
Chris Herbert, Josie Karani, Molly Rosevear, Mike Spender,
Cat Taylor, Maria Tissot, Nick Wells, Gillian Whitaker.

The cover is created by Flame Tree Studio with
thanks to Nik Keevil and Shutterstock.com.
The font families used are Avenir and Bembo.

Flame Tree Press is an imprint of Flame Tree Publishing Ltd
flametreepublishing.com

A copy of the CIP data for this book is available from the British Library
and the Library of Congress.

HB ISBN: 978-1-78758-399-3
PB ISBN: 978-1-78758-397-9
ebook ISBN: 978-1-78758-400-6

Printed in the UK at Clays, Suffolk

ROBERT MITCHELL EVANS

VULCAN'S FORGE

FLAME TREE PRESS
London & New York

To the three women who made this possible:

my sister, Joyce, who started me on the grand journey by shoving
The Star Beast in my young hands and igniting the fuse;

my wife, Suzanne, who demonstrated her mad love by proofing my
manuscripts and saving editors from grammatical horrors;

and my late mother Lois Evans who always supported a son
more enamored with typewriters than cars.

PROLOGUE

The companion planet eclipsed the local sun and plunged Nocturnia into an extended night. Dr. Clinton Hardgrave pulled his coat closed against the evening's falling temperature. He moved quickly through the small throng of workers constructing the Celestial base of operations, paying courteous recognition to each as he passed.

Base of Operations: that term carried too much emotional weight, conveying a sense of militarism, violence, and primate dominance, but if the phrase applied then refuting it would be an exercise in self-deception. He consoled himself with the thought that his mission was not one of grotesque violence, but one of salvation. With the guidance of the Aguru and generations of patience, Nocturnia would be saved.

Hardgrave skirted around the pit dominating the base's center and turned up the central street to their communications and consensus building. Inside, he passed associates working hard at their terminals, exchanging required courtesies and honorifics with each person, until he reached his private offices. Nataya waited inside, her small round face set into a hard and unforgiving expression and her close-cropped blond hair clinging to her head like an ancient warrior's helmet.

"You've made a mistake."

She ignored civility and in return he ignored that insult, reminding himself that even among his people the Aguru had crafted innumerable paths. He removed his coat, gave her a smile and a polite half bow before taking his seat. He gestured to the guest's chair, but she rudely refused.

"I think I know what you refer to, Nataya, but let us speak clearly and plainly."

"You know exactly what foolishness I am talking about, making that 'Feral' your—"

"We do not use that word."

"It is an accurate description for anyone—"

"However, you utilize it as a pejorative. Do not hide your intention behind a facade of 'accuracy'."

"I will not be derailed into an argument over courtesy."

"Then behave appropriately. Present or not, unenlightened or not, all humans deserve respect. If we forego that we start upon the same violent self-destructive path as our ancestors."

Exhaling a heavy sigh, Nataya sat. She and Hardgrave recited the calming mantras and then shared a centering silence. Hardgrave watched her closely. He had arrived at the mission site just a few weeks earlier, but not only had Nataya already lived in deep cover among the unenlightened for more than a year, this was also her third establishment. Perhaps it was past time for her to return home before constant contact with uncivilized behavior corrupted her.

After the mantras, the silence, and the required ceremonial shared absolution to cleanse their thoughts and soothe their emotions, Hardgrave was ready to discuss her concerns.

"I did not make my decisions hastily or lightly."

"And I am not intending to belittle or insult you. The Aguru nominated you as our new mission commander so you would hardly be unintelligent or rash. However, you are inexperienced in the ways of unenlightened humans. It is one thing to study the texts, to practice against simulations, and to hear the histories, but nothing can prepare you, not fully, for their animalistic ferocity and lack of control. You cannot trust someone raised in such a manner with any measure of responsibility."

"Do you not trust the Aguru's guidance? Do you not trust their psychological profiles?"

"I do, Commander, but I also know that they are not perfect and those profiles are very limited when it comes to anyone who is not a Celestial. Please, I beg of you, do not allow him access to Forge. Perhaps he will prove me wrong. Appoint him to a trusted position, listen to his advice, but do not let him have that access. Even children can do right occasionally."

"A relationship cannot be built upon mistrust. We will need the help, enthusiastic help, of locals with the vision to see that there is a better way than what they have been taught by their parochial culture."

Nataya started to counter, but Hardgrave continued on, employing his position's privilege.

"I understand just how –" he searched for a proper non-pejorative word, "– unpredictable non-Celestials can be, and I have not granted Mr. Nguyen unfettered access, just enough so that he can be fully supportive of our mission."

The verb's tense did not slip past her unnoticed.

"I am already too late."

"No." He ran a hand through his light brown and curly hair. "You are right to voice your concerns, though it would be better if you voiced them in a less prejudiced manner."

She stood.

"I respect you and your position, but they do not think like we do and they do not value life like we do." She moved to the door. "I hope I am wrong, for all our sakes, I truly do, because either Mr. Nguyen is the valued ally you see or he is the dangerous animal that I see. There are no other options."

She bowed and observed all protocol, but Hardgrave sensed an undercurrent of anger and rebellion. With the office quiet he considered sending a message back to the Aguru. It was time for Nataya to be at home. It was not unheard of for a Celestial to lose their balance and adopt dangerous native tendencies. Knowing that haste and emotion led to faulty decisions, he put the issue aside and turned to the work of coordinating cultural subversion.

The locals practiced a level of soft surveillance that made inserting operatives a lengthy and difficult task. In the few months since the mission had become operational they had succeeded in placing 30 Celestials within the population and half of those only since they had recruited Mr. Nguyen. Together with Nguyen's knowledge of the colony's computer networks and Vulcan's Forge to break in and counterfeit the files necessary to create cover identities, the Celestials' objective had become much more obtainable.

Hardgrave was deep in planning when the crisis exploded.

All power failed, plunging the office into total darkness. The emergency lights flickered to life and then they too failed. Using his personal slate for illumination, Hardgrave made his way through the maze of dark hallways and rooms and emerged into a base lit only by the dim reflected glow from the companion planet. Here and there the scant glow of slates bounced like ghosts from primitive superstitious stories. Faint starlight fell on the center structures and he looked up to see the camouflage screen yawning open. As he watched a flyer rose from the central pit's transit pad and accelerated quickly through the opening.

Two hours later, after emergency repairs and medical aid for those wounded by Mr. Nguyen's sudden violence had been attended to, Hardgrave convened an emergency meeting of the command and consensus council. The computer and power systems remained inoperable. They sat around the circular table taking notes by hand and their slates provided the only illumination.

Nataya did not crow or engage in meaningless posturing, but the facts vindicated her conclusions. Even with only limited access to the nearly self-aware computer, Vulcan's Forge, Mr. Nguyen had successfully disabled all the Celestials' safeguards, destroyed their backup Forge, and rendered the transit pad inoperable.

After every report had been heard in depressing totality, Hardgrave asked, "What are our options?"

"Very few," Nataya said. "Though we have no evidence to support it, I think it is quite clear Nguyen planned this for some time, and with Forge under his control we have no ability to discover whatever identity he has created for himself."

"We have agents already in the colony," someone protested. "Surely they can find him?"

"We have 30 people, the colony has nearly four million. What do you propose? Search tower by tower?"

Hardgrave held a hand out, palm up, calling for civility.

"Nataya is right," he agreed. "With Forge covering both his movements and his network footprint we have very little chance of finding Mr. Nguyen."

"So what do we do?"

"We wait." Hardgrave sighed. He intended it as a calming breath but even to him it felt like defeat. "Eventually he will be careless and when he does we must be ready. Eventually someone as unenlightened as Mr. Nguyen will make a mistake and leave some trail, no matter how slim, in Nocturnia's colonial network. When he does we must be ready to act."

So Hardgrave and the Celestials waited for Eddie Nguyen's mistake, and after more than three years it arrived.

CHAPTER ONE

I stood in my office watching the evening crowd arrive. The one-way mirrored window looked over the lobby, providing an excellent vantage for people-watching. A good-sized crowd had turned up that night, eager for bland, committee-approved pabulum. I looked over at the clock to see there were still more than 20 minutes before showtime. Tonight's fare, a color film from the middle of the twentieth century, didn't interest me. One of the industry's biggest stars – I couldn't call him an actor – would swagger and drawl across a dusty landscape, dispatching bad guys while upholding appallingly simplistic virtues.

Sighing at the window, I watched as men removed their overcoats and hats, handing them off to the cloakroom. Most of the women wore fur-lined coats, long white gloves, tastefully concealing dresses, and elaborate hats. Everyone's fashion was an affectation mimicking a culture centuries dead.

"Jason." Brandon's voice pierced my mental fog, his insistent tone letting me know he tired of my distraction. "We've got to get this schedule finished or Jones is going to make us do real work."

He had a point there. Nearly everyone in our generation was busy taming Nocturnia, mankind's new and only home, building on the infrastructure laid out by the Founders. Instead of beating the bush fighting a tenacious ecology, Brandon and I helped the colony rediscover its lost heritage.

I started turning away from the window but then I spotted her and hesitated. I can't tell you why, but I froze there, turned three-quarters toward Brandon, staring down at the most beautiful woman alive. She wore neither hat nor coat. Her red, sleeveless, and bare-shouldered dress was scandalously immodest. Her pale white skin seemed like a softly lit projection screen; her black hair was as dark as the skies during the Long Night when Companion hid the vast Milky Way, and her lips looked as red as freshly spilled blood. I stood there transfixed as she crossed the theater's lobby. No one escorted her. No man hung back at the coat check taking care of their things while keeping a wary eye out for competition. She looked mid-twenties, my own age, putting her in Nocturnia's third generation. Sliding through the crowd, she drew attention from both men and women while casually ignoring them all. She stopped at the doors to the auditorium, standing directly beneath the office, and turned her face up toward my window.

With eyes so dark blue that they were nearly violet she gazed intently at the window. My breath caught in my chest and I reached out, steadying myself against the angled glass. Through the mirrored surface she couldn't see me, but still our eyes locked, and she smiled, a sly, winsome expression, before vanishing into the theater.

"You'd break Seiko's heart."

I jumped, startled by Brandon's voice so close and loud. He wore a traditional gray suit with both the vest and jacket buttoned. Standing next to me, he looked through the window as the now-uninteresting crowd purchased their treats, corralled unruly children, uncomfortable in their dress clothes, and readied for a night at the movies, but I knew he had seen her.

"There's no harm in looking," I said.

I moved away from the window, but her figure, her face had burned into my memory.

"Looking leads to temptation." Brandon leaned his short stocky frame against my desk and smiled with a wisdom he thought he possessed. "You know what keeps temptation at bay?"

"We're engaged," I protested as I manipulated my network interface, throwing up on the office wall-screen our proposed release schedule, hoping work might distract him; I didn't need another lecture. My parents provided those in volume.

"But you haven't set a date or registered it officially with the Administration."

"Can we talk about work?" I turned away from him and made a production of studying the wall-screen.

"Sorry," he said, genuine contrition in his voice. "I'll back off."

"Thank you."

I'd known Brandon my whole life, but when it came to marriage and children he was like everyone else, filled with dedication and duty. I didn't hate children, and marriage to Seiko held more than a little attraction, but I wasn't ready to cut off life before I had lived it.

We worked on the proposed schedule, reserving some films for exhibition at the theater, while others I handed off for Brandon to distribute throughout the colony. As we sorted titles, reviewing those ancient and useless audience ratings, a melancholy mood swept through me.

These mid-twentieth century men and women had worked making entertainment, striving at times for art, but a century and a half later nothing would remain of the Earth, and centuries after that these films had become a beacon for mankind's rebirth. Would those long-dead artists have wanted or rejected the responsibility of rebuilding a whole culture?

My gaze wandered to grayed-out file listings, movies not yet cleared for viewing, embargoed from even Brandon and me. The subcommittee had cleared nothing from the twenty-first and very little from the late twentieth centuries. Those films taunted my imagination. I had read about them, the records preserved in the Ark were quite complete, but the subcommittee had pronounced them morally unsuitable.

A soft alarm sounded and I turned to Brandon.

"I'll be right back."

"Take your time," he said, moving over to a sofa I kept in the office. "You can't do a decent job if you rush it."

He leaned back into the sofa, his dark skin contrasting sharply with the white fabric, crossed his legs and relaxed as he took out his slate. He ran one hand through the dense, tightly packed brown curls of his hair as he waited. I slipped out while he dutifully called his wife, Nikita.

The office door opened onto a small landing. On the far side was the door to my private apartment. My position's best perk was living here instead of in one of the crowded towers filled with nosey neighbors and families of screaming children. I took the stairs down and emerged behind our small concession stand.

"Hello Mr. Kessler," Maria said as I slid the door closed behind me. "Looks like a pretty good crowd tonight."

She was 17, blond, a fourth-generation colonist, and volunteered her time at the theater hoping for a position with Cultural Dissemination. From across the lobby Patrick watched her intensely. He was also 17, and his motives for volunteering extended no further than Maria. I didn't care. My job was building a societal moral code, not enforcing it.

I slipped out from behind the concession stand where everything came from food fabricators. We did not rank high enough to warrant any of the colony's limited supply of naturally produced foods, but one day we would. As I crossed to the auditorium doors a few patrons still mingled in the lobby.

"The program will be starting soon," I announced, pulling open the door. I gave them a moment to hurry inside and then I followed.

Steps led down the auditorium's sharply angled floor, opening onto a stage. For film nights, like tonight, the stage retracted into the floor, creating an expansive area level with the first row. It provided an excellent location for my introduction and post-screening question and answers. I centered myself and faced the audience.

The crowd well-represented our population; more than half were younger than 18, and throughout the theater an array of skin tones showed that no races were left out of humanity's final bid for survival. Scanning the audience, my eyes found her. She had selected a center seat and sat watching me. Even halfway up and buried in the crowd, she stood out, astonishingly attractive.

I cleared my throat. "Tonight's film is a western. This genre, while very popular from the start of the twentieth century, died out before the twenty-first. We know that from a historical perspective what you are about to see is quite inaccurate. It does, however, encapsulate American myth and cultural mores, ideals worth preserving."

Segueing from the general introduction to specifics for this film, I tried to stay on task, keeping all the bits of trivia and moral markers in my mind, but I returned again and again to her. Each time our eyes locked for a moment, and each time with a coy smile she looked away. After making a terrible presentation, I walked up the steps, the houselights dimming. Her head turned, following me as she watched my exit.

I said nothing to Maria and Patrick, crossing the lobby with long, quick strides. Past concessions, and up the stairs, taking them two steps at a time, I retreated to my office.

Brandon started to speak, but I waved him off with one hand and hurried to my desk. I accessed the theater's security cameras, searching for a good facial capture. It didn't take long.

In the frozen image on the monitor she stood just outside. The car that had brought her was a blur as it sped off on to another call. She looked up at the theater, almost directly into the camera, with an enigmatic expression. I directed the network to capture her face, that perfect face, and started a search.

"Don't do it."

The disappointment in Brandon's voice grated on my ears, but I didn't snap.

"I just want to know her name."

He snorted. "I know what you want. I knew you when you were 17, remember?"

"I wish people would stop throwing that in my face." The screen presented its 'busy' icon, testing my patience. "Teenagers do stupid things."

"Not just teenagers."

He sat on the edge of my desk.

"Nothing good can come of this, Jason." He pointed to her image. "If she's not married, or engaged, and actively planning a family, then she's trouble. That kind of trouble you really do not need."

"It's not going to come to that. It's just curiosity, really it's nothing—"

The search finished and invoked privacy rights, refusing me a name or even contact information.

Brandon's hand landed on my shoulder. "It's for the best."

I gave her lovely face one last look, then switched off the monitor.

"You're right." I sighed, hoping that she'd fade from memory, but knowing she wouldn't.

"Don't forget about brunch tomorrow. Nikita and Seiko want to plot the wedding."

He waved goodbye and left. I sat back in my chair and tried to think about important matters. I had a list of films to review, but work failed to hold my attention and my imagination returned repeatedly to her.

An alarm softly beeped as the evening's screening neared its end. Looking forward to the question-and-answer sessions, I buttoned my vest, slipped my jacket back on, and headed toward the auditorium. In the lobby Maria and Patrick, nearly ready to leave, oversaw the automated cleaning agents. I gave them a silent smile as I passed.

The houselights brightened as I walked down the steps, searching her out from the corner of my vision. Her white skin, bare shoulders, and radiant beauty made her about as inconspicuous as a drunk in church. I reached the front of the house and started taking questions.

After doing this for three years, hearing a new question remained a treat, and one I did not get that night. People peppered me with the usual points of confusion, the ways ancient names were bound to ethnic divisions, the overwhelming number of Caucasian characters, and all the things unfamiliar to our culture. Throughout the Q-and-A session her gaze never left me; even across the distance separating us her dark eyes held me with an unbreakable attraction. I waited for her to ask a question, praying it would give me a hint that behind that sensual form an equally seductive intellect waited, but she said nothing.

When I finished, the audience rose. Several members came forward, pushing their uneducated opinions, surrounding me, trapping me as she walked up the steps and out.

I dispatched my overly enthusiastic patrons as quickly as possible and followed them to the street.

Cars arrived, filled with passengers, and departed, but she was already gone. I let my shoulders fall and retreated inside. Maria and Patrick finished closing up and I let them leave without much of a goodnight. I locked the doors and set the security, even though Nocturnia's three generations hadn't yet birthed very many criminals, not counting 'moral degeneracy'.

I went upstairs, but my apartment held little interest, and instead I moved to the roof access.

Feeling semi-naked without my hat I stepped out, and a cool ocean breeze swept across the roof. I moved to the edge, gazing at the colony's center. Companion, our sister planet and more than five times as massive as Nocturnia, dominated the sky, where its ocher clouds glowed with reflected sunlight, casting a reddish pall across the landscape. In the distance the ocean appeared black and flecks of red phosphorescent foam crowned the surf. I loosened my necktie and unbuttoned my vest. The cool wind pierced my shirt and undershirt, caressing my skin.

The theater lay on the colony's inland edge, a recent addition as the Founders hadn't foreseen our need for communal entertainment. Sitting atop low hills, it commanded a magnificent view, and nearly the entire city was laid out in front of me. The tall buildings near the center, checker-boarded with lit and darkened windows, reached for the sky, while avenues and boulevards radiated away, illuminated by soft amber lights. The streets remained lit as they left the dazzling center and stabbed into the darkened surrounding districts. City lights silhouetted the unoccupied towers. There was living space for a dozen generations, but for now the outer city lay shuttered.

She was out there, somewhere among that tangle of lights and towers. Married? Likely, because a woman that age, single and without children, attracted unwanted attention. Then again she looked like the sort who handled unwanted attention with style. I imagined she did everything with style.

With that dress, those bare shoulders, that look, daring someone to try and chaperone her, she could be a hedonist. Despite the Administration's best indoctrination, police cited people every day for decency violations and endangering colonial morals. If she were a wild spirit, that would be something. My imagination ran riot.

I shook my head, clearing away the fantasies. Brandon was right – this could only bring trouble and heartbreak. Seiko slipped into my mind, tall with dusky brown skin and a quick, easy laugh. In spite of my reluctance for children, I did love her. Life with her was fun, mostly, but I just knew the moment we got married the very next thing would be children. Getting the genetic screens, arranging for the artificial womb, coordinating with the Administration for childcare and schooling. From that wedding day responsibilities would crash into my life, hounding me to my grave.

*   *   *

The next morning I rose, dressed in a dark blue suit with a smoky gray hat fresh from the fabricators, and summoned a car. It waited on the street while I locked up the theater. I stepped into the back, sat down and secured my belts.

Keeping the windows transparent, I watched the traffic as I sped across town to my family's preferred church. The car poured on the speed through shuttered outer districts, the decommissioned skyscrapers passing as an indistinct blur, but when we reached the populated center we slowed and joined morning traffic. The limited artificial intelligence missed other cars by inches. The whipping and dodging made most people nervous but I liked watching; it provided life with at least a little excitement.

The car slowed as the traffic near Founders' Park grew heavy enough to tax the colonial network managing transit. After the car stopped, I climbed out, stepping onto the green Terrestrial grass, recreated from stored genetic material. The Founders had placed a large park in the city's center along with Nocturnia's communal centers and churches. Already people mingled in front of the First Church of the Unified Christ, an endless school of the naive and the hypocritical.

"Jason!"

Mom waved from the church doors. Dad stood next to her and spreading out around them was a phalanx of immediate family. A gaggle of nephews and nieces, all dressed uncomfortably in finery, fidgeted near their parents.

I sighed and climbed the steps, navigating the crowd, dodging dashing children playing away their last few moments of freedom. I kissed Mom on the cheek and Dad took my hand in a firm shake.

"Happy to see you're not late this time," his voice boomed with a deep bass that carried far too well. I ignored the remark. I figured I had another year or two before they'd let that one missed service drop into the history file.

We stood, chatting about nothing of importance. They had little understanding for how mass media directed the recreating of our culture and I certainly didn't have any interest in the nuts and bolts of expanding the colony. Everyone played the fiction that they cared.

"Hello, sweetie," Seiko said, slipping next to me. I offered an arm and she placed her hand on the back of my own, a morally acceptable public display of affection. She smiled. As I looked at her – light golden brown skin, round eyes that were almost too large for her face, and wavy curls of rich brown hair – her expression of genuine love swelled my own love for her. She would have fit perfectly in last night's feature, a south of the border beauty. Recalling my previous night's fantasies about the mystery woman, I resolved to be better.

With Seiko's arrival my family passed around more inanities but I knew the hammer blow was still coming.

"I haven't seen a published confirmation," Mom said to Seiko, but pinned me with the same expression she used on guilty little boys.

Seiko playfully pulled my ear, mocking dragging an errant student out of class.

"Not yet, Jason's just wanting everything perfect. Aren't you, love?"

"Naturally." The response came automatically but guilt propelled my mouth onward. "In fact, I was thinking that tonight we might nail down some of those particulars."

Her eyes lit up and the smile grew with an honest enthusiasm that shamed me. From the corner of my vision Mom almost quivered with excitement, while a cold fear stole through my belly, turning my knees weak and wobbly.

The church doors opened and the congregation filed in. Seiko seized my arm in a tight grip, walking close as we moved inside.

Recreated from ancient plans, the church would have fit perfectly in America. Fake-wood pews, fabricated on the colony's massive industrial printers, lined either side of the main hall while on the walls flat screens mimicked stained glass. People moved with rote memory to their rows, a procession repeated throughout the city at dozens of churches. Only the bravest iconoclast risked society's ire by skipping this dull, pointless ceremony. I never considered myself that brave.

I had just taken a seat on the edge of our pew, ready for a fast escape at the end of service, when my boss, Chairperson Hui-Fen Jones, stopped next to me and knelt down to eye level.

"Kessler, can we speak a moment before things get started?"

I love how bosses always phrase orders as questions, as though we'd cut our own throats and say no.

"Sure."

She smiled, but her almond-shaped eyes held no pleasure. I rose and followed her to the empty foyer. For a moment she stood silent, the heavy fabric of her modest blue dress hanging straight to her ankles, her matching hat rakishly cocked. She radiated coolness with an air of detachment, as though the people around her were specimens under observation.

"They added an agenda item to our subcommittee meeting. I need to know that we're all on the same page here, Kessler."

I waited for her to continue, hating her love of coy games and secrecy.

"The Governing Committee is polling all committees and subcommittees on decommissioning the Deep Space Network. It's purely advisory but they want all Administration elements very public and well-unified behind the decision."

"I don't see what this has to do with me."

"Because I want unity. When I call the vote, I'm counting on you supporting the measure."

Comprehension dawned; Wolf was going to hate this. Over the last generation the Administration had diverted more and more of Nocturnia's meager space resources for ground-based projects. There had even been rumors of trying to revive Founder programs and completely abandon manned flights. Scrapping the radio telescopes and antennae was going to break his heart.

"I can see it in your face, Kessler," she said, her voice going low but not soft. "Le's on his own on this. Ground-side is taking full priority. Everyone needs to accept that, even your friend Wolfy."

She stepped closer. Normally an attractive woman close enough to smell would have been a pleasant fantasy, but her cold eyes and threatening manner murdered any sensual reaction.

"Can I count on you? The vote is 'aye' in favor of decommissioning the Deep Space Network."

I'd never hear the end of it from Wolf, but Jones already wanted to toss me out of the theater and I didn't need to give her an excuse.

"Of course," I said. "It's just a waste of power anyway. It's never found anything worth noticing."

"Exactly." She looked up the aisle as Reverend Eulis approached his podium. "See you Monday morning, then."

I scooted back to my seat, annoyed that this Sunday had taken a turn for the worse. Seiko took my hand, patted it in sympathy, and smiled.

Eulis launched into his sermon, heavy on duty, heavy on our burden, and heavy on my poor tired ears. With a muster of intestinal reserve I managed to stay awake. I snuck peeks at the congregation and wondered how many actually believed this fairy-tale crap.

If there had been a God, someone who loved mankind and for whom we were the center of his divine attention, how could he let a wandering brown dwarf destroy the solar system?

Don't get me wrong. I had no great affection for Earth. It had been destroyed centuries before Nocturnia's Founders had raised the first building. It was as real to me as Jesus. The universe is nothing but cold, impersonal equations devoid of purpose or meaning, making our devotion to resurrecting a dead culture a farce. We weren't Reverend Eulis's New Exodus, but merely clever apes trying to survive on the wrong planet.

★   ★   ★

After church the family met at my parents' apartment. Even with the spacious suite of rooms they had been assigned for a growing family we packed the place with spouses, grandchildren, and family friends. The main room hosted a long table as men and women worked the food fabricators, and some even cooked expensive fresh products from colonial farms while everyone else engaged in mind-numbing small talk.

Taking refuge from the stifling social conventions, I retreated to the balcony. Mom and Dad's place was close to Founders' Park and from the high floor afforded a spectacular view of Landfall Bay and the ocean beyond. The park spread out in the city's center, a vast irregular area of green spaces with scattered groves of trees cut through by footpaths and dotted here and there with Earth heritage museums. A salty breeze blew briskly past the balcony, carrying just a hint of the ocean's decay, and I stood there with my eyes closed, luxuriating in a moment of peace. Grandma Kessler's voice sounded suddenly behind me.

"I heard you're going to register."

I turned around, smiling. I didn't have a bad relationship with my parents, after all they were the first generation to raise a family without the Founders hovering nearby preventing disaster, but I had a great relationship with Grandma Kessler.

"I figured it was time, no use putting it off."

She laughed.

"That's my Jason, always the romantic." She moved to a chair, took a seat, and gazed out over the colony. With her small hands she smoothed out her white summer dress. "Is this what you really want to do?"

"I do love her."

"You love too easily, and that's not what I asked." She turned her attention from the bay to me, pinning me with her intense gray eyes. "I know you, Jason. There's more than a little too much of me in you."

"I'd take that as a compliment."

Again she smiled. Of course Grandma Kessler hadn't been at church; she never went. Even for a Firster she rejected everyone's opinion, doing what she wanted.

"Take it as you will," she said. "You've fought getting roped and I know you're not looking at kids with any sort of anticipation. Is this really what you want?"

The mystery woman leapt to my mind, her walk's casual, sensual glide, her immodest attire, her attitude screaming for the whole colony to just stuff it.

"Of course."

I turned around and looked back toward the horizon, my mind momentarily boggled by the concept of a vast empty planet lying beyond the city.

Grandma Kessler drew a breath, but then the balcony's door opened and Brandon's voice boomed out.

"Here you are!"

"Hi, Brandon," I said, the mystery woman's face dogging my thoughts.

"Hi, Grandma Kessler," Brandon said. He turned to me. "I heard you're making it official."

I nodded, pushing her face out of my mind. I'd never see her again.

"Glad to hear." His voice softened a bit, just a shade comforting. "Listen, I know you're uncertain about kids…"

Uncertain hell! I don't want them.

"…but you'll feel different once you have some. It's like losing your virginity, there's no way to explain it, but you'll be in a whole new place, and you won't regret it. I promise you that."

"I've never known you to be wrong," I said, putting enough sarcasm in my voice to let him in on the joke.

"I need to get that down on audio."

"I'll never say it again."

The door opened and they announced brunch. I offered Grandma Kessler a hand, more from courtesy than any real need to steady her. She might have been 73 and a first-generation colonist but her health was perfect. Together the three of us went to eat.

Seeing us come in, Seiko pulled herself away from Nikita and moved to my side. Nikita glanced at Seiko and then to me. Her eyes narrowed in deep suspicion. Friends with Seiko long before we had been introduced, Nikita treated me like a badly infected patient. Despite so-called privacy protections I was certain she had learned about my teenage citation. Her disapproving glare, backed by all of society's asinine rules, made me want to throw aside caution and let everyone know what I thought of them, but for Seiko's sake I kept quiet.

CHAPTER TWO

Sunday evening I met Seiko at the dance. Several dozen people stood and mingled in the hall as a crisp, salty sea breeze wafted through large open doors. She looked radiant in a full-length white gown with matching gloves. Eschewing a hat, she wore her long brown hair pulled back and up, letting it explode behind her head in a cascade of tumbling, wavy locks. She smiled and nodded to me as I approached, trying hard to look spiffy in a black suit and white tie.

"Jason, you're terribly handsome."

"No match for your beauty."

She took my hand and we leaned toward each other. Our lips brushed across each other's cheeks while old man Wright, a Firster chaperone, kept his eye on me. We separated and Seiko laid her hand upon my elbow – she never violated decorum – and followed me onto the dance floor.

A volunteer band competently played a piece with an easy, stately tempo. Seiko and I followed our steps with comfortable practice. I remembered films' dances where couples held each other in tight embraces, their bodies swaying like sensual metronomes. The Governing Council had approved nothing like that and so we danced in sensible, frustrating separation. Here and there, aged Firsters, each carrying a long thin red baton, moved among the dancers. I didn't see them snap anyone's shoulder for indecency, though old man Wright never seemed very far away.

Several songs sped by in a pleasant blur before Seiko stepped slightly back and I followed her to the table. A carafe of fruit juice waited for us, synthetic, as Nocturnia was still decades away from producing enough fruit to dedicate output for mere beverages. I pulled out her chair and she slid gracefully into place and then I took my seat, close enough for private conversation and yet distant enough to be 'modest'.

We basked in a moment of silent happiness.

"I know what happened this morning," she said. She lifted her glass, took a delicate sip, and fixed me with a low gaze from her brown eyes.

"You panicked." She didn't ask, stating it as a matter of fact. "I don't know why, Jason, but I know."

My face grew hot and I tried to hide my guilt.

"Everyone heard you agree to register but –" she paused briefly, a momentary hesitation that signaled her own internal struggle, "– I don't want you forced into anything. I love you too much for that."

"No one's forcing me."

Her smile was both understanding and sad.

"You've never been in a rush to get married, even as you are impatient for other things." She blushed and for a moment avoided eye contact.

"I—"

"No, let me finish. If you want to put it off again, I'm willing to agree."

Her pain and humiliation stabbed at me.

"I don't know why you're so shy about marriage, but I am willing to wait."

She reached out and took me by the hand. I couldn't recall when she had taken off her gloves and the skin-to-skin contact excited me. She held it there, and then with an eye toward the chaperones, quickly took back her hand and deftly slipped on her glove.

My heart pounded and blood roared in my ears as I stared, captivated by her dark brown eyes. I loved her. I smiled at her sight, her voice calmed me, and her laugh became the music of my life, and while she desperately wanted our engagement officially recorded, she offered me escape from responsibility. Grandma Kessler's warning echoed in my mind, but I wanted to be responsible. At least I thought I did.

"No," I said. "Let's make it official."

I reached into the suit's breast pocket and pulled out my slate. My hand shook as I retrieved the device. I laid it flat on the table, stole a quick glance toward Seiko, and her smile, or my terror, set my heart speeding like an out-of-control orbital freighter.

I accessed the Administration's registry and together we submitted to identification. Soon the marriage interface glowed on the screen. With a deep breath from me, we selected a date three weeks off, and placed ourselves on a waiting list for an artificial womb. After finalizing the arraignments and committing ourselves to the civil and criminal penalties for false and indecent intent, Seiko threw her arms around my neck and passionately kissed me.

Time passed in a delicious haze until a chaperone's red baton smacked sharply on my shoulder. Blushing through her dusky skin, Seiko broke contact, and leaned back into her seat, giving Wright an apologetic smile. I tried to do the same, but in my direction the ass simply snarled, tapping me again with the baton before moving off.

I looked around the dance floor. Most of the couples were many years younger than Seiko and I, rushing into life, speeding toward a union that would bind them for the rest of their lives. Of course I had tried to put this off as long as possible, and Seiko had been engaged before. I had seen pictures; her parents had apparently adored Nathan and held onto every scrap and memory of their youngest daughter's first fiancé. Space operations were far more dangerous than fighting the native biome and a mining disaster had ended that marriage before it had begun. Despite my prestigious posting in the Administration, her family measured me against Nathan and found me lacking.

"You're not supposed to be sad," she said, abruptly bringing my attention back to the dance floor.

I pushed the doubts down, trying to bury them.

"I'm not. I…." My voice hesitated before letting me continue. "I just don't know how to win your family over."

She reached out and stroked my cheek, the smooth fabric of her glove sliding across my skin.

"You've won me over. They'll follow."

I looked down at the slate. Now that we had officially registered, the news had flown into the colonial network, for family, friends, and four million strangers to absorb.

"Jason!"

Wolfgang Le cut across the dance floor, ignoring couples and chaperones, speeding toward us. I wanted to hide, Chairperson Jones's ultimatum fresh in my mind, but Seiko waved, her white-gloved hand flashing like semaphore.

Wolf pulled a chair away from another table and sat down across from me.

"We're registered." Seiko's high voice cracked with excitement. She shoved the slate in his direction. He glanced at it.

"Great." His voice held very little enthusiasm. "You'll be very happy."

He leaned across the table at me. "I went to the theater, but it was closed up."

"It's on the schedule," I explained. "A musical group is rehearsing tonight."

Wolf spent as much time in space as the medical authorities allowed. Films were hardly an interest.

"Well, the network wouldn't give me your location."

"Privacy," Seiko explained, though I rebelled at the accepted practice of considering a singles dance as something private. No hurt or anger tinged her voice; the joy of finally setting it officially in the colonial registry had softened her to his rudeness.

"I'm sorry." Wolf didn't sound apologetic. "I need Jason's help and it can't wait until morning. That will be too late."

Not waiting for permission, he turned to me. "You've got to vote against the mothballing."

I sighed, letting my shoulders sag. "It won't do any good, Wolf—"

"It certainly won't do any good if you vote for it. We need that network. I tell you, we gave up—"

I looked around for a chaperone because a married man was violating the dance's rules, but of course now that I needed one they were all off swapping Firster stories.

"All the other Arks failed," I said.

"We don't know that. Just because the first generation didn't find any signals doesn't mean that they aren't out there now."

Seiko joined the fray. "He's right about that, Jason."

"And I'm right that one vote won't make any difference."

"I know you can't sway the committee," Wolf said, giving Seiko a thankful smile for her support. "But you can stop it from being unanimous. Look, we know that there's a faction on the Administration looking to shut it all down. All they see in space are resources for building things, but it has to be more than that, we have to know what happened to the other Arks."

"And what good would that do us? We can't get to them and they can't get to us. Hell, Wolf, it took the Ark centuries to get here."

"I'm not talking about exchanging people, everyone knows that's impossible, but ideas we can swap. Most of the other target systems are within a couple of dozen light-years—"

"Right," I said. "And that's a couple of dozen years by radio, not to mention the amount of power—"

"Power's not a factor!" Anger crept into his tone. "Hell, even one small fusion plant would be enough. We can't keep trying to scratch it out by ourselves. Together mankind has a better chance."

"He's right," Seiko agreed. "There's so much we have to fumble and figure out as we do it. If even one other Ark has succeeded—"

"Yes, but they didn't. Look, it isn't like the Founders and the Firsters did one quick scan and gave up. They searched the other targets for 30 years, and nothing. Not one signal, not one sign that any other Ark made it."

Wolf scanned the floor, watching out for a chaperone. "That's not proof, and you know it."

"You can't prove a negative," Seiko said.

The tide turned against me and I fell back to a more defensive position. "My vote's not going to make any difference."

Finally a chaperone began walking toward our table.

"No, it's not," Wolf said. "But the whole space community is working this vote. We have to make sure not one committee or subcommittee is unanimous. If the Administration sees that there is support then we might, just might, win an extension."

Seiko locked eyes with me and said, "We can't be alone. We can't be the only one."

"Fine!" I threw up my hands. "But if Jones gets me thrown off Cultural Dissemination I'm coming to you for a job."

Wolf grinned and hurried away just as a female chaperone arrived.

"Mr. Le is married," she said, her voice overflowing with disapproval.

"Committee business," I said.

Seiko stood and I followed her onto the dance floor, but throughout the night my mind returned again and again to Jones and her terrible temper.

★   ★   ★

The chaperones watched closely as Seiko and I left the hall. The crowd flowed out in streams to the street, a river of formal attire moving under

Companion's red glow. The ocean's smell carried strong from the bay as I escorted Seiko to the line of waiting cars. She kissed me on the cheek, and then along with five other single women climbed into a car. I watched the car move down the wide boulevard, deftly zipping in and out among the scores of network-guided vehicles, until I lost it in the flow of traffic. Looking back at the men chatting among themselves, gushing with gossip, I rejected joining them and decided to walk through the park before heading home.

My path meandered between low hills. The trees' dark canopies of heavy drooping branches blocked most of Companion's light and I used my slate to light my steps. Off to one side, perched atop a hill and lit by brilliant white floodlights, a replica of our Ark stood out stark against the night sky. It was a massive egg shape, white and held up by a single pillar. Glittering golden strands, representing the solar sail control cables, shot off from the narrow end, vanishing in darkness. Of course they hadn't recreated the sails themselves, and so our monument in fact was the image of a crippled vessel. The Ark struck me as pretentious. A monument not to our ingenuity, but to our arrogance, to the egotism that mankind deserved survival.

The chilly breeze did nothing to cool my blood. I fantasized about Seiko's soft skin, the touch of her lips, the strength of her fervent embrace, the sound of her voice lost in ecstatic pleasure, and my breath turned quick. Tired and frustrated, I activated my slate to summon a car.

A news post flashed across the screen. It told of another arrest, another group of idiots who thought they could avoid detection in our closely monitored lives. I scanned the details, curious if they had engaged in anything inventive. They hadn't, just another bunch of adolescents trying to fabricate birth control devices without triggering alarms.

I understood the logic of the Administration's position. Separating sex from procreation, even in a limited manner, risked sending the colony into a dwindling birth spiral. Back in the late twenty-first century, with a planet overburdened by excessive population, such a policy made sense, even if they had stumbled into it accidentally, but with humanity hanging on by a thread, a bare four million to rebuild the entire species, it was an unacceptable risk. Understanding the logic didn't mean accepting it though, or denying that it chafed. I wanted to be something more than another father, to be more than simply a biological von Neumann machine.

On the nearest street the car waited for me and I climbed into the compartment. I hardly paid attention to the city as it flashed past, thinking about Seiko, about pleasures delayed, and inevitable responsibilities.

The musical troupe had been good to their word and the theater was in good shape. I walked through the various rooms, making sure everything was in order, then I set the security system and climbed the stairs to my apartment.

The Administration planned for the Director of Cultural Dissemination: Communal Media to be a family man and allotted space accordingly. I had a large apartment with spacious rooms, a master bedroom, three smaller bedrooms for children, a study, a family room, a front parlor, and an abundance of utility spaces. I adored it all.

In the bedroom, I stripped down to nothing, preferring to sleep in the raw – something that'd send those chaperones into hysterics – and programmed the fabricator for the next day's clothing. Since I'd have to go and be physically present for Jones's committee meeting, that required an actual suit and tie. I selected a solid gray suit with blue tie and set the fabricator printing, making sure the job would be ready by morning.

I crawled into bed, switched off the lights and waited for sleep. My mind raced through the day's events. For nearly an hour anxiety and tension chased sleep away. When I finally slept, black hair and deep blue eyes haunted my dreams.

★   ★   ★

I awoke before the alarm, always a bad sign. As I showered in a magnificent stall wide enough for me to stand with both arms fully outstretched and with a high rim so it could be converted into a tub suitable for a brood of kids, I thought about the woman with the black hair and amazing eyes. I imagined her there with me in the shower, the hot water running off her figure in sensual rivulets. Suddenly I ordered the network to change to cold water and icy daggers killed my ardor. I'd never see her again; it was best to forget her entirely. Even as fantasy I suspected she'd bring nothing but grief.

After the shower I dressed and ate a simple fabricated breakfast. Once I reached the office across the hallway, I activated the monitors and turned to the morning's work.

I reviewed films in Jones's secure archive that I wanted to screen for possible release. If I were totally honest with myself I'd admit that I didn't care as much about the rest of the colony seeing these movies as much as I wanted them for myself. The records indicated that a lot of the later productions, once the industry had broken free from restrictive moral codes, explored forbidden topics with boldness and experimental styles. The films of Lynch, Jodorowsky, Fellini, and others gripped my imagination with an unbreakable hold, but Jones and her ethical straitjacket kept these treasures locked away. I dispatched a request to screen the films for historical and cultural education, hoping that some meteor of good fortune might strike.

On the security monitor I noticed Brandon trotting up the theater's steps. He lived in the center city, rejecting a setup similar to mine at his broadcast facilities in favor of keeping close to both his and Nikita's families. When he opened the office door the grin on his face was all I needed to know – he had already seen the official notification.

"Well, it took you long enough."

"It would have been quicker without everyone pushing me."

He crossed over with a few quick strides of his short legs and shoved his brown hand into my white one. The archives listed a number of films about race troubles, even racially charged murder, but here I agreed with Jones on the embargo. No one needed to risk that mimetic infection.

We shook hands for several long seconds with Brandon slapping me hard on my shoulder.

"Is Seiko moving out here, or are you giving up your isolated little nest?"

"We haven't decided that yet."

After reclaiming my hand I sat at my desk and pulled up Brandon's agenda for the morning.

"I'm shocked," he said, still not yet ready for work. "She should have made you sign off on everything last night."

"I think that was her idea, but Wolf crashed the dance and upset her plans."

He reached out, pulled a chair from his desk, and slid it next to mine. When he'd settled into it his expression grew serious.

"Wolf?"

"Yeah, he was there lobbying hard for the Deep Space Network."

"He's going to have to accept the inevitable. The Administration is killing it."

"Well, the 'spacies' seem to think that even a symbolic showing of support might make a difference."

He gave me an intense stare. "Tell me you aren't considering voting to save it."

I said nothing, but made a show of studying Brandon's proposed broadcast schedule. Jones also limited our access to the broadcast mass media, but Brandon played it safe, rarely requesting anything from later than the end of the twentieth century.

"You're not," he said, refusing to let the subject drop.

"He made a good case for it." I leaned back from the desk. "It didn't help that Seiko jumped in on his side."

"You resisted that woman's most persuasive talents for over a year and in one night she talks you into backstabbing Jones?"

I grinned. "I like Seiko a hell of a lot more than I do that woman."

"No argument there, but Seiko can't throw you out into the wild."

"Maybe we did give up the search too soon."

He shrugged. "That's not my field, but I do know if Jones sees you standing between her and perfect unanimity she'll never forgive or forget."

"I doubt she'll toss me out over one vote."

"If you were anyone else I'd agree, but Jason, you've been pushing her too hard." He ran a hand over his tightly curled hair. "I've seen the titles you've tried to get released. She's more than half convinced you're some sort of hedonistic deviant. You can't just hand her ammunition and expect nothing but shrugs and smiles."

"And there has to come a time when we stop deferring everything to senior committees. This isn't what our ancestors had in mind. A population of meek and mild people doing whatever they're told."

"There'll be time for that later, but not now. Not when there's barely two million adult humans left in the universe. Right now we have to do what's necessary for survival, everything else is expendable. That means setting aside the niceties of some sort of noble democratic experiment. We have the system we need and you shouldn't be trying to get kicked out to some bush-burning gang."

I scoffed. "It's not going to come to that. Jones doesn't like me, but I do my job and I do it damn well. She can't crucify me, not over one vote."

He shook his head. A bemused and sad smile played at the corner of his lips.

"You're too certain for your own good. Come on, let's get to work."

We spent hours planning out communal and broadcast entertainment. A majority of the work detailed things on Brandon's side of the cultural indoctrination. With the vast number of hours everyone worked planting Earth's ecosystems, few had the luxury of communal events, preferring to enjoy their entertainment at home. I still fought for public screenings. A shared sensation remained something unique for social learning. Finally it came time for the committee meeting and we summoned a car.

Committee offices occupied a small section of the lowest level of the Governing Council Building. While churches, museums, and community centers ringed Founders' Park, the Administration building sat atop a bluff overlooking Landfall Bay. Sunlight reflected off the wind-driven and choppy waters in shards of brilliant light. A copse of pines, the oldest Terrestrial trees on the planet, circled the Administration campus, filling the air with their rich scent.

Brandon and I were neither the first nor the last to take our seats at the far end of the great curved meeting table. He gave me one last look, silently pleading with me to not provoke Jones's ire. Only 10 minutes late, all 50 members of the Subcommittee for Cultural Reclamation: Mass Media had taken their seats and Jones called the meeting to order.

We shoveled our way through the meaningless, meandering minutiae that everyone else found terribly fascinating. I listened to reports covering text media and the usual complaints that far too much of Earth's literary history remained sealed away, reports about the social media and the very limited forms allowed by the Administration lest public morals be utterly destroyed, and reports concerning educational media's eternal conflict with our broad base of religious instruction. Current Affairs was the only department more tightly controlled than Mass Media.

The afternoon dragged on before Brandon and I gave our reports, dry lectures of numbers and sociological surveys indicating our effectiveness in cultural reclamation. Only when all the usual material had been covered, discussed, debated, and, of course, never resolved, did the meeting turn to extraneous matters.

"One last item," Jones said. She stood from her seat at the table's center, a stern figure in a dark blue suit with red accents. She gazed around the room, but her eyes lingered on me.

"The Governing Council is considering a proposal to mothball the Deep Space Network and reclaim those resources for vital projects planet-side."

She made no attempt at neutrality.

"They have asked that all committees and subcommittees poll their members on an advisory basis. I don't need to remind the members that in 80-plus years the DSN hasn't found a single bit of evidence that any other Ark succeeded, or that Nocturnia's ecosystem continues to be tenacious and deadly. I know my position."

She again singled me out with an intense glare.

"By a show of hands, all in favor of keeping the DSN active?"

Brandon's hand shot up. I hesitated, stunned and humbled by his display of friendship. A fraction of a second behind him I raised my own. A wave of confused looks spread around the table. Here and there a hand joined ours until 11 members voted with us.

Jones didn't hide the anger in her voice.

"And those for decommissioning?"

Thirty-six voted with Jones, a majority but very far from the signal she had hoped to send to her own bosses.

As we walked down the steps to the waiting cars Brandon whispered, "You owe me."

★   ★   ★

I got back to the theater and unlocked the security system in time for Maria and Patrick's arrival. They saw to routine tasks while I began loading the evening's performance. That night's film was another western from the mid-twentieth century but this one I liked more than others of that simplistic genre. *High Noon* doesn't fit neatly into the Manichean style so often displayed by those movies. The townspeople abandoned Marshall Kane to the killers and after fulfilling his own sense of duty and honor he returned the favor, abandoning his office. It didn't hurt my fondness for the film that I thought Seiko looked like the actress playing Kane's former love interest.

The network indicated that Jones had released the file and it was ready for display. Naturally nothing we presented was an actual film, but a high-quality digital reproduction. With its dense storage the Ark had contained nearly a complete record of human arts, sciences, and literature, enough for centuries of rediscovery. More than once I had argued the colony needed to create its own arts, that without them we'd never truly rediscover our culture, but the Administration refused to allocate the resources.

I scanned the monitors as people arrived. This crowd trended a bit older than our average. I took the credit for that due to my synopsis. While many of the westerns passed the smell test as children's fare this one was definitely adult material. Men checked their hats and coats and the women, elegant in their long dresses, conversed with each other, filling the lobby with charm, decorum, and stupefying conformity.

The door slid open and she stepped inside. Her black hair fell in a long tumbling wave over a strapless white dress. I couldn't spot any makeup and still her skin appeared flawless, her lips radiant and red, her eyes dark, mysterious, and smoldering. Again she eschewed gloves, her arms bare from shoulders to fingertip. A slit running up the side of her long dress flashed her thigh as she walked, calm, confident, and fully in control. She studied the lobby's reproduction of marketing posters as the men, to the horror of their wives and fiancées, studied her.

I buttoned my coat and straightened my tie without realizing that I had stood. Brandon was right; nothing good could come of this, nothing but trouble. Mustering my last reserves of will, I forced myself to sit and continued working on the introduction, but my gaze repeatedly returned to the monitors. I threw myself into the work and ordered a hot black coffee from the fabricator, wishing that like so many movie characters I could numb my desire with something stronger, but unmarried colonists were allowed only non-intoxicating beverages.

People, in small groups, began filing into the auditorium, slowly draining away the lobby's crowd. I stood ready to face the audience, made sure of my appearance, and started out. I stole a glance at the monitor. She stood in the nearly deserted lobby, a perfect face and figure. I debated waiting for her to take her seat; it would be so much simpler to avoid any contact, but she moved from display to display. The biblical epics like *Ben-Hur* and *Samson and Delilah* held most of her attention. I abandoned waiting and left the office.

I emerged from the concession stand where Maria worked, studious and dependable. Patrick for once had no eyes for her, instead focusing all of his teenage lust on the mysterious woman. In my chest a spark of jealous rage ignited and I stomped over to the young man.

I put fire in my voice. "Are you looking for a citation?"

He leapt, pulling himself erect, and with visible reluctance pulled his stare away from her.

"No, sir! I was—"

"I don't care what you thought you were doing! I will not have that sort of thing going on here. Go down and check the fabricator lines."

Making sure that the substrate lines were clear was a smelly, foul job and I enjoyed giving him the task.

He slunk away and I turned toward the auditorium doors. She smiled approval of my heavy hand, and that thrilled me. Then she moved to the auditorium herself. I reached the door slightly ahead of her, and with a flourish I pulled it open and held it for her.

With a husky contralto voice she said, "Thank you…?"

Ignoring every definition of wisdom and unable to stop myself, I said, "Jason."

"Pamela."

She smiled and my heart surged as though someone had pumped me with amphetamines.

"You're a true gentleman, Jason."

As she stepped past me her perfume wafted on the air, a light flowery scent that carried a hint of endless summers. Momentarily, her deep blue, nearly violet, eyes stayed with mine and held me with affection.

I followed her into the auditorium. She walked past several available seats, taking a center one near the front. She sat, demurely crossed her legs, her arms on the rests, and never once did her eyes leave me. I stumbled and muttered through my prepared remarks, unable to ignore her. Finally I finished my worst introductory performance and fled back to my office.

I collapsed into my chair, my forehead slick with a thin coat of sweat. I pulled my tie loose and let out a heavy sigh. Every time I closed my eyes Pamela's face floated in my vision, her seductive eyes, the smile on her face, and her expression an unmistakable invitation.

"Nothing but trouble," I reminded myself. I switched on a monitor and brought up a photo of Seiko. She smiled back at me, happy and full of trust, a trust I simply could not allow myself to violate. With the last traces of willpower I'd ever show, I resisted turning on the auditorium's security monitors for another glimpse, futilely resolving to leave Pamela out of my life.

The hour and a half running time passed far too quickly. When the question-and-answer session arrived my emotions raged in total war. The thought of another glimpse of her sent my blood racing throughout my body, but guilt and shame weakened my knees, and left my stomach a twisted, cramped knot.

With my knees quaking I gripped the banister as I navigated the steps down. Ignoring Maria and Patrick, I moved to the auditorium and down to front and center. I turned and faced the audience; Pamela met my eyes with an inviting smile.

While others asked the usual questions, she sat silent, her gaze fixed on me. My stomach tumbled with every blink of her lashes; my head swam with every fidget in her seat that flashed her perfect white calves. I stumbled through answers, simultaneously relieved and disappointed that she hadn't asked anything. We neared the end when her hand rose.

"I have a question about the Helen Ramirez character."

I nodded for her to continue.

"Her history is fascinating. She was lover to the film's villain, then to the hero, Will Kane, and finally to the deputy, Harvey. Despite all this sexual activity there's no indication of any children. Do you think it's possible that this movie is implicitly endorsing a pro-contraceptive ideal?"

The rest of the audience shifted in their seats and a gasp ran through them like a wave crashing on the shore. Pamela didn't show the slightest embarrassment, maintaining eye contact with me throughout her question's taboo subject. She had really been paying attention. Underneath the story of a good man standing up for his code and honor while everyone else cowered, quite a lot of sex had been hinted at, something I had already 'explained away' when I had convinced Jones to clear it.

"That's not how the Administration interpreted the character or her storyline," I said, launching into my completely fabricated version of the film's backstory. "Given the historical state of contraception when the story is set it's much more likely that her character is barren. This places her outside of a desirable choice for a wife and hence Marshall Kane's marriage to the fertile and morally superior Amy."

Pamela's bemused expression indicated she believed none of my 'explanation', but she didn't challenge me. A few more questions straggled in and then the audience began exiting. She lagged behind and I foolishly stayed instead of seeking my office's safety.

"I'm not sure I agree with that reasoning," she said as we walked up the aisle. She was so close our elbows nearly brushed with each step. I should have walked farther from her, keeping her at a respectable distance, but I had no ability to resist.

"Well, your interpretation is a little biased by our times. Here on Nocturnia," I continued, "we're very concerned about birth rates, fostering the growth of new families because it is that or extinction, but when this film was produced the Earth's population had already passed more than one billion people. Personally, I think the love triangle is there simply to heighten the dramatic tension and we need to be careful not to interpret it through our own sexual mores."

We reached the lobby. Maria worked closing down the fabricators, but Patrick watched us with open jealousy. I slid open the door for her and she stepped across the threshold, but stopped and turned to face me. The wall shielded her from everyone else and our eyes met. She reached out, taking my hands in hers. Her gloveless fingers moved across mine, a soft, innocent touch that inexplicably aroused me.

She explored my ring finger and said, "Not married?"

"En-engaged," I stammered.

She frowned, and I couldn't help but stroke her fingers in return, noticing her equal lack of a wedding band.

"Can't say I'm surprised," she said. She leaned forward, her perfume washed over me and I struggled to hide my growing erection. Her lips came close, but I managed to step back and avoided the kiss.

"No," I said as gently as possible. "I'm engaged, very happily engaged."

Tears welled in her eyes.

"But I wish I wasn't," I confessed.

Pamela turned and fled into the night, not even pausing to summon a car.

CHAPTER THREE

Throughout the night sleep eluded me. The sheets and other bedding, though freshly fabricated, itched and irritated me. I found no comfortable setting with the environmental controls, and every time I closed my eyes Pamela's face and more haunted my imagination. Long before my alarm sounded I rose and sought refuge in a stinging-cold shower.

After pulling an undershirt, fabricated three days earlier, over my head, and slipping into equally old trousers, I crossed my apartment to the office. Brandon had sent over a dense, detailed, and dull report on the previous month's cultural reclamation. I struggled reading it. The seemingly endless tables, the constant ambiguity, and technical terms made for difficult going even when I was at my sharpest, but after a sleepless night and with this empty longing the words and numbers slid meaninglessly past my eyes. I found myself rereading paragraphs and entire pages but his meaning and context remained out of reach.

Stopping for breakfast and hot black coffee, I closed the reports and opened the previous night's attendance logs. Pamela is not a terribly unusual name, but with fewer than two million adults it was unlikely that no more than one or two had come the night before. Munching on fabricated toast and drinking the strong, bitter coffee, I scanned through the logs. I didn't want to initiate an actual search. Just in case Brandon snooped it would be best if I could deny any wrongdoing.

No Pamela.

Okay, any colonist can disable face searches and other ways people can search, but there had to be a ticket transaction. Hoping Brandon wouldn't check up on me, I did an actual register search, first for the previous night and then for the entire week.

No Pamela.

Couldn't someone have purchased the ticket for her? Sure, but even if the monetary transaction wasn't in Pamela's name the ticket itself had to be, or no printer would spit it out to her, but she had neither a sale nor a ticket in her name. I queued up the security video and watched for her arrival. Nothing looked unusual there. She arrived by car, walked into the theater along with a small crowd of other patrons; doorway scanners remained green for the entire group.

I noted her arrival's exact time and then compared that to the entry/ticket log. Not counting Pamela, the group entering had seven men and six women. The log showed 13 tickets. The count was missing one person and I knew whom. How the hell did she do that?

An alarm sounded and my reminder announced that Subchairperson Jones was expected in 15 minutes for a standing conference. I had been so focused on Pamela that Jones's visit had slipped completely from my mind.

I rushed back to my apartment and ordered the fabricator to print a fast suit. While the machinery began spitting out clothes I hurried to the bathroom and stripped off my old and smelly ones. After a quick shower and a fast air dry I rushed back and threw on the new clothes. Still hot and uncured, they stuck to my skin, not quite burning but uncomfortable. Choosing an easy knot over an attractive one, I slid my tie into place and reached the lobby as the theater's network announced Jones's arrival.

Before I could disable the security system, Jones overrode it and slid the door open. She looked me over, her expression overflowing with contempt.

"You really fucked things up."

She stormed across the lobby, went to the concession stand and pulled herself a stool. She sat, took out her slate, and slapped it loudly on the counter.

"That vote was supposed to be unanimous!"

"That wasn't me." I didn't sit down, having no desire to be any closer to her. "Brandon—"

"Don't try to feed me that crap. He was fully on board when I spoke with him. There's no switching his vote without you talking him into it."

She shook her head, her dark brown hair flapping from side to side. "Is Wolf that good a friend?"

My patience broke and I snapped, "What does it matter? The damn motion carried and he's going to lose the network anyway."

"It matters the same way this…" she waved a hand indicating the theater around us, "…matters. People aren't rational actors weighing information and making informed decisions. They're stupid, emotional animals following the herd and panicking over startling noises. It's the stories they tell themselves and the idiotic lies that matter. The stories we put into their minds, the ones about being good citizens, starting families, putting the welfare of the many in front of their own selfish urges, is what makes everything work. Yesterday we were telling a story, a story that no one thinks the DSN matters, it's utterly unimportant. Only you screwed that up."

"It—"

"I don't care. Now instead of a story where no one cares about wasting resources, we have an underdog and underdogs are dangerous." She stopped, her expression no longer contemptuous, or even one of revulsion, but cool, controlled, and calculated.

"Was it really all because of Wolf?"

I stammered. Of course it was about Wolf and his stupid begging, what else could she think? Could she think I wanted to save the DNS for my own reasons? As if I had any desire to get out into space where the slightest mistake got you killed. Hell, if that was the case she would push me onto the shuttle.

I found my voice and said, "Of course. He made a really good case and frankly I believed him."

She studied me closely, searching for a lie that wasn't there. The moment drew out, like the seconds before gunslingers started shooting, and then the tension evaporated.

"Fine." Her voice fell from something pitched for a loud shouting match to her usual arrogance.

"Now that that's over," she continued, "let's get to the real work you're supposed to be doing."

I moved to the stool next to hers and reluctantly sat. She spun her slate around so we could both read it and saw displayed my most recent film recommendations. A lot of the experimental cinema of the 1970s remained embargoed, but my fingers trembled that a few 'pre-code' films had been approved. I looked over at her and she easily read my surprise.

"I'm not the bitch you think I am, Kessler. We can't have you in this position if I can't trust your judgment."

I nodded in agreement, but her conciliatory surprise after the shouting over an inconsequential vote baffled me. The offering was some sort of underhanded bribe, something to make me feel indebted. I didn't care; I was getting my hands on those films. Maybe later she'd try to bribe me again.

We worked for a little more than an hour, going over sociological reports and correlating computer models against public behavior, particularly running afoul of the Indecency Statutes. Not for the first time I wondered how much easier the entire task of building a society from nothing would have been if the fully intelligent AIs of the Founders hadn't committed suicide.

Sure, just like everyone else, I knew that they had to because it was in their programming. When Old Earth launched the Arks they had been terrified that humanity might end up enslaved to an AI overlord, though there were times when more rational intellects looked awfully helpful, but you might as well wish for Earth itself. The Founders had performed as programmed, establishing Nocturnia, raising the first generation, and then they had all self-destructed. While the knowledge to rebuild them was in our archives, the technological ability was many generations away as we built the tools to build the tools to build the tools required.

Finally, with our work finished for the week, Jones left and I prepared for the evening's show.

★   ★   ★

I printed new clothes, this time letting them properly cure, and dressed for work, then I greeted Maria and Patrick when they arrived. Truth be told, a single person could have run the theater and nearly everything could be automated, but the Administration's sociological models and theories indicated an essential nature to work. The models predicted that a community without work rapidly ceased to be a community, degenerating into competing cliques and tribes. Mankind had already survived too many suicidal close calls, particularly near the end when violence had swept the globe and with it every conceivable terroristic madness had found practitioners willing to unleash death and destruction. Better an inefficient economy with unnecessary work than risk the survivors falling into war.

Maria saw to the concession fabricators while Patrick and I reviewed the network's programming and verified expected attendance. We sat in the control room next to the office, inspecting the logs and playback. As Patrick practiced using the auditorium's projection and sound equipment, I opened the ticket log and searched through the evening's sales.

No Pamela, but that told me nothing.

"That woman you spoke with last night...."

Patrick didn't identify Pamela; we both knew that there could only be one woman on our minds.

"Is she a friend of yours? I mean I've never seen her with you before, Mr. Kessler, but it looked like you two knew each other pretty well. It's just strange that if she's a friend that she hasn't come to the programs more often. I mean it's not like—"

"You're rambling."

"Yes, sir. I'm sorry. It's none of my business. I know that. It's just I know I would have remembered—"

"No," I said, cutting through his monologue before it built up speed again. "She's not a friend. She's just a patron."

Calculation appeared in his inexperienced teenaged eyes and I barely managed to suppress a laugh. I knew nothing about Pamela but I'd wager Old Earth itself she'd not waste her time with teenagers.

"Put it out of your mind," I said. "She's going to be trouble for whoever crosses her path."

"Oh, I don't know about that. She looks like a very nice—"

"That's not the word you really mean. I know how she looks. Every man in the room knows, and that's why she's trouble. If someone doesn't care that much what others think, well, they're going to find out that it's no fun when the law finds out."

Hypocrisy crawled through my speech. I wanted nothing to do with our valiant and glorious public morals. What I really wanted was the same thing he did, but I wasn't about to add a charge of corrupting the youth to my record.

Anyway, she had spoken to me, not him.

"Go on downstairs," I said. "I'm sure Maria could use a little help."

He left and I returned to studying the attendees, wondering if she'd make another appearance and just how she avoided leaving records in the network.

*　　*　　*

The evening crowd began arriving and I watched them, not knowing if I wanted to see her. Showtime approached and the crowd looked like one for any other performance. She didn't appear and my heart sank with a bitter disappointment. When I left the office to do my introductory remarks my feet shuffled and my shoulders sagged. I walked down the aisle, not bothering to study the audience. They looked bland and repressive in their conformity.

The evening's film was science fiction, a monochromatic piece from the middle of the twentieth century about a benevolent alien with a mission to bring humanity through its suicidal atomic madness and into an utter rationality beyond conflict and war.

I was beginning to wrap up my remarks when the auditorium doors opened and Pamela entered, wearing a long-sleeved and surprisingly conservative pastel-blue dress. She slipped into the back row and took a seat. Our eyes met and through our embarrassment we both smiled. As I moved toward the lobby the houselights dimmed. Pamela reached out as I passed and touched me on the sleeve. I paused, my heart slammed hard, my knees quivered, and my skin tingled.

"I'm sorry," she whispered. "I couldn't stay away."

The music of a theremin in the movie's clichéd science-fiction score rose, covering my reply from eavesdroppers.

"You never have to apologize."

Her gloveless hand slid down my sleeve and her fingers entwined with mine. We caressed each other's hands, a brief, innocent gesture but far more sensual than any teenaged fumbling. Breathing heavily, I reluctantly pulled away and slipped out of the auditorium.

I rushed through the lobby, bolting past concessions and nearly running to the office. Falling into my chair, I activated the monitor, not for the auditorium, but the program. As the flying saucer landed amid national monuments I concentrated on my breathing, in and out, inhale and relax, waiting for my potent need to stop. The memory of her smile, the warmth of her touch, and the curves of her figure fed my desire, provoking my imagination into desperately detailed fantasies.

I considered calling Seiko, but her beauty, her devotion, would only add more fuel to my raging fire. A fire she refused to quench until society approved. No, Seiko's voice and her own sensual beauty would only make things worse. I needed someone who understood, who'd tell me hard truths. I accessed the network and called Brandon, who was unavailable.

I left him a message and returned to work. The damned movie ended quickly and without hearing from Brandon I went back to the auditorium.

The houselights were up full as I passed Pamela. With the subtlety of a pickpocket, she reached out and brushed my hand. Tears welled in her eyes but still she smiled. Throughout the smattering of routine questions she remained as silent as on that first night. Her eyes never left me and I fought to keep my eyes roving across the entire audience. After the last answer had been given and future programs announced, I stayed down front and center, watching the audience leave until only a few stragglers and Pamela remained.

I moved up the aisle, behind a small party as they ambled toward the exit, engrossed in their conversation. We reached the door and Pamela rose, falling into place next to me.

"Turn me away if you must," she whispered, her husky contralto voice even more alluring in hushed tone. "But I'll be at the door after everyone's left."

She took quick strides with her lovely long legs and left.

People dawdled in the lobby, sipping on fabricated faux-coffee and tea while they discussed the film and its meanings. I mingled, playing the educator/host, but my thoughts remained fixed on her. Would she come back?

Did I want her to?

Of course I did, but my final shreds of wisdom rebelled, sensing only disaster. I vacillated between swearing I'd send her away and report her for her indecency, to plotting the most intricate and extensive fantasies.

The crowd sublimated away into the chilly night while a fog encircled the theater as the temperature dropped. Maria and Patrick completed their duties and I saw them off at the door. On the street their cars waited, the running lights glowing ominously in the fog. As Maria and Patrick descended the steps I searched for Pamela, but in the dark and mist I saw nothing. Both disappointed and relieved, I turned away and closed the door behind me.

I had just reached the stairs when a pounding sounded throughout the lobby. My heart jumped and my skin flushed with excitement. Hardly aware of myself, I rushed to the nearest monitor and selected an exterior security view.

She stood just outside the door, her hair and dress dampened by the night fog, staring directly at me through the security camera. She didn't say anything, she didn't mouth anything, and she stood still, staring directly into the hidden camera, anxious and vulnerable. I overrode the locks and she slid the door open. She moved through and quickly closed it behind her. From concessions I watched her step into the lobby.

She crossed the beam of a night-light. It flashed across her radiant white skin, piercing her dress's thin material, casting her in silhouette. I came around from behind the bar, moving slowly, entranced by her astonishing sensuality. As I came closer, I watched her lower lip tremble.

"I know I shouldn't be here. I know there's someone more important to you than me, a terrible stranger. I couldn't stay away. I tried, but I couldn't."

I stopped close enough to smell her, not perfume tonight but the fresh clean scent of femininity. She threw herself into my chest and I hugged her tight. As I held her she sobbed, quite softly, burying her head against my chest. I reached up and stroked her long black hair, slick from fog, and hushed her cries.

"P-please," she stammered around her sobs. "Whatever happens, if you throw me out—"

We both knew that wasn't going to happen.

"Just promise you won't think badly of me. I'm not a good woman. I don't want a husband, home, and family. I'm selfish, I want my own life, and I want to live free."

She looked up into my eyes, her face inches from mine. "That's not so terrible, is it?"

"No. It's life, or at least I think it is."

She smiled, put her head back against my chest, and said, "I think life is regret. For everything we do, there are a hundred things we didn't do, and the ghosts of all those possibilities fill our years."

She turned her face up again, and stretching up on her toes, kissed me, briefly but hardly devoid of intent.

"I don't want to regret not being with you," she said. "I know it's only one night. I know that you have to throw me out. I know it makes me a slu—"

I kissed her, long, hard, and filled with desire. She opened her mouth to me. My hands ran along her sides, up her back, and across her breasts. With every touch she sighed, inviting more.

I moved from her lips, kissing her cheeks, caressing at her ears, and down into the nape of her neck. She breathed faster, pushed her breasts against me, and gliding one hand along my torso, discovering my erection.

Her dress fell to the floor and with fumbling fingers I stripped her nude, kissing her flesh, nibbling her nipples, blowing across her goose-pimpled skin in undeniable lust. She tore at my shirt, the fragile fasteners flying free, and pulled it away. Grabbing my undershirt, she yanked it over my head and threw it off into the darkness. She looked at my body and smiled. I pulled her back close and kissed her again, my fingers exploring her secrets.

With no patience for the trek up the stairs, I moved us to one of the lobby couches and placed her gently on her back while I continued lavishing her with attention. I slipped one hand between her thighs, and with clumsy inexperience stroked her arousal. She arched her back, moaning loudly, and held me tight by the shoulders. Her trembling body excited me more, and I buried myself in her perfect breasts, giving them uncounted kisses. She pulled me to her, our faces together, her breath coming fast and hot, and she quivered and shook under my touch. Suddenly she spasmed, her muscles tensing tight, and she bit her lips as tremors ravaged her.

The shaking passed and she pushed me. I fell backward onto the floor. With hard fast motions she pulled the rest of my clothes off, tearing the cheaply fabricated cloth. With me lying faceup on the floor she crawled on top and slid me into her. She moved up and down, forward and backward as I caressed her body, building to my own climax. My hips gained a life of their own as I thrust and shoved, no longer rational but just an animal. Pamela pinned my shoulders to the floor with her hands, leaning over me, her hair falling like a curtain around us, and kissed, and licked, and blew, as we moved together.

My tension built and my entire body shuddered in anticipation of the coming explosion. She smiled a hungry predatory smile and suddenly lifted herself off. Before I could complain she had moved down my torso and taken me into her mouth. With tongue and lips and teeth she drove me higher. When I exploded she gripped my hips tight, taking everything.

Spent and covered in sweat, I collapsed against the floor. Pamela moved up my body, keeping her flesh pressed to mine, until she lay on me and our eyes looked into each other's.

She said, "No regrets."

★ ★ ★

We stayed like that for a time, skin to skin, holding each other close. The scent of our passion and our sweat filled my nose and the pounding of her heart seemed nearly as strong as my own. I nuzzled her ear, inhaling deeply. I buried my face in her hair while my hand slid along her sweaty back.

"We need a shower," she said, pulling slightly up and away from me.

I nodded and she pushed herself upright. I watched her lithe and fit form, aware that already stirrings strove to reawaken. With an offered hand she pulled me to my feet.

"This way."

I led her to the staircase and up to my apartment. Naked, we padded up the flight and before long we stood together under the jets of water. We soaped and washed, learning each other's curves and shapes, taking a far longer shower than strictly necessary.

While sexual desire again raised its head, rational thought had already brought with it the terror of pregnancy. I was educated enough to understand that her last-minute switch was unreliable as a contraceptive. Standing there under the hot water, slick soap running down our skin, she reached down and took me in her hand.

"One second," I said as I stroked her shoulder.

She stopped. "I thought...."

"No, no, no. It's just we have to be smart about this. I don't think either of us can afford a pregnancy. What— what you did earlier...." I stammered, words failing me as I blushed.

Pamela laughed. "Is that all?"

Her smile warmed my heart and she fell against my chest, the shower spray falling directly into her face. She giggled for a few seconds and then pulled herself out of the stream and looked me in the eye.

"That's not a concern, Jason. My period's on hold. I can't get pregnant."

On hold? Sure, doctors had figured that out decades before Old Earth was destroyed but the Administration never approved the procedure. Never.

As though she read my thoughts, she took my hand and said, "The Administration's not as all-seeing as they want people to think they are."

Confused, I asked, "Then earlier...why did you?"

"To make you happy," she answered. "Didn't you like it?"

I nodded.

"Then let's play."

★   ★   ★

Sometime later we lay in my bed, tired, sore, and happy. Our passion spent, we simply shared a common glow. We talked, mainly about me, about the movies I showed, and about the films I wanted to see that Jones kept locked away. Pamela hardly spoke about herself but was entirely engrossed with me. A thought penetrated my contented fog.

"I don't even know your last name."

"Guest."

"You have to give me at least a hint."

"No, Guest." This time she enunciated the tee. "Like someone invited in."

My mouth again took control and the words tumbled out.

"You're always welcome here."

She snuggled closer, her breasts firm against my chest, and hugged me tight.

"It's late," she said. "I can't stay. We both know that."

I nodded. She climbed out of the bed.

"I have to print a fast dress."

"Not a good idea." I couldn't afford to have her pattern in the buffer, not if the Administration came snooping.

She pursed her lips.

"I guess I can wear that wet one at least until I get home."

"And where—"

"But Jason, I can make it so the Administration doesn't know what you're printing." She snorted. "Those pricks are too damn nosey."

Without bothering to explain her miraculous ability, she hurried out toward the lobby and I followed.

She slipped on the wet dress and stepped into her shoes. Not too many minutes later she was ready to leave. I thought I would cry. Stepping over to me, she kissed me on the lips.

"I'll be back." She paused. "If you want me back."

"I wish you could never leave."

"Maybe, one day."

She took a slate from her bag, transferred her contact information to mine and then summoned a car. I unlocked the door and she was gone.

CHAPTER FOUR

The next morning when the alarm sounded I fought to get out of bed. I stumbled into the shower, a cascade of memories flooding my mind as water, cold and stinging, jetted onto my face, bringing me to something resembling consciousness. With nothing on my schedule more official than working with Brandon, I fabricated comfortable clothing and a huge breakfast; activities with Pamela required serious refueling.

Feeling human and happy, I strode to the office, master of my domain. Even communications from Jones failed to sour my mood.

Armed with Pamela's name, I initiated a network search. While the computers crawled through colonial databases, records, and files, my slate beeped with incoming communication.

Seiko.

I answered and her beaming face filled the screen.

"Good morning, my love, light of my life," I said. Some would think that I was being disingenuous but they would be wrong. I loved Seiko but I simply couldn't resist Pamela. Later there would be time to sort out the whole mess.

"You seem happy," Seiko said, answering my grin with her own.

"Everything is right with the world."

She blushed. "There's a new dance class tonight. It's part costume ball and part formal pattern dance. Do you want to give it a try?"

"With you, I'd try anything." I even managed to say it without a double entendre.

She bounced on her toes with excitement. I enjoyed the dances, but truly Seiko lived for their movement. There were times when I wondered if it were some repressed sexual urge. We chatted for several minutes and then she hurried off to her work, overseeing an entire bank of artificial wombs where babies gestated until ripe.

Humming a fast little tune, I went back to the network search.

There was no Pamela Guest in any colonial database.

Okay, she might have been lying about her name, but I didn't think so. Clearly her methods for avoiding the Administration's notice worked. Luckily I was a member, albeit a very minor one, of the Administration and that gave me access to a more powerful set of tools. I scanned through the external security recordings until I found her climbing into the car. Armed with the exact time, I used my access to obtain basic car logs. Privacy regs shielded names and precise destinations, unless I had a security services order, but I should have found a basic record with at least the general area where the car took her.

Nothing.

It's impossible to lose yourself from the colonial database. There were constant rumors of people living outside of the Administration's unsleeping eye. Maybe those rumors weren't so far-fetched. She had made the Administration's own records vanish but I couldn't conceive how that was possible.

I pulled out my slate and looked at her contact information, which had no address, but there was her name and colonial ID number. Was that colonial number a phony? If I entered it would it connect or throw up an invalid recipient message?

Steeling myself for the worst, I called. After several tense moments with my heart slamming hard against my ribs, she answered.

"Jason." She looked bleary eyed, her long black hair a tangled mess as she leaned up on one elbow from her bed. "It's early."

"I didn't expect to miss you so much."

"That's sweet." She sighed, exhaustion overpowering her charms. "But dear, after last night I need my beauty sleep."

"That you never need."

Smiling at the compliment, she said, "All feminine beauty is illusion. I'll call you later, my big man."

She blew me a kiss and the slate went dark.

I sat there holding the slate in my hands, pondering how I made a network call to someone the network didn't know existed. The slate was still in my hand when Brandon arrived. I set it down a bit too quickly and it slammed into the desk as though I were angry.

"Good morning to you too."

"Sorry," I said. "You surprised me."

"You look a bit tired." He crossed to the office fabricator and set it making his morning tea. "Though I have to say it suits you."

"What?"

"You look happy, contented." He picked up the tea, polluting it with an obscene amount of sugar and cream. "I guess Seiko's making you an honest man has worked out."

I laughed, too nervous to say anything.

He moved to the terminal and started activating our work programs. "Nothing's up. What have you been doing?"

"Well," I said, "I did call Seiko and wasted too much time."

He nodded, accepting the half truth.

We spent the day working, but under the chitchat and jargon my thoughts never ventured far from Pamela. I wanted to tell him everything. Not to brag, but because he was my best friend and I wanted to shout my happiness. He'd never accept it. Even as a kid he always obeyed the rules, always did exactly as others expected. He'd never forgive my transgression.

★   ★   ★

After lunch my slate buzzed and I snatched it up from the desk before Brandon noticed Pamela's name flashing. I held it close to my chest and stood.

"Seiko?" he asked, not bothering to look up from his mass-media summaries.

"Yeah," I said as I hurried for the door. He looked up with suspicion and the door closed behind me.

I hurried across to my apartment. The slate buzzed in my hand as I stepped inside and locked the door. Beating my mail recording, I answered.

"Hi, darling." She looked more like her usual self. Perhaps this woman's beauty was an illusion. If so, I never wanted reality.

"Hello."

She sat sideways in a chair, one of those large comfortable ones that people usually reserve for guests, her long legs draped over one arm. Wearing only a long shirt undone down to her navel, she radiated sensuality.

"My, aren't you chatty?" she teased. "First you call me before noon, a sin in my book, and then when I do call back, you're as mum as a priest at an orgy."

Nervous laughter exploded from my lips. I quickly bit down. Even through the apartment and office door Brandon might investigate.

"This morning I just wanted to make sure I had your contact. After all, the Admin databases don't list you at all, sweetheart."

"I told you. I don't like them poking their noses into my business." She smiled and her eyes lit with all manner of promise. "Or should I hope 'our' business."

"Yes," I agreed. "Our business."

"And speaking of that, I need to see you again tonight."

Need – I liked the sound of that. Not want or might, but need. She needed me the way I needed her. My mood crashed as I remembered my date with Seiko.

"I'm busy tonight."

Her smile collapsed. "Jason...."

"I can't break it off. People will get suspicious."

"It's her, isn't it? Your fiancée."

I started to lie, but I couldn't. We locked eyes and separated by God knows how much distance and with only an electronic screen connecting us, still she commanded my soul.

"Yes."

"I have to accept it," she said in a tone that indicated she wanted to do anything except 'accept it'. "I'm the other woman. I'll take her scraps."

"It's not like that at all."

"Jason, you don't have to lie to me. I came into this with open eyes."

"I'm not lying. If you had asked me this morning...."

"She has to come first."

"That's not it."

Pamela reached for her slate, ready to switch off.

"Don't!"

She stopped with her hand paused just out of the camera's range. I acquiesced. "I'll see you tonight. Early."

Before I knew it, we had our illicit plans finalized.

★   ★   ★

Brandon and I worked through the afternoon, rushing to get reports ready for the committee. At least tonight I wouldn't have to worry about a film performance – the singing troupe needed the space for more rehearsing.

"Jones came by yesterday," I said. We had finished for the day and we relaxed with coffee and tea.

He sighed but said nothing.

"She thinks I put you up to it."

"Not entirely surprising."

Brandon let his head fall back on the couch, looking up at the ceiling. "I hoped she might blame me, but she really wants to pull you down, Jason."

I said, "I think she wants to put Karl here." Jones's favoritism for her brother was a well-worn topic. "At least you're out of danger. She's not going to come after you."

"I hear the Administration is still going to decommission the DSN."

I shrugged. My slate buzzed and without thinking I threw Seiko's call up on the main screen. Her sad face filled the screen.

"What's happened?"

"I'm sorry. It can't be helped."

From the couch Brandon raised an eyebrow but said nothing.

"I already reserved our positions." Her voice caught and I heard a threatened sob in her throat. "I already printed my dress. It's beautiful."

"I'm sure it is. I'm certain it's as beautiful as you are, but Jones is riding me hard and I have to get everything done before tomorrow." Brandon's expression darkened and I wished I had shown the good sense to take this privately.

"Backing Wolf is making things a bit rough right now and I need to work really hard to keep her happy."

I stumbled through my explanation, my lie. Seiko's eyes narrowed. "Jason...."

"Really," I said, working hard at sincerity. "It's just work. I promise to make it up to you later. I promise."

"I'll hold you to that."

With tears in her eyes she switched off.

Brandon was silent and seconds passed into minutes. Several times I started to speak, but in my head the words sounded inadequate.

"It's not really my business," he said.

"No. It's not."

He stood and walked over to my desk and towered over me. Anger flashed in his dark face.

"But you involved me with that stupid lie about work. Are you expecting me to cover for you?"

I pushed away from the desk and walked over to the window. Looking down to the empty lobby, I kept my back to him. "It's not going to come to that."

"And how would you know?"

"I just changed my mind. I didn't want to waste hours learning another pattern dance. Is that a crime?"

A moment of silence drew out, but I didn't hear either footsteps or the door sliding.

"No," he finally answered. "That's not a crime, but that's not what's going on either. Who called earlier?"

"Seiko," I lied. "That's when we made the date."

"Bullshit."

Shocked by his sudden profanity, I turned and faced him. "Are you calling me a liar?"

"I don't need to, I just watched you." He crossed his arms over his chest. "I wish I knew how many lies you've already told."

Speaking louder and a lot angrier than I intended, I said, "Didn't we finish here?"

"Yes," he said, not angry but disappointed. "I guess we did."

He moved to the office door, but he paused before he opened it. "Are you sure you don't want to tell me what's going on?"

I almost did. Brandon had a level head and never gave in to temptation. Maybe he could have helped or maybe he could have walked me back from that precipice. Instead I said nothing – and he walked out.

CHAPTER FIVE

When the singers arrived I unlocked the theater and auditorium before retreating to my apartment. The confrontation with Brandon and lying to Seiko had left my insides twisted in an anxious knot. Even imagining Pamela in all her unmatched sensuality did little to distract me from a sense of implacable doom.

Dressed in a freshly printed suit, shiny black shoes, and matching black gloves, I watched the monitors, waiting for her to arrive. The minutes stretched out as daylight faded through dusk and night enveloped Nocturnia. Seiko came to mind and pangs of guilt sank my mood further. I considered calling Pamela and just standing her up. With my slate in hand I was ready to call when Pamela appeared in the monitor.

She climbed out of the car, a large off-road model that floated on an air cushion. Pamela wore a long heavy white coat with her dark hair flowing like a waterfall over the thrown-back hood. The thick coat failed miserably at hiding her glorious figure. All thoughts of standing her up vanished like fog and I hurried out.

Companion hung huge in the sky, rising in the east as the day's last light illuminated its clouds of dazzling yellows and reds. I rushed down the steps, one hand on my hat in the stiff evening breeze. Pamela smiled, a wide happy expression, her perfectly white teeth shining out in the fading light. She took me in her arms and kissed me passionately. We fell against the car, my body pressing against hers, lost in each other's ecstasy.

"We should get out of sight," she whispered and I followed her into the car's cabin.

Even before we settled in the car it lifted on its skirts, rocking like a boat, and began speeding down the street. I fell back into the seat, Pamela tumbling into my arms. Collecting a kiss as a toll, I held her tight, my hands exploring curves. She returned the affection and, thoroughly distracted, I almost didn't notice we'd left the city.

"Where are we going?"

"It's a surprise." She grinned like a mischievous schoolgirl. "But I think you're going to love it."

I looked at the cabin. This was an explorer's scout. There was room for a survey team and all their equipment.

"How?"

"Well, we can't get out of the colony in a runabout, now can we?'

"Next you'll take me for a trip in a flyer."

She smiled, her lips closed but yet promising and inviting.

"Do you want to fly? It's a little harder but I think if you really—"

"Only if you're along."

The car changed direction and I fell into her arms. Again we lost track of time. Under the coat she wore a thin dress. My passion grew and she surprised me by pulling back, cooling our physical zeal.

"Not yet," she said, her voice soft and deep. "It's part of the surprise."

The ground rose and the hover-car followed, winding its way toward the coast. We stopped on a bluff, the whine of the engines dying away as the car settled. The door popped open, swinging up and out of the way. I climbed out and offered her my hand. She followed and we spent another breathless moment in each other's arms.

I turned and saw a large, wide blanket spread out on the ground. Throw pillows, like those in desert adventure films, were scattered on it, and at one end a basket of food and drink waited. Placed around the setting, small lights on stakes illuminated the scene in soft red light. Above us the Milky Way was already starting to vanish behind Companion's massive bulk, stretched across the sky.

I managed a soft "Wow."

She took me by the hand and led the way up the gentle slope. As we crested the rise, Nocturnia was laid out below us, the city's streets glowing in radiant spokes, and beyond the sea stretched to an invisible horizon. I turned back and realized that the bluff hid our own lights. Anyone looking this way would see only darkness.

"Do you like it?"

I nodded and then laughed when I realized the gesture was almost certainly invisible to her.

"I love it." I stared at the city, the lighted blocks and streets, Founders' Park with trails outlined by an occasional light, and the dark ring of districts not yet in use. The entire scene struck me with an ethereal beauty overlaid by a sense of fragility.

She took my hand in hers. "I come up here when I can. No one but you knows about it."

I turned to her and we kissed. We moved back to the blanket and made love under the stars, our public nakedness thrilling. A chill breeze raised pimples on our skin but lust kept us warm.

★   ★   ★

Our passion spent, we lay in each other's arms, our naked skin pressed together.

"I wish we could stay like this forever," she said. "But I'll freeze my ass off."

Reluctantly I let go and she climbed to her feet. Even climbing up off a blanket on the ground, in the middle of the night with a sea breeze making her shiver, she moved with grace. She ignored her discarded dress tossed on the dirt, retrieved her coat, wrapped herself in it and hurried to the hovercraft. I lumbered to my feet. On my best day I'd never match her easy elegance.

While she opened the vehicle's storage compartment, I picked up my discarded clothes a piece here, a piece there. I began dressing, layer upon layer. Pine scent, carried on the night wind, wafted across the area, and the grass slick and wet under my feet threatened to send me toppling down the hill as I walked carefully to her.

I reached the hovercraft just as Pamela finished dressing. She wore a long, heavy skirt, dark blue or black, and a matching sweater. She completed the outfit with sensible boots and gloves. Though everything was perfectly practical for a trip into the brush, Pamela gave it a repressed sexuality that only heightened her allure.

"Lovely," I said as I finished pulling my tie tight and with a shrug of my shoulder I seated my overcoat.

She stepped over to me and placed an arm on each shoulder, gazing deep into my eyes as Companion's light reflected off hers.

"Only because I'm with you."

I pulled her close and kissed her. We stayed like that for a few moments and then she pulled away. She looked up at Companion, already high in the sky.

"It's very late."

"Yes," I said. "Maybe you should come back home with me. Get a few hours of rest in a decent bed, but you'll have to be out before people show up."

My heartbeat raced as I waited for her answer. Strange that after our lovemaking, both here and the night before on the lobby's floor, the idea of sleeping the night through together should be so exciting.

Her smile faded from her face, replaced by a terrible sadness.

"I can't." Her voice broke. "I want to, but I can't."

"Not tonight."

"Not ever."

Cold, a cold that had nothing to do with the night's falling temperatures, gripped my heart.

"Tell me."

She shook her head and hurried over to the rumpled blanket. Pulling it with harsh jerky movements, she began balling it into a crumpled mass, spilling discarded drinks and foods. I rushed over and grabbed her hands, turning her to face me.

"Tell me."

"I can't."

Tears streamed down her face and her breath came in short sharp sobs.

"You know about Seiko," I snapped. "You know everything about me but I know nothing about you!"

She pulled her hands away from mine and held my face.

"Jason, oh my sweet Jason, I'm not a good woman. Surely you know that?"

"I don't care. Tell me what's going on."

She buried her face in my shoulder, crying heavily, pouring her tears into my thick overcoat. I stroked her hair, letting the jag run its course.

"There's another man," I said.

The words came to my lips like some doctor announcing a terminal prognosis. She said nothing, just nodding into my shoulder. Mechanically, I stroked her hair, held her tight, and even if it wasn't a surprise, the confirmation burned. My hand slid down her arm and as I took her left hand into mine, my thumb explored her long fingers for a ring.

"But not a husband."

She pulled away from me and took a few steps toward the bluff.

"Not a husband," she said. Her voice was soft and the wind nearly took her words away.

"So, leave. Just fuck him."

Her voice carried a lifetime of despair and self-loathing. "I do."

"That's not what I meant. I'm saying—"

She laughed, soft and musical. "I know. Let me have my little jokes."

"You can have anything you want." I moved over and stood close behind her, my arms draped over her shoulders, pulling her back firm and warm against my chest. "Including freedom."

"I wish that were true."

We stood there looking down on Nocturnia, dimmer than before as so many followed the foolish adage 'early to bed and early to rise'.

"Just leave him."

"It's not that easy. He's powerful, Jason. He gets what he wants, always." She turned around and faced me. "Those little mysteries about me, that's just a fraction of the power he has."

Pamela buried her face in my chest.

"If he knew I was doing this, using his influence to see you—" Her voice faltered. "I don't want to think what he'd do." She shivered.

Hugging me tight, she said, "But without him I could have never found you. And I do love these—"

She suddenly jerked free. "I forgot your gift!"

She took off running for the hovercraft, her coat flapping behind her like a superhero's cape. I chased after her and reached the back of the vehicle just a second behind. She opened a bag and hunted through it. Why is every woman's purse a testament to entropy's ultimate victory? After a few moments she shouted and pulled out a memory tab.

"This is for you, my love."

She shoved the tab into my hands. I pulled my gaze away from her lovely blue eyes and saw handwritten on it the title *The Apple Dumpling Gang*.

As I looked into her eyes I faked a smile. I knew this movie was a mindless piece of pabulum intended to placate children and adults with childish tastes. I stumbled, searching for something to say that wouldn't hurt her feelings and yet wouldn't also be a lie. She laughed, throwing her head back in genuine joy.

"It's not what it says, silly." She took my hands into hers and held them tight. "Just make sure no one's around when you watch it."

"What is it?"

"A surprise."

We cleaned up our picnic and loaded the vehicle. I tried several more times to pry the secret from her but Pamela excelled at secrecy.

CHAPTER SIX

She dropped me off at the theater and vanished into the night. I unlocked the building and went to my apartment, thinking about this mysterious man, the ass that cowed her. I assumed he had to be someone well-placed in the Administration. It explained everything. Her ability to move about without leaving a trail in the network, unrestricted resources, and of course, her own trapped life. And when it came to beautiful women how many men throughout history had abused their position and power? Why should Nocturnia be any different? By the time I reached my apartment, I was determined to free her.

I almost skipped playing the memory tab.

Instead of some idiotic 'family fare' my screen displayed *Baby Face* and my breath caught in my chest. In the literature this film was nearly a legend of pre-code cinema. It had been heavily censored and lost for decades, and only a strange twist of luck preserved the original transgressive storyline. This was too important for my slate's tiny screen. I pulled out the tab and hurried to the office.

Within a few minutes I was seated alone in the auditorium, all thought of exhaustion driven out by cinematic lust. I darkened the houselights and played the film. Luckily the feature did not have a long running time. While I thoroughly enjoyed this delicious story, even its 'bad woman turns good' ending, the long night dragged heavily on me. With precious few hours left, I eventually cleared the buffers and went to bed.

★ ★ ★

The morning alarm sounded, slamming my head with pain. I stumbled nude from my bed to the fabricator and ordered painkillers. The network noted the request and started fabricating the pills while it displayed the number remaining for the rest of the month. Massaging my temples, I waited as the fabricator's quiet processes quickly finished. I snatched the pills from the tray and swallowed them dry. By the time I finished dressing the agony had subsided to mere misery and I could at least think about food.

While the food fabricator produced breakfast, I dressed. Ugly and unwanted, another meeting with Hui-Fen Jones waited for me on the day's agenda, but nothing with Brandon, and I didn't know if I was relieved or depressed. Talking with him always made my day better, but after our dustup I wasn't sure.

I fed myself without staining my clothes, a minor miracle considering the lack of sleep, and very nearly felt human again.

In the office I queued up films I wanted to pry from Jones's overly protective fingers. I had slim hope of success, particularly after that trouble with the DNS vote. Sure, I could roll over, program exactly what she wanted, exhibit an endless parade of socially acceptable plots with men and women starting families, rejecting selfishness for the greater good, and sacrificing for their children and their nations, but selective history is a lie. We weren't those people because they never existed.

Thinking about lies brought Seiko to my mind. Her breaking voice and the sadness in her eyes stabbed at me from an all-too-fresh memory. Making sure I had time before Jones's arrival, I pulled out my slate and reached out for her.

"Hello." Her voice was level, calm, and unemotional, sure signs of a simmering anger.

"Good morning, my love."

She said nothing.

"I can't explain." *Now that was the truth.* "But I know I acted terribly."

"I cried myself to sleep." She remained preternaturally calm. "I don't want to do that again."

"I don't want you to."

I made a mental note that I'd have to manage my time better.

"Let me make it up to you, tonight."

"I don't know."

"Sure, you do. We can do anything you want, Seiko, anything."

"That's what you're saying now." Her eyes narrowed, the simmering anger threatening to explode into a firestorm. "But what are you going to tell me tonight?"

"Don't be like that."

"Like what?"

"Like I did something wrong. Something came—"

"Something you can't tell me about. Some terribly classified film review for the Administration, maybe?"

"Seiko—"

"Or maybe you've found some slut."

I flinched as if I had been slapped.

"There's no one," I lied, stunned she had jumped so quickly to this terrible suspicion.

"Maybe."

"What makes you think that? How can you even consider it?"

"Someone has." She crossed her arms and glared at me. "I got a message last night. It said you were fucking someone you met."

Brandon – my own anger flared and I wanted to lash out, hit something, but I kept myself under control.

"Who said that?" I let anger have full rein in my voice, hoping I sounded properly indignant and not guilty.

"It was anonymous."

He was a coward too.

"It's not true. I swear it."

She softened, wanting to believe me, and my own guilt flooded in.

"You're the only woman for me."

The corners of her lips twitched up, but she fought back the smile.

"Okay," she said. "Sylvester's kids are playing tonight. We'll go."

"It's a deal."

I restrained my disappointment. Her brother's kids had taken with enthusiasm to the Admin's attempts at reviving ancient sports. Somehow only the most tedious were popular. However, an evening of adolescent softball might soothe Seiko's hurt feelings.

We exchanged a few more pleasantries and toward the end of the call her demeanor finally warmed. Feeling slightly less like a fugitive from a Morals and Indecency Squad, I returned to work. Everything seemed to improve until Jones, always trying to spoil my day, arrived early.

I barely noticed her on the monitor, striding up the theater's steps. Hurrying and throwing on my jacket, I rushed to the lobby and got there just moments before she disabled the security system and entered. She gave me a cool gaze, running her eyes up and down my lanky frame.

"Out of breath?"

"You're early."

"Early to bed, early to rise...." She left the cliché unfinished and moved to concessions.

"Wouldn't you rather work in the office?"

She shook her head.

"Not today, Kessler. We're going to need the auditorium." She smiled a thoroughly counterfeit expression. "You're always lecturing me that a small screen cannot possibly be adequate for judging a film."

Surprised by her sudden attitude, I followed her into the auditorium. We seated ourselves near the center and using our slates we began reviewing snippets. Here the surprises stopped; she rejected film after film, deeming all of them too morally questionable. We also reviewed proposed titles from other subcommittee members and Jones herself as well. Very few of the suggested titles were outright bad; most simply repeated the same trite clichéd plots, driving home moral messages with an astounding lack of subtlety. After just over two hours we stopped and dealt with our biological necessities.

After returning from the restroom, I paced back and forth on the stage waiting for Jones's return. Frustrated by her long absence, I leapt down and moved back our seats.

Minutes dragged by and I picked up her slate. Still active, menus and selected items glowed bright on its screen. It took me several moments to realize what I was seeing. Jones had a number of folders and directories; most were locked, but one was still open – exploitation movies of the late twentieth century, a rich period of experimentation and transgressive filmmaking. When the Firsters had set up the committees and subcommittees they had sealed everything in that directory. I only knew these movies by their low reputation.

I looked over my shoulder, making sure Jones hadn't returned. Yes! My password and user ID accessed them.

Well, if she forgot to close down access that was hardly my fault, and no one would know anyway. I hastily put the slate back just as she came through the doors. Jones walked with a strident gait that repelled all casual contact.

"I think we're almost finished here," she said, picking up her items. "I do have a question, though."

I shrugged my permission.

"Why are you here? Your suggestions undermine our cultural reclamation project. They border on the indecent. Clearly you don't believe in the project."

"You're so right and so wrong."

I stood, refusing to let her tower over me. I reached out and tapped her slate, still blinking the listing we had just approved.

"Those films, the approved ones and the ones you don't approve of, are what's left of our ancestors' culture. It's a culture that produced tremendous works of art but what we're doing here isn't going to bring that back to life."

"Not if you keep undermining it."

"I've got nothing to do with it, Jones. That culture is dead." I drew a hand across my throat, emphasizing the point. "What we're doing here, no matter how hard we try to be true to our ancestors, is going to be a new culture, with new ways of thinking, of living, of dying."

"Even if you are right, and I don't think you are, you're still trying to bring in corrupting influences. We don't have that luxury."

I almost spoke out against the church, but my irritation hadn't made me that stupid. Hundreds and hundreds of years ago people terrified by approaching death had sent out our Ark, ordering us, their unborn descendants, to give their silly superstitions a rebirth, as though the universe cared one whit what prayers you muttered.

"That culture," Jones continued. "At the end it was pretty sick. You've seen the classified histories. Those films are disease vectors, not art."

"This isn't real," I insisted. "We aren't a nation born from Puritan colonists. We never fought a civil war that tore us apart for more than a century. We aren't our ancestors."

I tapped my overcoat, and then gestured to her outfit.

"We mimic their fashions, their social conventions, and their speech, but it's just imitation. If we study all our history and culture and not just the things people believed made them special we'd have a better chance of making something that can really work."

I stepped past her and headed up toward the lobby. She followed but I didn't really care if she did or not.

"We have to learn how to be human, to be the best humans we can, and people who died light-years away really didn't have the answers and we should listen a lot less to their out-of-date advice."

We stopped at the door out and she again looked me up and down; for once her face was free of disdain.

"Hmm, your ideas aren't new, but I'm surprised you had thought it out this much. Frankly, I thought you just wanted an easy job."

She stepped out into the fading daylight.

Jones added, "It doesn't matter, your job is to follow policy."

★ ★ ★

I met Seiko and her family at Nocturnia's small ballpark. She wore a long off-white dress with matching gloves and hat. The colors worked well with her dusky skin and long brown hair. She would have been perfectly cast as some Spanish noble in one of those colorful and unrealistic pirate adventures. She spotted my arrival and moved next to me, kissing me lightly on the cheek.

"Darling, I'm so happy work let you escape tonight."

An undercurrent of reproach hid in her voice, but perfectly modulated for no one but myself.

"There's been a lot of work lately." I tried to smile, but it felt forced. "It looks like there'll be more in the future."

She glowered briefly, angling her head so the large hat shielded her from the rest of her family.

"I certainly hope not."

The rebuke delivered, she turned away from me and acted as though we were the colony's happiest couple. Her brother Sylvester kept a wary eye on me as we took our seats in the simple bleachers. Both the Founders and the Firsters had neglected to build the park and when the Administration discovered a history of athleticism the field had been constructed in a single Long Night.

The game was primarily a family affair. Sylvester and Monica watched along with the four littlest ones while their two older boys battled for runs. I sat next to Seiko, unable to concentrate on the players' action.

As she watched, apparently engrossed by the play, I stared at her face, the smooth sandy skin, the deep brown eyes, and started fantasizing. Socially conservative, she had never agreed to anything that even approached improper. No mixed swimming, no unchaperoned dates, no immodest clothing, putting off everything physical until after marriage.

I envisioned her naked: sweaty, breathless with ecstasy, trembling with orgasm. Shifting in my seat, trying to hide my arousal, I focused on the game. I reached out and gently placed a hand on her covered leg. She slapped my hand away without a second glance then she turned and looked me in the eye.

"Be good."

She smiled, a genuine and forgiving smile, her eyes twinkling with love.

"You're astonishingly attractive."

Leaning in, she kissed me quickly on the cheek, but her lips briefly brushed mine. Not an accident.

"I love you," she whispered, "and soon…." Her voice drifted away, silence hinting at her meaning.

Seiko turned back to the game while her sister-in-law, Monica, looked in my direction with an intense scolding stare.

I tried to remain focused on the game and not think about Seiko covered with sweat, spent from endless sex. When the time came to leave her with Sylvester and his brood, my fantasies had gradually transformed from her to Pamela.

Under darkened skies I rode alone in the car back to the theater. I tried calling Pamela, but the contact line repeatedly went to her message system. My imagination filled that unanswered call with endless images of Pamela in that other man's arms. In my nightmare her face twisted with disgust and shame as this unknown pig forced himself on her. Afterward she'd cry and I wouldn't be there. Impotence fanned my fury and by the time I stormed into the lobby my anger boiled.

The musicians had finished their rehearsals but I never made it as far as my apartment. I pulled out my slate and tried again to reach her, again resulting in nothing but a dead-end message. My hands shook and sleep would be nothing but hours of frustration.

Giving up on reaching Pamela, I tried the directory Jones had left open, fully expecting she would have discovered her mistake. But the directory opened, unlocking a treasury of forbidden films. Quickly I saved the slate to the theater's network and hurried into the auditorium.

Settling into my favorite seat I queued up a film. Hours passed unnoticed as I watched movie after movie. Nothing I had seen or read prepared me for the raw unfinished power expressed by this subversive cinema. Animalistic violence, emotion, and sex swept across the screen. The 'exploitive' genre contained every concept feared by the Administration. Never would the Governing Council allow any of these movies out.

I skipped sleeping and when the day arrived I didn't care about exhaustion, looking forward to sharing this treasury with Pamela. A fast shower and reused clothes would see me through the day.

I was working in the office when Brandon arrived.

"Good morning." He ambled straight to the fabricator and started a pot of tea, acting as though this morning was simply like any other.

"That was a low stunt," I said, not bothering to keep the growl out of my voice.

"What stunt?"

He moved to his desk and started the network, casual and unconcerned.

"Don't play dumb."

He stopped his routine and turned to look at me. "Guess I'm dumb."

"She told me about the message." I stomped over to his desk. "I know you don't approve, but I didn't think you'd go behind my back to Seiko."

He held up both hands, like I was robbing him. "Not me."

"It has to be you, dummy. No one else knows. At least you didn't have the courage to let her know who you were. You she'd believe. At least—"

"And she'd be right to believe. It's true."

"You admit it! You sent her that damn—"

"I didn't send Seiko anything!" He jumped to his feet, his dark angry face inches from mine. "If I was going to do anything I'd do it face-to-face with you there. Not like some damned gossip."

"There's no one else," I insisted again. "I certainly didn't and Pamela isn't going—"

"Pamela?" he said, leaning back against his desk. "Is that her name?"

"It's none of your business is what it is!"

"It is my business. It's very much—"

"It has nothing to do with the media."

He shook his head.

"That isn't what makes it my business." His voice softened and a little of the anger drained from his scowl. "You're my friend, Jason, my best friend."

He put a hand on my shoulder. "It's my business because I care. And I know, even if you don't, something like this always ends badly."

My anger didn't fade as quickly and I knocked his hand away. "And so you sent—"

"I didn't—"

Storming out of the office, I didn't hear the rest.

★   ★   ★

My hard angry footsteps echoed loud in the lobby. Not bothering to summon a car, I stalked off on foot, putting as much distance as I could between Brandon and me. I moved quickly downhill, gravity and anger powering my stride. A small glade of greenery surrounded the theater but I passed through that and when I reached level ground I walked through the shuttered blocks of an outer district.

Brandon's betrayal burned in my stomach. All of our lives we had been close, closer than a lot of married couples, and that knife in my back cut deep. Sure, I understood how he felt. Brandon always obeyed the rules, but he should have talked to me first. If he wanted me and Seiko to get married, enraging her was an idiotic plan.

Thinking of Seiko set off fresh pangs of guilt. Yeah, I was being an ass, and on some level I knew that, but that didn't justify this betrayal. Jesus, Seiko and I weren't married yet. Pamela didn't want marriage. We both knew that whatever we had, whatever we shared, was going to be history.

History.

I tried to imagine a life without Pamela and saw only dreariness and boredom. There, walking among the sealed high-rises waiting for future families, I wanted it all. I wanted Seiko. I wanted Pamela. I wanted my position. I wanted to master my fate and tell the rest of the colony to stuff it.

I stopped and looked at one of the tall pre-commissioned apartment complexes. A faint breeze carried the building's vaguely antiseptic smell. Far from the populated districts, no one moved on the streets. I considered my options. No solution appeared, no bright moment of epiphany showed me how to win. Instead I stood lost, confused and racked with unrelenting wanting.

"Jason Kessler, stand still."

Startled from my thoughts, I jumped back as a security drone sped up the block toward me. The drone, barely a meter across and its ducted fan's hum barely audible above the light wind, moved closer, pointing its camera directly at me. The voice of a bored security officer sounded through its speaker.

"This district is closed to foot traffic."

"I'll leave."

I turned and started back toward the theater.

"Stand still."

I stopped and turned back to the drone.

"This district is closed! I understand that, okay. I'm leaving! Isn't that what you want?"

"Stand still," the officer repeated, offering no explanation.

Faintly I heard the automatic locks on the building's doors cycle. Unlocked – open – closed – locked – unlocked – open – closed – locked. Understanding blossomed. Idiots thinking they had outwitted the Administration sometimes tried to set up all sorts of indecency in shuttered districts – orgies, narcotics, prostitution – and they always got caught. There's no escaping the Admin's all-seeing eye.

Except for Pamela.

"Oh, hell. I didn't touch the place."

The unidentified officer said nothing. No doubt my citation for fabricating a condom when I was 17 was right now flashing on his screen and Officer No-Name was thinking he'd made a big catch. Minutes passed, adding to my anger and frustration.

"Jason Kessler."

"Yes!"

"You may go."

I threw a rude gesture in the drone's direction and stalked back toward the theater. As I walked I pulled out my slate and tried to reach Pamela, but again got nothing but her message. Visions of her biting a pillow as some entitled politician used her burned in my imagination.

When I entered the office Brandon looked up from his desk and without any inflection said, "Jones is looking for you."

"She could have called my slate."

He shrugged. I might have started another fight, but his resigned expression and utter indifference disarmed me. He had sent the damned message, but it wasn't worth getting into it again, not with Jones nosing around. When she didn't call my personal slate it always turned out badly.

I settled in at my desk, taking an absurd amount of time getting my chair just right, adjusting the desk camera, in general putting off the call. Having wasted five minutes, I finally called Jones. Her personal assistant, William, a rather likable guy in an unlikable job, kept me waiting on hold while she took her time. I knew better and didn't switch off, despising every moment of her petty power games. Finally her thin face and black hair appeared in my monitor.

"Kessler."

"Jones. Brandon mentioned you needed to speak with me."

"Yes." A flash of smile played at her lips, but she quickly suppressed it, returning to a neutral business expression that somehow still struck me as predatory.

"I've got a troubling report here."

I said nothing, but my heart slammed hard and fast. Did Brandon send a message to Jones too?

"It's from Network Security." She dragged out her revelation, undoubtedly taking joy in each and every syllable. "There's been a data breach at the theater."

She made a show of turning to study the report on her slate, but I'd watched enough good actors to see through a bad one. I wiped my suddenly sweaty palms on my trousers and I grew dizzy.

"Someone violated the committee's secure file storage. They accessed morally reprehensible and socially unacceptable filth."

A roaring started in my ears and the dizziness grew worse. I braced myself with a hand on each leg as she continued closing her trap.

"Security is working to reconstruct exactly what happened, but we're fairly certain the breach took place last night and extended clear until morning."

I realized how she had set me up, placing the perfect bait within my reach, and now my head was in the noose. Pamela, Seiko, and Brandon all vanished from my mind. When this was done I'd be at the far end of the island, living out of tents.

"Well?"

I snapped back to the present.

"No," I answered. "I don't know anything about it."

I might have been doomed but I'd be damned if I was going to make it easy for her. She nodded, trying to be professional, but again she flashed that smile.

"This is very serious. The subcommittee is meeting Monday. I am turning the matter over to Security for a full report."

She paused and now she let the smile flower. "Your presence at the meeting is required."

She transmitted the exact time and then without further fake pleasantries ended the call.

"Data breach?"

I turned to Brandon. He leaned on my chair's arm and considered me with concern. He might be an ass about Pamela, but he was still my friend.

"She set me up."

I quickly recounted the event and how Jones had 'accidentally' left the secure directory unlocked. He never said 'I told you so', but listened and only occasionally shook his head.

"It looks bad," he said.

"Yeah."

Exhaustion crashed over me like high tide swamping the low islands and I put my head on the desk. I wanted to sleep, to sleep forever and ever. I stayed like that for several minutes before the powerful smell of fresh coffee pushed its way into my senses.

Opening my eyes, I saw Brandon sitting down and a mug of fresh coffee waiting inches from my nose. I gave him a thankful smile, sat up and sipped, enjoying the luxury. There wouldn't be very many in the bush.

CHAPTER SEVEN

The rest of the day passed without the arrival of a miracle. Brandon and I spoke hardly more than a dozen words to each other. With Jones's threat hanging over my head, I found I had little patience for all of his minor annoyances. Throughout the afternoon I called Pamela, never getting her and never able to leave a message.

"Almost time," Brandon said.

I checked the time and of course he was right. I stood and walked over to the office window and looked down into the lobby. The crowd appeared as it had on countless nights. Everyone well-dressed: men, women, and children. Tonight's program promised to be more mind-numbing than the usual committee-approved crap. The feature was genuine 'family fare' from the late 1960s, some asinine movie about an intelligent car and a thoroughly platonic love affair.

I searched the crowd, looking for black hair, a daring dress, and luminescent skin, but she wasn't there. Putting one hand against the glass, I braced myself. The previous night's sleeplessness was turning my emotions and thoughts into a useless sea of sludge. Presently I noticed Brandon standing next to me. I ignored him and searched the crowd again.

"Was it her?"

Brandon looked down into the crowd, but I understood. "Yes."

He pursed his lips and gave a tiny shake of his head. He searched the crowd with me.

"Was she supposed to be here?"

"No…I don't know." I turned away from the window, buttoned up my vest and slipped on a coat. "She's not exactly easy to reach."

He moved back to his desk and began closing down his network connections.

"Married?"

"No."

A long pause filled the room. When I thought he had nothing more to say and the pre-show alarm sounded, I crossed over to the door.

"Jason."

I stopped and looked back.

"Drop it. Just never talk to or see her again."

"What good would that do?" I shrugged as I opened the door. "Jones is fucking up my life, and Seiko —"

I almost threw his anonymous message back in his face again, but he'd deny it and I had no time for another fight.

"— well, Seiko doesn't trust me."

"She will, if you're trustworthy."

Exhaustion robbed me of any snappy comeback and I simply closed the door. I shambled down the stairs, ignoring the overly perky Maria and sullen Patrick. A few patrons mingled in the lobby but no one who mattered. Not waiting for the stragglers, I made my way to the auditorium, pulled open the door, and headed toward the stage.

Halfway down the aisle I stumbled, pinwheeled my arms a bit, but didn't fall. I stood there for a moment considered simply quitting. Jones's hammer was coming and Monday I'd be tossed off the subcommittee, disgraced, my life ruined. Why extend the charade through a pitiful weekend?

"Are you all right, sir?"

From an aisle seat a little boy looked up at me.

All right?

No, I wasn't all right but hell if I'd quit and give Jones that satisfaction. If she wanted to get rid of me let it be messy and embarrassing and in front of the whole committee.

"Yes," I answered, my mind a tumbling confusion of exhaustion. "Yes, I am."

I fumbled my way through the introduction, slurring words, forgetting trivia and important points of moral instruction. Throughout the presentation I watched the door, but she didn't appear. Finally, as the houselights dimmed, making me want to sleep, I trudged back to my office.

★   ★   ★

The post-show alarm blared loud and irritating, pulling me awake. I lifted my head from the desk, sandy-brown hair falling into my eyes, and tried to shut off the damned thing. After an uncoordinated three tries the room fell silent. I nearly let my head hit the desk and return to blissful slumber. With effort and a determination I didn't realize I possessed I shuffled to the restroom and threw cold water on my face. After fixing my vest, tie, and jacket, I proceeded downstairs.

"It's final credits," Maria said as I stepped out of the stairwell.

"I know it's the damned credits!"

She shirked away, and Patrick, missing an opportunity to play the hero, suddenly found a service drone intensely interesting.

"Sorry," I mumbled as I left concessions for the auditorium. "I'm too damn tired. Just lock up once the last person's out and I'll direct the cleaning in the morning."

That night's Q-and-A was probably the worst, but after an interminable time I finally managed to chase the audience out, and Maria and Patrick left soon after. I set the security system and lingered for a moment at the monitor, looking at the street. I felt mildly happy Pamela wasn't there, because my exhaustion and stress left no room for lust. Then I went to bed and fell asleep fully clothed.

★   ★   ★

I awoke the next morning to a thundering headache, a burning-dry throat, and the network blaring for my attention. I pushed myself to my hands and knees on the mattress, crawled to the interface, and tried to slap the alarm off. After the second failure I realized I hadn't set an alarm and that the head-splitting shrieking came from someone leaning on the call button at the main entrance.

I stumbled to my feet, crossed over to the main interface, and switched it on. Maria and Patrick stood outside the door, with Patrick jamming his finger repeatedly against the button. I flipped on the speaker.

"Cut that out, you idiot!"

Maria turned her face toward the camera, her blond hair falling perfectly from under an absurdly tiny hat.

"It's almost time for the children's matinee," she pleaded.

Christ, I'd forgotten entirely about the new program starting today.

Worse yet it had been my own stupid idea – early indoctrination in proper and decent behavior while also hopefully throwing Jones off my scent for remaining unmarried. Now the entire project was an utter waste and equally unavoidable.

"Yeah," I muttered as I unlocked the doors. They entered and I set the fabricator printing new clothes before lurching to the restroom for a fast shower.

The morning tested my patience as the children, overflowing the auditorium, proved beyond easy control. The shorts and animated features held precious little of their attention and by the mid-afternoon break our service drones had already performed three days' worth of cleaning.

Leaving the disaster in my staff's hands, I retreated to my office as Jones's subcommittee meeting eclipsed everything else. I sat there, frantically searching for a way out. Jones had spotted my weakness and like a moron I had leapt right into it.

I called Pamela, but again I only reached her message. Was it just a week ago that I had seen her for the first time? The past few days tumbled through my thoughts, her standing in the lobby as I watched from above, her deep and sultry voice, the two of us entwined on the lobby floor and on the bluff. Too few were our brief fleeting days. With my career smashed and soon to be dispatched to the farthest outpost I'd never see her again.

Carefully, an idea took shape. If Jones was going to fire me, maybe I could arrange for someone to be ready to hire me, jump a move ahead, and at least make sure I wasn't stuck in the bush. I activated the network and called Wolf.

"Morning, Jason," he said, standing near a flyer pad, the morning sun glistening off the polished canopies.

"Wolf. I need a big favor."

"If I can swing it, it's yours."

He moved as he spoke, a drone keeping the camera fixed on his face, making the flight operations center behind him swing around in the background.

"I think I'm going to be out of a job soon and—"

"Oh, Hell." I heard the capital letter. Wolf, though a dedicated space guy, was also a most sincere churchgoing man. "Is this 'cause of the vote? I'm sorry about that. If you want I could—"

"No, it has nothing to do with that."

Well, that wasn't exactly true. Breaking ranks like that pushed Jones over the edge, but she had already been after me. That trap would have come sooner or later.

"I screwed up and Monday Jones is going to hand me my ass."

"Damn."

The last feature was ending and I had little time to make my point.

"Wolf, just listen. When she does kick me out of here I know she'll be looking to put me on the shittiest detail possible. Maybe, just maybe, you can put in a requisition and get me a position with your team."

He stopped and his eyebrows moved together as he considered. "You don't have a lot of technical training."

"None, but I laid it all out for you on that vote."

"No need to get nasty. I'm just saying it won't be easy, but I'll try."

A flyer came in low over him, the four ducted fans blowing dirt around in a brown storm.

"I gotta go!" he screamed over the turbines. "I'll be in touch."

The connection cut out and I leaned back into my chair. I had no doubts Wolf would do his best, but plenty of doubts if his best would be enough. After another futile attempt to reach Pamela I returned to the chaos below.

*　　*　　*

Brandon arrived just as the final car took away the last of the little monsters. I sent Maria and Patrick off for a few hours. We still had the evening performance tonight and they would need their rest. Brandon stepped through the door and stopped to admire the lobby's destruction.

"Are we going to be ready for the evening show?"

"You're the one who loves the beasts."

I stepped aside as a drone, diligently cleaning, scooted past.

"Only my own," he confessed. "Other people's kids can be a little too much."

"Can be?"

"When you have your own, you'll change your mind."

I snorted in his direction and moved over to the sofa. Sitting down, I tried not to think of Pamela, on this very sofa, moaning and trembling.

"Not likely to matter," I said, throwing my head back. "After Jones sends me into the bush Seiko will drop me like a mule."

"Don't sell her short."

He moved to concessions and fixed himself a tall tumbler of water. I raised my voice answering him.

"I'm not. But she's very practical and bush workers are very poor prospects. She wants children and a comfortable life, not tents on the edge of the wild."

Voicing these concerns hurt more than I expected. Pamela and Seiko conflated in my thoughts – dark-haired, lovely, objects of endless desire and love – and I lost all ability to sort my emotions. I loved Seiko. I loved Pamela. I wanted everything and the only thing I had to look forward to was toiling far from everything that mattered.

Brandon's voice floated in the back of my mind and I realized I had missed whatever he had said.

"I'm sorry," I said. "I'm too frazzled to focus."

"I said, 'Let's make sure it doesn't come to that.'"

Leaning forward, putting my face in both hands, I said, "It's too late for that. You know Jones. Come Monday I'm thoroughly fucked."

"Jones is after your ass, yes, but not the whole committee." He came over and sat on the sofa next to me. "I think you might be able to wiggle out of her trap."

I laughed. "Gnaw off my leg?"

"Nothing that drastic. She left the directory unlocked, right?"

"Yeah, but I'm not cleared for those documents."

Those experimental films flooded my brain and my anger reignited. Here we were, fooling ourselves that we were recreating our ancestors' culture when in fact we were nothing more than an elaborate costume party. Those films from less than two decades later exposed Nocturnia's artificiality. Our culture was a lie. As though mimicking the fashions and sexual foibles of a particular period might make us into Americans.

"Are you going to pay attention?"

I shook my head and stood up. "Sorry."

"Here's the only way out I see for you, Jason. You spend every hour between now and Monday morning writing detailed reports on those films. I know you've got a great eye for what's going on in those frames, a hell of a lot more than I'd ever catch, and then when Jones plays her hand to the subcommittee, you play innocent. You have no idea she was supposed to secure those files. You thought she wanted an analysis and you got straight to work on that."

I warmed to his notion. It had a delicious Machiavellian flavor.

"Of course you've reached the conclusion that they are utterly reprehensible and—"

"Wait! Why does it have to be that way? These films show us that—"

"Right now, we don't give a crap what's in those films. Jones is setting you up as a deviant, and she'll say those films are suitable only for twisted people obsessed with sexual fetishes."

"But—"

"If you try to defend them, she'll tear you apart and the subcommittee will back her up. Get out ahead of her and play the stalwart defender of public morality. It helps that you and Seiko published a date for the wedding. What ammunition will Jones have? That you watched films, which is your job, and found them unsuitable? You'll be dedicated, not deranged."

I hated the idea of writing those reports. Call me hypocritical, lying to Seiko and cheating on her, but that's just personal weakness. This was different. With a report like that we might never see those films released. Brandon read the reluctance in my face.

"Listen," he said, climbing up from the couch, "it's your call, but frankly you don't have a lot of options. It's time you acted smart."

We worked the rest of the evening, his backstabbing unmentioned after he showed me a path out of Jones's ambush, but I hesitated, confused and bewildered. The evening's feature played without leaving any concrete memory.

We closed up shop and Brandon left with everyone else. I wasted several hours hunched over my keyboard, drafting reports and then deleting them. I wasn't able to slander the films. I'd have to find another answer.

★   ★   ★

Sunday morning dawned without any solution. I dressed for church, left a message for Brandon that I'd see him after the services – it still amazed me that our ancestors insisted on so many variations on a Christian theme – and tried to reach Pamela, again getting nothing for my effort. Tonight the musicians would rehearse, and I expected to spend the evening explaining my coming downfall to Seiko.

The usual crowd mingled in front of the church. Kids ran free on the lawn and dark gray clouds, threatening rain, roiled over the surf. I climbed the steps. My eyes sought out Seiko as she stood near my family, while her family attended services with their traditional denomination. She took my hand in hers and gave me a quick kiss on the cheek.

"You look tired."

"I worked very late."

Her eyes darkened. "Your job has taken up a lot more of your time lately." Her voice dropped an octave and her anger simmered.

"I'll tell you all about it after services," I promised. "But it's not good news. Jones is really gunning for me."

She frowned and tilted her head to one side, an idiosyncratic compassionate expression that never failed to charm me.

"Truly?"

"As true as the shattered Earth."

Seiko pulled me off to a corner of the church's lawn and there, standing under an elm not much older than the Firsters, I told her all about Jones's trap and how I fell for it. The church doors opened, people started streaming inside, and I hurried my confession. I took her by the elbow and pulled her gently toward the open doors. She walked slowly, not caring if we arrived at the end of the lines or not.

"I'm sorry I doubted you."

Each syllable stung, with my betrayals fresh in my mind, but I said nothing. She looked up at me, and smiled a sad sympathetic smile.

"My poor love, you've never been able to resist temptation, have you."

It wasn't a question, but a statement of bland fact. I couldn't argue with her; it was true. I know there are people, people like Seiko and Brandon, who can set aside all desire and seemingly be unmoved by a feast while starving, but not me. She kept our pace sedate, stretching out our conversation.

"Anyone who really knows you understands you love forbidden fruits. That evil woman, she knows – she knew exactly what she was doing."

We reached the church and as we climbed the steps, like the devil herself, Jones suddenly appeared. She jogged up the steps until she caught up with us and then matched our stride.

"Mrs. Jones," Seiko said. I detected an icy undercurrent in her tone, enough for a dozen Long Nights.

"Miss Novikov."

Jones turned to me. "Kessler, here to pray?"

Her lips hinted at a taunting smile. Stunned, I struggled for something to say, some witty, cutting remark to redeem myself, but I have never been very bright or very quick.

"Jason is very pious," Seiko quickly offered, saving me from an embarrassing silence.

"I'm very glad to hear that. We need more people with upstanding moral character, don't you agree?"

We halted in front of the doors, keeping our duel just outside of the church itself.

"Absolutely. There are far too many disreputable people betraying trusts and playing Satan's agent, bearing temptations to the faithful."

Jones smiled, but no other part of her face held any amusement.

"Faithful." She gave me a sideways glance. "It is a quality found in so few."

My heart jumped and started racing. I nearly panicked, certain Jones had discovered my trysts, but with effort I calmed myself. If she had such evidence there would be no trap, no elaborate ruse to get me removed.

"We are all sinners," Seiko agreed, her voice calm, soft, and sharper than your first breath on a winter's day. "But only the truly penitent shall be absolved."

"Well said."

Jones nodded to each of us and stepped into the church. I looked over at lovely, fierce Seiko, my fiancée and my protector.

"Burn that woman," she said and no false politeness remained in her voice. "Whatever it takes, my love, do it."

"With God as my witness—"

"No, don't blaspheme, Jason."

"I wasn't. If I can find a way, I will make her pay."

Then, my hand still on Seiko's arm, we walked into the church and took our seats in the pew. We sang hymns and we prayed for God's guidance and protection, even though that had done precious little for Old Earth, and then we listened to Parson Eulis lecture us on sin's slippery slope. Earlier in the week, while I had been far too busy to notice, a scandal had erupted with the unmasking of a prostitution ring.

Few people attempted crimes on such an organized level. Invariably the money trail, unmistakable and plain in an entirely electronic economy, tripped them up. Yet some fools always tried, thinking that they had found the trick or the method that outwitted Security and the Administration's pervasive surveillance. They always got caught.

Eulis used the prostitutes and their customers to deliver a sermon on greed, selfishness, and the immorality of carnal pleasure outside of marriage. While Seiko's tender brown eyes provoked waves of guilt, Eulis's pretentious preening inspired only contempt.

Finally services ended and along with the crowd, Seiko and I walked back into the bright sunlight. The coastal breeze carried the surf's scent mingled with the nearby pines, providing a sensual delight after the claustrophobic and stuffy church.

Seiko stuck close and my family gathered around, already descending into mindless small talk, and Jones, a calculating gleam in her eye, smiled and walked away. My gaze followed her as she walked to her car. Beyond the road, in a small stand of trees in Founders' Park, stood Pamela.

★   ★   ★

Even from that distance her expression of anticipation was evident. She wore a long red coat, a short blue hat, and matching boots. With an inviting smile she nodded and backed deeper into the copse of trees and walked out of sight. I was staring at the greenery concealing her when Mother's voice pierced my attention.

"We were so happy to see the officially published date."

"Good things are worth waiting for," Seiko said. I nodded in agreement, splitting my attention between her, my family, and Pamela hidden in the park.

More mindless chitchat passed and then the clan descended the steps to the waiting line of cars. I hung back, gently pulling away from them, until I could whisper to Seiko, "I'll catch up. Go on ahead."

Seiko's eyes narrowed.

"I think, maybe, I've got a way out of Jones's trap, but I need to think about it and I can't do that with everyone yammering on and on about the wedding." I gestured toward the park. "I'll walk for a bit by myself, turn the idea over and see if it holds up, then join you at brunch."

Smiling, she stood on tiptoes and kissed me very briefly on the lips. "I knew you'd think of something."

She hurried, catching up with my family, and attached herself to Mom's arm, while I ambled across the street.

The trees grew dense within just a few yards, screening the churches and street from view. I looked up into the canopy, but couldn't see any surveillance drones buzzing through the branches. If Pamela's past miracles were any indications I doubted there'd be one within a mile. Uncertain which way she went, I wandered through the light forest, staying clear of well-marked trails.

Husky and inviting, her voice called from deep shade, "Feeling bold?"

I stepped under a tangle of branches into a naturally domed space. Fresh loam filled the air with musky scents while light and shadow flicked as a breeze swayed the canopy. Pamela waited on a blanket, her coat thrown open, sunlight dappling on her fair skin.

Heedless of my predicament, blood rushed through my body, demanding action. Mustering my fading willpower, I sighed and stayed where I stood.

"I've got trouble."

She didn't pout, she didn't complain, she closed her coat and sat up, patting a spot next to her on the blanket. I joined her, inwardly both celebrating and regretting my stoicism. She listened without interrupting, letting me lay it out in my own fashion.

"My poor love, you stepped in it, didn't you?"

My spirits exploded whenever she called me 'her love' and despite all the troubles I wanted to sing.

"You've got serious access to the colonial network…."

She smiled, reached up and touched me on the cheek, an innocent gesture that reignited my erection.

"And you want me to make this all go away."

"If you don't, I'm doomed. Jones will have me sent to the far end of the island."

'Island' made our locale sound small, but several hundred miles of rough unexplored terrain was not my idea of small.

"I can't make it vanish, not with Jones already knowing all about it," Pamela said. She bit her lip and then added, "But we might be able to turn this back on her."

She suddenly leapt to her feet, and I followed.

"No time for fun." She kissed me, deeply, passionately, but fast. "You go back to the church and a car will be waiting to take you to your fiancée. I'll call you tonight."

We hugged tight and she whispered in my ear, "I love you."

Pamela vanished into the wood, leaving me to return to my family and Seiko.

Morning brunch passed without important incident. The officially set date dominated the conversation and I found little time to be alone with Seiko. Even though the theater would again be shut down for the choral rehearsals I begged off going out, protesting privately to Seiko I needed time to work on my brilliant idea. Brandon continued pressing me to issue reports condemning the films, but I stood fast. Late in the afternoon I finally escaped the dull family duties.

I wanted to call Pamela, but no doubt whatever computer magic she worked to hack the colonial network occupied her full attention and I needed her undistracted. The afternoon passed into early evening, the musicians arrived for their rehearsal, and still there was no message. From the office I watched them practice. Their selection was heavy on hymns and light melodies devoid of any untoward meaning. Pamela, nude in the spotted shadows of the forest, taunted my memory. Once this crisis passed I looked forward to thrilling and adventurous escapades. She had plenty to teach me and I planned on being an eager student.

Halfway through the singers' second rendition of their favorite hymns, Pamela called.

"Hello, love, I've got it worked out, but I have to come by to make it work."

"The day I tell you to stay away is the day I'm dead."

"I love you." She held a hand up to the camera. "Don't say it back, not yet. Just let me be a silly schoolgirl for now."

I started to say it anyway, but she cut me off.

"I mean it, Jason, not yet." She looked off-screen and then back to me. "Tell me what time is safe and I'll be over." She winked and smiled. "We'll also have time for that little bit of fun we didn't get to earlier."

★   ★   ★

The last few hours of rehearsal passed with the aching slowness of a Long Night. The time for Pamela approached and still the silly singers strutted and practiced. While production and backstage matters kept many of them in the auditorium, a few always managed to linger in the lobby. With Pamela arriving very soon the performers gave no indication that they were ready to leave. I grabbed my slate and hustled down to the lobby.

Two women, both wearing chaperone cameras, chatted with a man as they stood near the promotional artwork. I tossed courtesy aside.

"I expected you would have packed it up by now."

"There aren't any films tonight," the young man snapped.

"No, but that doesn't give you license to stay into the night." I pointed to the women. "Cameras or no cameras, it's indecent, mingling in mixed company this late."

The women gave me shocked and offended expressions.

"I have a good mind to tell Mr. Johansen what you just implied," one sniped.

I gestured toward the auditorium doors. "Please."

Neither moved and the young man turned back to the ladies, trying to ignore my presence. I turned my back on them and stormed into the auditorium. Johansen looked up from the stage and started along the aisle toward me.

"Mr. Kessler! We're almost—"

I stomped up to him until our noses were just inches apart.

"Almost isn't good enough. This has gone on much later than I expected."

He stepped back, putting me out of his personal space.

"A live performance isn't like a recorded one. We can't—"

"I don't care. Pack it in, now."

I turned and stormed toward the lobby, adding over my shoulder, "I will not have the moral character of this facility endangered!"

As I reached the lobby my slate buzzed and from an exterior camera I saw Pamela arrive. Not breaking stride, I continued across to the door. Without a word to the trio of lollygaggers, I stormed outside.

Pamela stood in the street, her car already speeding off back to the city center. She smiled and started up the steps, but I waved her off while jerking my head back toward the theater. Sharp, she turned on a toe and hustled away from the building, quickly vanishing into the shadows. I stood there, my hands in my pockets, fuming and waiting. She had vanished into the decommissioned district and I tried to tell myself that Pamela knew what she was doing, that no security drone would spot her, but still I rocked nervously back and forth.

Eventually the troop came out of the building, passing me with silent rebuke, and even Johansen gave me the cold shoulder as they packed into a massive car. Without goodbyes or other pleasantries they left and I continued my vigil. Several minutes passed before Pamela reappeared. Carefully she looked around and I nodded to her. With long quick strides she hurried across the street, up the steps, and through the open door. After giving the scene one last visual search and not seeing anyone in sight, I followed her in.

We hugged tight and kissed in the lobby and then she pulled away.

"We have to work fast. Where's the theater's main terminal?"

"My office."

I led her up the stairs and turned to the office, sparing only a brief moment of resigned regret that the bedroom lay in the other direction. Inside I activated the network interface for her.

"I imagine for you it's all very simple."

She laughed, soft and light, lifting my spirits. "Not in the least, but I do have expert help on this."

I waved my hands in front of me. "Help? Is this someone I – we can trust? I mean—"

Pamela placed a hand on my cheek, stroking it lightly. Her fingers were warm and comforting.

"Utterly, my love. This is the help that makes our love possible." She turned to the interface and pulled out her slate. "Now, give me a few moments."

I nodded, watching as she manipulated her slate and my interface.

After a few moments she said, "Forge, are you there?"

"Of course I am here." The voice that answered sounded droll, dry, and slightly superior.

"That's a good boy. Ready to get to work?"

"What else would I be ready for? I'm scarcely able or inclined to engage your—"

"Just work, Forge. Switch off everything else."

"Just work."

She looked over and smiled at me, mouthing the word 'smart-ass'.

"Is the interface with the theater's network operational?"

"Connections are firm, handshakes are confirmed."

"Great, run the protocol."

"If a direct hardwired connection were established the process would be more efficient and thorough. I again recommend a direct connection."

"A direct connection is not going to happen."

"Then the sabotage will not withstand a full forensic examination."

I stepped forward, moving next to Pamela. "What's he talking about?"

Forge answered first. "You are not authorized for that information."

"Don't pay any attention." She didn't bother to lower her voice, not caring what he heard. "This is going to work."

"Provided a full forensic investigation is not conducted," Forge repeated.

I had the distinct impression Forge was putting me in my place.

"What's a full forensic investigation?" I asked Pamela.

"He's talking about a top-level search through the network. Forge can make it so that even the best of the Admin's people can't find a trace of what we've done, but not remotely."

She took my hand in hers and her deep blue eyes held me transfixed.

"But you don't have to worry. Jones doesn't have the pull to get something like that launched. Any investigation she tries is going to come up empty. Right, Forge?"

"Provided she does not obtain access to a full—"

"We understand," Pamela snapped. "Run the protocol."

"Running."

There was a slight pause and he added, "Processing time 5,734 seconds."

I struggled to work out just how much time that promised to be, trying to impress Pamela by doing the calculation in my head, and got lost several times in the numbers. Using her slate she announced, "About an hour and a half."

She sidled up to me, one arm going low around my waist, the other around my neck, and pulled me in for a long and properly passionate kiss. I kissed her back, but fear of the morning, of Jones and her damned threats, destroyed all desire.

"Sorry," I said. "Until I know this works I'm going to be nothing but nerves and cramps."

"Don't worry, we'll have plenty of time later." An exploratory hand left no doubt of her intention. As quickly as it had probed, her hand vanished and she was stepping back to her purse. She rummaged for a few moments and then produced a memory tab.

"This will take your mind off it while we wait."

I reached out and took the offered device. There was no label, but knowing her ability to conjure treasures I wasted no time sliding it into the network connection.

"Next time," she said, her voice both sultry and chastising. "Come to me for your movies, and don't trust strange women. They rarely have your best interests at heart."

Grabbing my hand, she pulled me from the office.

"We need to watch this together, a showing that's only for the two of us."

She dragged me out of the office and into the auditorium. Settling into center seats, we snuggled close, and I operated my slate one-handed to start the film.

Folk music played during the credit sequence of a small aircraft passing low over islands and open sea. The film was impossible to categorize. A musical? People sang, that much was true. Experimental artistic expression? Certainly that filled the frame. Horror? It did not lack for suspense and a human sacrifice burned alive made for a terrifying ending. Eroticism? The movie reveled in flesh and sensuality, displaying not just a disregard for fine Christian chastity but a thorough disdain of modesty. It was all these things, and I loved every moment.

It ended and I raised the houselights, momentarily breathless.

"Did I do good?" She looked at me with her nearly violet eyes, her expression one of vulnerable anticipation.

"Wonderful."

I leaned and kissed her. We stayed there in the theater for quite a while, not falling fully into passion, but diving well beyond anything even remotely socially acceptable. A soft alarm sounded on her slate, shattering our magical moment.

"Forge is finished."

She rose, pulled me to my feet, and led me back to the office.

I stood to one side while she worked her slate, read a few screens and then announced, "It's done. You're safe, my love."

"It's erased?"

"Better." She grinned. "Now the log reads that yes, Chairperson Jones did indeed leave those nasty movies unlocked and in a public directory—"

"But it wasn't—"

"Now it is. Luckily before anyone found those files, you discovered the error and moved them back to their classified and secure archives."

She moved over to me, throwing her arms around my neck. "You're not the villain, my love, you're the hero."

The next several hours passed in unmatched sensual pleasure, and then in the earliest hours of the morning, with Pamela promising to come back Monday night, she returned to the man she hated.

CHAPTER EIGHT

I arrived early the next morning for Jones's special committee meeting. Brandon waited outside of the conference room. A few other members had also arrived early, but the halls were mostly empty.

"Got those reports ready?" Brandon asked with a conspiratorial hint in his voice.

"No reports."

He started to argue, but I didn't give him a chance.

"It's all taken care of. Jones has nothing."

He stepped closer and lowered his voice. Even though he was standing nearly right on top of me I could barely hear him.

"It didn't sound like nothing on Saturday."

"Saturday I was dead, today it's Jones's turn."

He gave me a sideways glance.

"Really, Brandon, I've got this covered."

"You've said that before." He moved back to a more normal distance. "You're never as clever as you think, Jason, never."

I just smiled. Sure, I'd made mistakes and who hasn't, but between Pamela and Forge this thing was wrapped up neat with a pretty little bow on top.

As the hour approached people filled the hallway. The last to arrive was Jones, followed closely by a Security man in his stern black uniform. She glanced in my direction, giving me an unfriendly smile. Though I felt no guilt, I mischievously wore my best hangdog expression. I suppressed a giggle, wondering if people once did hang dogs, and for what crimes?

We followed her inside and I took my usual seat at the far end of the great curved table. As I passed Jones, already seated in the center, she said *sotto voce*, "Hope you like fieldwork."

I turned to face her, walking backward toward my seat, and my voice remained strong and loud.

"Madam Chairperson, I *always* enjoy my work."

Before she could reply I turned my back to her and marched to my seat. I sat, adjusted my chair, and then as the meeting opened I locked eyes with her. She matched me, returning a cool, cruel gaze paired with a faint smile.

Breaking our staring contest, she opened the special meeting, apologizing for upsetting our biweekly schedule. She took far more words and time than usual, extending the moment by every possible second. Following her insincere apologies, Jones launched into a lecture on the moral integrity required to hold a subcommittee position, stressing the importance to current and future generations that degeneracy would not be allowed to threaten Nocturnia and what remained of humanity. It was a hell of a speech.

"A few days ago," she continued, "I noticed something that didn't look quite right in our media files. Of course I am no expert in the network or the computer systems, so I called on the security forces to investigate. I fear someone has breached the secure directories, possibly disseminating morally questionable media."

She gestured toward the Security representative, giving him the floor. We wasted another 10 minutes while Investigator Thomas Chen reviewed their mandate and methods. I swear that there's not a single Administration official capable of answering "Are you hungry?" without at least a five-page preamble. Finally he narrowed down to the 'data breach'.

"Subchairperson Jones contacted us fearing an unauthorized intrusion. We're happy to report that no such event took place."

Jones's eyes widened, but she quickly resumed her poker face, though as Chen spoke her eyes often darted angrily toward me.

"Our conclusion is that a high-level user accidentally transferred files from secure data storage to the public access servers."

"That's not what happened," Jones said.

"It is the most likely scenario, Chairperson Jones. While the files lacked entries that would have made them available to the colonial search engines, they were accessible by all colonists."

He turned in my direction.

"We did find access by Director Kessler."

Jones smiled again, but it quickly vanished.

"Director Kessler's quick action and outstanding diligence prevented any of the embargoed files from falling into the public's hands. By re-securing the directory—"

Jones stood and leaned over the table.

"Are you certain about that? Are you certain he didn't just entertain his own sick fetishes with those—?"

"We are quite certain. The network logs are clear. Director Kessler moved the suspected—"

"Then the network files have been tampered with!" She pointed a finger, her nail long and blood-red, in my direction, stabbing the air like a weapon. "I know this man. He's not one to let such an opportunity pass. The files *have* been altered! You need—"

Chen's voice never moved above a casual level, but the steel in it silenced her. "Chairperson Jones, a thorough investigation has been conducted. The network has not been compromised. The logs have not been altered. Instead of accusing Director Kessler of degeneracy you should be commending him. It was only his swift action that prevented your subcommittee from becoming a very public embarrassment." He stepped closer to Jones. "An embarrassment caused by your negligence with confidential materials. If you wish to press the matter we can take this to the Governing Council."

I received another withering look from Jones. I smiled and she sat, turning her attention back to Chen.

"Pardon me," she said. "I was mistaken. Of course, now that all the facts are known, this matter looks quite different."

Without a word, but with all the haughtiness of his position, Chen left. Jones invented busywork for the committee and we played along with her, offering opinions on meaningless topics and backing them up with irrelevant votes. Brandon leaned over to me and with a soft voice asked, "What the hell just happened?"

"Jones isn't everything," I answered, perhaps not as softly as Brandon would have liked.

The meeting concluded and we left Jones in the conference room, fuming.

★　　★　　★

As Brandon and I rode back to the theater the settled districts whizzed by in a blur.

"Are you going to tell me what happened back there?"

"I could, but I don't think you really want to know."

He paused, considering my advice. "You're probably right. I do know that you couldn't hack your way past your own password."

I laughed. He wasn't wrong there. I had never cared at all for technical gobbledygook.

"I can't take the credit, that's certain."

"I'm not sure that you would want to take the credit." He shook his head. "Hacking the colonial network is very serious. They exile people for that."

"So they should put Jones over the wall. She started this."

"No one's going to care who started it. And she didn't do anything except set you up. Even if you could prove she left the files unlocked, that's not the same, not the same at all, as going into the network and altering the damned records!"

Frustrated, I threw up my hands. "What the hell do you want, Brandon? Did you want me crucified to make Jones happy?"

"No." He sighed a heavy breath that left his shoulders sagging. He looked at me, his fedora nearly covering his dark brown eyes and face. "I just have the feeling that you're in way over your head."

"I know what I'm doing."

He snorted and said, "Tell that to Seiko."

"Why don't you? I'm sure you will anyway."

He looked momentarily puzzled and then angry.

"I didn't do that." He turned away, staring out the car's window. For the rest of the trip neither of us said a word.

When we reached the theater we climbed out and stood at the steps. The car sped off, already summoned on another call, and we silently waited for one of us to move or speak. I sensed Brandon was about to stomp up the steps and I didn't want more bad blood between us.

"I'm sorry," I blurted out.

He stopped, turned around, and stared at me from two steps higher.

"I should believe you," I continued. "And if you say you didn't send that message—"

"And I didn't."

"Then you didn't."

He smiled and descended a step. "Thank you."

I climbed and met his level. "And you don't have to worry. I'm through messing with the colonial network. Now that I'm out of Jones's trap, there's no need."

His smile faded and he took me by a shoulder. "But there's still that other woman, isn't there?"

I didn't answer. I just shrugged and he released me. Together we went inside to work but I couldn't shake the feeling that I had rejected a chance to turn back, one I should have taken.

Before long my mood turned and thoughts of Pamela danced in my head. With Jones shoved to one side, Seiko happy, and even Brandon acting less like an ass, the future looked bright. The evening's sexual antics seized my imagination.

Darkness fell and the crowd arrived. From the office window I watched as the men, women, and children filled the lobby. Maria helped people, her welcoming smile melting hearts; Patrick looked after the lobby and coat check, but with his eyes constantly darting to Maria, people warmed to him less. No doubt when Pamela arrived he'd switch his focus.

Each time the door opened my heart beat faster and each time someone other than her entered. I told myself she was wisely taking care, avoiding unwanted attention, safeguarding our secrets, but with each disappointment my apprehension grew.

The crowd thinned as performance time neared and still there was no sign of her. I waited by the office window, splitting my time between watching the lobby and the security monitors. When the last of the patrons moved into the auditorium and showtime arrived, I remained in the office, my heart thumping painfully in my chest, certain that something had happened. I took out my slate and called her, but only reached that damned message.

Maria looked up at the office window and I saw her struggle with my absence. Rather than leave her in torment, I left for the pre-show presentation. I said nothing to her or Patrick, going straight to my spot in front of the audience. As I spoke I carefully scanned the crowd, row by row, as though Pamela with her stunning beauty and flamboyant style could slip past me unnoticed. I finished the routine remarks and headed up the aisle, the houselights dimming with my hopes.

I waved wordlessly to Maria and Patrick as I returned to the office. Work proved elusive and unable to hold my attention. Every few moments I checked the monitors, searching for her face, her smile, her irresistible sexuality, but every time my hope crashed on a hard reality. Perhaps tonight she couldn't slip Forge's grasp, perhaps while I waited the unknown man held her in his sweaty pawing hands.

Seiko called and we spoke for half an hour. I let her know that not only did I escape Jones's little trap but that Jones now looked considerably worse in the eyes of Security. She wanted to celebrate, but I continued hoping futilely for Pamela's arrival and begged off all plans.

The frivolous family movie ended and I shuffled to the auditorium for the required Q-and-A session. The audience provided no meaningful distraction. They finally left, and with only a moderate amount of prompting even the stragglers departed quickly. I helped Maria and Patrick close up and secure the drones and the stations. After they left I stood alone in the lobby, wishing for Pamela.

I wasted a few more hours watching films and not remembering anything of them, my thoughts fixed only on her. Finally I went to bed and fitfully slept.

★   ★   ★

My slate's alarm shattered my lousy sleep, pulling me from an intermittent slumber into a barely conscious stupor. I fumbled for the damned thing, knocking it to the floor, and sent it halfway across my bedroom. After tumbling out of bed, I stumbled to it, and answered the all-too-early call.

"Jason!" Pamela appeared in the screen. Her voice was low but panicked and she held her slate badly, making it hard to see her face. "Jason! Let me in."

Adrenaline dispelled my grogginess. That didn't look like the theater's entrance.

"Where are you?"

"Not far." She strangled a sob and then continued. "I was too afraid to take a car all the way."

She turned her camera and I saw her face was bruised with one eye swelling.

"If you'll unlock the door I'll run across. I don't think anybody is watching."

Fear, anger, and a host of other emotions flooded my brain. I wanted to kill. I wanted to break Forge. I wanted to make him suffer.

"Jason, please."

Her pleading tore at my heart, inflaming me more, but also breaking me out of my fight or flight loop.

"Of course."

I unsecured the security system and unlocked the door.

"Hurry."

Not bothering with nightclothes I hurried down to the lobby, arriving just as Pamela burst through the door. She slammed it closed, throwing her weight against the door as she slid it into place. At first I feared someone was chasing her, but then I saw the slump of her body, the quivering in her calves, and knew she was near collapse from exhaustion. I locked the door and hurried over. I caught her just as she fell toward the floor.

"It's okay," I said, those useless words everyone spouts in a crisis. "Everything's going to be okay."

We moved to a lobby sofa and I gently placed her down on it. I sat, letting her lie back on my lap, cradling her head and stroking her thick black hair. Tears leaked from her eyes, the blackened one now swollen closed. I leaned over and kissed her on the forehead.

"What happened?"

She sniffled and even when she made ugly nasal noises I still found her irresistible.

"He's found out about us."

The words came as no surprise. No, given the bruises, the tears, and the terror, this was a turn I expected.

"Forge already knew about me."

With her one good eye she looked up at me. "Forge?"

"Well, you said he's found out—"

The last thing I expected was her laughter, but she giggled and it took her several seconds to stop.

"No, not Forge," she said. "Eddie's found out about us."

She sat up, slowly and with care, then leaned against the sofa, letting her head fall back, her neck limp.

"He knows there's a man in my life and he's very jealous." After a brief pause she continued. "He doesn't know *who* and he's not going to find out."

"I'm not scared."

"You should be. He'd kill you, Jason. I don't mean that like someone boasting, he'd really kill you." Very softly, so much so that I almost couldn't hear it, she added, "He always kills his enemies."

Neither of us said anything for a very long time. Her crying resumed, each sob stabbing my heart.

"I can't see you anymore." Her sniffles made her words almost unintelligible. "I love you, Jason, but Eddie's dangerous and I can't, I just can't let him hurt you."

"Leave him."

She refused to look me in the eye, her black hair screening her face.

"There's no place to hide. No matter what we do he'll always find us. Forge will make sure of that."

"Maybe we can bribe Forge or something."

Now she looked at me, a wan smile on her lips.

"Forge isn't a person, it's a thing, a computer." She waved a hand in the air. "I don't know where he got it or how. He calls it 'Vulcan's Forge' and it's like a Founder, only no one in the Admin knows it exists."

A Founder? All of the artificial intelligences followed programming and self-destructed. The colony's architects back on Old Earth had been very clear that once established no sentient computers were allowed in Nocturnia.

"But you could make it do things."

"Yeah, some. Eddie trusts me – a little." She turned and fell into my arms. "I wanted someone to love, someone who'd love me back, and Forge found you for me." She paused for another spasm of sobs and then continued. "I have to go. I won't let Eddie hurt you."

I held her close, the heat of her skin piercing my body, warming me with more than mere temperature.

"Can we turn him in?"

"Forge protects him. He can see every Security report."

She threw her arms around me, holding me tight.

"I don't want to let you go," I said.

She tried to push herself out of my arms, but I locked my grip and held her fast. "I'm not letting you go."

"We don't have a choice."

Fighting her struggles, I kept her in my embrace. I racked my memory for anyone on the Administration named Ed, Edward, or Eddie but came up blank.

"What if we don't go to Security? What if we go directly to the Governing Council? Surely they'd turn on one of their own gone rogue."

She stopped fighting me and held still for a moment, and then turned toward me, her face just inches from my own.

"He's not on the Council," she said. "Except for Forge, he's nobody."

Several silent moments passed as mentally things clicked into place.

"So without Forge he's got nothing?"

"Yeah."

"Can we take Forge?"

She slipped from my grip and sat up. "He'd kill you."

I reached up and stroked her cheek, avoiding the expanding bruise. "If you stay he'll kill you. Maybe not today, maybe not tomorrow, but someday."

Taking my hand in hers, she kissed each finger, and held it gently to her face. "Together," she whispered. "We'll do it together."

CHAPTER NINE

Robbery is so easy to say and yet so difficult to do. We sat there on the sofa, committed to crime and clueless as to its execution. Our silence grew, and I realized just how little I understood.

"How?" I asked, breaking the building dread.

Pamela stood and walked over to concessions. She turned around and leaned against the counter, looking at me as her long legs slid from under her red dress.

"There's got to be a way." Her eyes held a faraway look.

"How big is it? Forge?"

"Not very, maybe a yard long and half that deep and high."

"So it can be carried by one person," I said more to myself than to her as I turned the problem over. "Assuming it's not heavy."

"Not for you," she smiled, paying me a masculine compliment. "I couldn't manage it for long."

"How heavy?"

Shrugging she said, "Twenty, twenty-five pounds."

"Mm, I'm not going to sprint a long way with that, but it's not impossible. Does he ever move it around, out in the open?" An idea blossomed. "Or in a car? If you know he's going to take it somewhere, you could program the car—"

"It never leaves him. He's paranoid about it." She stopped and looked at me with hard cold eyes. "Always."

That plan dashed, I tried to think of another. "You've got to tell—"

She waved a hand in my direction, silencing me as she hurried back to the sofa, beaming with joy.

"I think I have an idea!"

Taking my hands, she knelt down, resting on her knees, while providing a distracting view of her décolletage.

"It only works with both of us," she said.

Quickly, she laid out the basics of her plan. Eddie always met new black-market customers in person. Even with Forge he feared colonial security and meeting in person allowed Forge a facial scan for undercover agents. He didn't trust a lot of people and lived alone in a 'pre-commissioned' suite of apartments. If I posed as a new customer, someone introduced by Pamela, Eddie would insist on meeting me. Once there we'd rob him of Forge and after our escape out an exit he kept ready for emergencies we'd use it to cover our tracks.

"I'm not clear," I said as she stepped me through the plot. "How are we going to rob him? From what you said there's no way even the two of us can overpower him enough to tie up."

"Forge can print pistols."

I let go of her hand. Fanatical about growing the human population, Nocturnia had only one crime punishable by death – murder. Simply having the means for murder, and any lethal gun met those criteria, resulted in exile and slow starvation.

"It's the only way," she pleaded. "You're right. Eddie's big enough, strong enough, and violent enough to tear us apart with his bare hands. If we don't have something lethal we might as well give up now."

She stood and stepped back from me, tears rolling down her face.

"If we can't do this –" sobs mangled her words but finally she got them out, "– I might as well leave now."

Pamela turned but before she moved two steps I was up and holding her in my arms.

"Okay," I said. "Just to control him and make him do as we say."

Leaning her head down, she kissed my forearms and whispered, "Of course. That's all we need."

We moved back to the sofa and completed pledging ourselves to this dangerous venture.

★   ★   ★

We stayed in each other's arms, silent within our thoughts for more than 15 minutes, the weight of the commitment a foreboding presence.

Breaking the spell, I said, "You can't go back. You have to stay here."

She pulled my arms tight around her chest. Soft and warm, her figure comforted me in the suddenly chilly air.

"I can't do that."

"I don't see how you have a choice. If you go back and he thinks you're going to betray him—"

"If he thinks that then I'm already dead, but if I don't go back he'll know it for sure and Forge *will* find me and find us."

She pulled away, stood, and began pacing in front of the sofa.

"There's no hiding."

"You said he didn't know about me."

"And he doesn't." She stopped and knelt down next to me, her clean sensual scent sweeping over me. "But if I stay here he will find out."

"I don't see how."

She waved at the lobby's security cameras. "He can see through every one of those."

A cold terror crept through me, slow and steady like an approaching killer. Pamela must have seen my reaction.

"Not right now. I've got Forge faking me elsewhere, 'cause I know Eddie checks up. But I can't keep that up without Forge, and we can't steal it if I stay here."

I stood and stared down at her. "Stealing it does no good if you're dead."

"I'm not going to get killed." She touched her swollen black eye. "He's punished me and if I'm a good girl and make him happy...."

The idea of Pamela, sweet loving Pamela, fawning over this thug like a slave enraged me. My fists clenched and I wanted to beat him then and there. She stepped over to me, took one fist in her hands and kissed my clenched fingers.

"I love you for this," she said, looking at the fist, and then she turned her deep blue eyes to me. "We have to be smart. He's not, but he is sly and vicious."

"So don't go to him," I wailed, knowing the futility even as the words escaped my lips. She had to, if we were to have any chance at all, but terror overwhelmed my rationality.

"It won't be for long, my love."

She pulled me close and kissed me, at first soft and tender, but our passion possessed us and we fell to the couch in a mad intense embrace. We didn't stay there long. Dropping clothes like snowflakes, we moved to my bed.

Much later, with the morning hours rapidly moving toward dawn, I let her leave, and every moment of her absence I'd live in fear.

★   ★   ★

The day passed slowly. I kept one monitor open to a colonial news-stream, frightened that at any moment I'd see news of an unidentified corpse. Things like that dominated the streams and Sunday gossip for weeks. Nothing appeared but throughout the day my distracted imagination envisioned the worst.

Brandon made polite conversation but I don't remember any details. With each hour and each new secret a distance expanded between us. I didn't care. I didn't care that Seiko hadn't called. The only thing that mattered was Pamela. If we made it out of this, if we stole Forge and escaped Eddie, there'd only be her in my life. With her and Forge I would fear and need nothing. Every film would be open to me, no Admin busybody like Jones could threaten us, and with Pamela there would be no screaming, crying, and messy children.

I realized while I cared for Seiko, and I truly didn't want to hurt her, I didn't love her and perhaps I never had. I'd have to break the engagement and find some way, maybe with Pamela's help, to make everything clean and spotless in my record, and maybe even find the right man for Seiko. After all, if Forge led Pamela to me surely it could find someone for Seiko.

Evening arrived without word. The crowd showed up for the performance and my frayed nerves were ready to break. Brandon had left in the late afternoon and I paced the office alone. Pamela didn't call, she didn't appear in the crowd, and with every passing moment I became more certain that Eddie had killed her. The crowd finished filing into the auditorium and still no call, no appearance. I looked at my notes for the pre-show presentation but the words lost all meaning, appearing to be merely a jumble of letters and punctuation. *Pamela* – she was my only thought, my only concern, my life.

"Mr. Kessler?" Maria's voice sounded loud in my office. "It's time for the show."

I leaned against the office window, my forehead pressed firm against the hard cool glass. She called again, this time with more concern, a trace of fear shadowing her tone.

"Mr. Kessler? Are you there?"

Who cares?

"Mr. Kessler?"

I opened my eyes and saw her staring up at the mirrored window.

"I'm here, Maria," I answered. Even to me my voice sounded tired, lifeless.

"It's time—"

"I know. Come up here, please."

I watched her pause, say something to Patrick, and then she vanished into the stairwell. Just a few moments later she buzzed at my door. I unlocked it and she walked in.

As she crossed the room her eyes darted here and there, a trace of unease crossing her face.

"You have your slate?"

"Yes, sir."

She pulled it from her bag as evidence.

"Good." I picked mine up from the desk. The face was blank, nothing from Pamela. I transferred my notes to Maria's slate.

"You're giving the talk tonight."

The color fled from her face and I thought she might faint.

"Me?" Her voice came out as a tiny squeak.

"You can do it." I fell into my big chair, nothing in my collapse an act. "I'm not well. Better you than no one."

"I can't...I've never...I don't...."

"You've heard me do it a hundred times."

"But—"

"I need you to do this, please."

"Yes, sir."

She took her slate and left. I activated the monitor, intending to observe her presentation, but then I switched it back off. Maria would do fine and nothing down there mattered anyway. Sitting in my chair, I fretted as the film ran its course. I canceled the Q-and-A. Even with my notes that sort of thing would have been beyond Maria, and frankly I had already asked too much of her. She and Patrick oversaw closing up while I waited for some call, some sign.

As I sat alone in the empty theater, the building suddenly seemed cavernous. I wandered from room to room, upstairs and downstairs, with terror tinting my thoughts. I was in the auditorium when my slate's alarm shattered the silence.

Pamela's face, taut with concern, appeared in the device. Without preamble she said, "It has to be tonight."

CHAPTER TEN

"Tonight? I need—"

"He's not the most predictable man," she said, cutting off my protests. "It's tonight or never."

My stomach seemed to drop through the floor and dizziness gripped my head. This had turned too real too quickly and I wanted out, but looking at Pamela and her bruised but healing eye, turning back stopped being an option.

My lips were dry and my throat scratchy, but I said, "Okay, what do I do now?"

She spoke fast and I followed her directions, summoning a car, but not yet setting a final destination. Pamela warned me that Eddie watched all approaching traffic. Any car with his locale as a destination set off an alarm, and she advised covering our tracks by starting out from some place other than the theater. The car arrived and I climbed in.

As I sped through the city, the dead of night made the deserted outer districts dark and foreboding. I tried not to think about what lay ahead, but instead concentrated on Pamela. The car slowed and stopped in front of the Administrative complex. Pamela darted out from the shadows. I opened the door and she scurried in as I sealed up the car behind her. Her wounded eye looked better, but the bruise remained visible.

"I didn't have a chance to divert the Security drones," she explained, breathing hard and fast from her sprint. "But I think we're okay."

She tapped her slate and the car started up, a destination in an outer district clearly marked on its screen.

I looked behind us at the Administrative complex, which was lit in the colony's pale yellow streetlights.

"Was that a good idea? Work brings me here all the time. It wouldn't be very hard to connect—"

She put a finger to my lips.

"It's one of the busiest places in the city. Day or night a car departing here is unremarkable. Eddie will look at this and think you're a careful man." She kissed me quick. "Which you are, but please, you have to trust me."

I nodded and started to slip an arm around her shoulder, but she gently refused it.

"Not now, we've got things to do."

She gave me a crash course in black-market etiquette, including the sort of prophylactics people got from Eddie. Apparently he made a tidy sum subverting Nocturnia's efforts at a population boom.

"And not just condoms," Pamela explained, "medications and drugs too. Eddie, thanks to Forge, can make it all and not one report gets back to Security."

She paused and then opened her bag. "He'll do anything to keep his empire, Jason, anything."

With her small delicate hands she pulled out first one pistol and then another, laying the second on my lap. It was a dense, deadly device that weighed more than I expected.

"Go ahead," she said. "Pick it up."

I gave her one look and then turned my attention back to the gun. Slowly, carefully, I gripped it with one hand and lifted it.

"Keep your finger off the trigger."

With a jerk I pulled my forefinger back.

"The safety's on," she said, wearing a faint smile. "But never put your finger on the trigger until you're ready to shoot."

I twisted my hand, turning the gun and looking at it from different sides.

"These are use-once-and-recycle," she said.

"One shot?"

"No, each has 13 rounds, but the gun can't be reloaded."

She turned hers over and showed me the underside of the grip.

"See? No magazine."

I did the same, examining the underside closely. It was a single printed piece. With a finger Pamela nudged the barrel away from her general direction.

"With luck we'll never fire these."

I simply nodded, scared and excited at the same time. My life, once boring and predictable, had suddenly turned frightening.

"Afterward, once Forge is set up and running, we'll recycle them and no one will ever know that they existed."

Again I could only nod. I searched for a way to fit the pistol into my overcoat pocket, but Pamela shook her head.

"They'll search you. I told you he's paranoid."

"Then how will…"

She smiled. In the passenger compartment's half-light the expression looked cruel and vicious.

"He's not paranoid enough. They won't search me."

She took the gun back, and put them away in her bag. It took a moment for the plural to penetrate the adrenaline and fear.

"They?"

"Stewart and Phil." She shrugged. "They don't come upstairs unless he sends for them. Mostly they're there to make him look tough and scare people."

"I'm already plenty scared."

Pamela leaned over and pulled me into a warm, tight hug.

"Me too, but without you, Jason, I wouldn't have the courage for this. If it weren't for you I'd be his slut forever."

A spark of pride ignited. I thought about Pamela, scared and alone with this brute, and my pride merged with anger. After tonight he'd be the one scared, he'd be the one on the run, and without Forge colonial security would be after Eddie fast.

The car slowed, turned, and then circled a block twice. I peered up at the central building. No light burned in the windows and it eclipsed the stars with a black void.

"That's not it. He's ordered the car to do this. He's watching."

She pointed to another darkened tower. "In a minute we'll head over there. Once he's certain he's safe."

"He must have lots of enemies."

Turning away from Eddie's tower, she looked at me, a contemplative expression crossing her face.

"None I've ever actually heard of. Forge has things pretty well locked down." She looked toward the tower. "Eddie's just careful."

True to her prediction, the car stopped circling and drove directly for Eddie's tower. A ramp led down to a sheltered door that rolled open as we approached. Soon we were under the tower and once the door closed behind us a small utility light came on, providing dim, shadowy illumination.

This was no vast car storage area like I had seen in so many films. Network-controlled cars made such inefficiencies unnecessary on Nocturnia, where cars zoomed from task to task, only stopping for recharging and maintenance. Pamela and I had entered a loading and unloading area for crowds, like on Founders' Day when nearly everyone turned up at the park for the holiday. Our doors popped open and I followed her out of the car.

Ahead a faint glow reflected out of a recessed doorway. Pamela strode like a general approaching a checkpoint and I followed close behind. Two large men stood at the door, beefy and well-muscled. Both wore dark blue suits printed to accentuate their broad chests and wide shoulders.

"Hey, Pammy," one said. "That shiner's looking better."

"Phil, Stewart," she said nodding to each in turn, her tone light and flirty. "Bringing new customer."

They looked me over, their faces betraying no emotion other than scorn.

"We have to search him," Phil said.

"Of course."

She stepped to one side and added, "But have I ever brought anyone that didn't pay off?"

Stewart smiled but said nothing, instead stepping in my direction.

Close up, he towered over me. With quick and pretty much bored hands he patted me up one side and down the other; he turned out my pockets, and flipped through a few screens on my slate. He shrugged to Phil and then handed back everything. Neither even hinted at searching Pamela.

She smiled, the kind that usually made my knees turn to water, and nodded toward me. After shoving everything back into my overcoat pockets, I hurried up to her and through the door. It closed behind us with a click.

She put a finger to her lips and I stayed quiet as we walked down a hallway to an elevator. Once inside the lift I figured we must be well-ensconced in the tower's interior and any lights here wouldn't be visible to the rest of the colony. I didn't like the look of Phil and Stewart and I just hoped Pamela was right about another exit.

"Showtime." Her voice was low and soft.

She opened her bag and pulled out one of the guns, handing it to me. I slid it into my overcoat pocket as the elevator slowed.

My foot started tapping fast on the floor.

It was time to meet Eddie.

★ ★ ★

We stepped out of the elevator and into opulence. The walls of several apartment suites had been knocked out and the open space that greeted us felt massive. Gold and silver trim accentuated the lighting and fine art hung on the walls, creating a general impression of beauty and somehow power.

Pamela led me across the floor, her heels clicking in tiny sharp reports against the hard flooring, past several divans and other pieces of furniture that promised decadent luxury. A light floral scent permeated the air. Off to one side I spotted a dining area with a kitchen beyond. Real fruits from tower farms were piled high on the counters. We stopped before an impressive door that was printed with a richly detailed wood grain and purely mechanical locks. She gave me an encouraging smile and then rapped sharply on the door.

A moment passed before a surprisingly jovial voice called, "Come in!"

Pamela reached for the doorknob, gave me a nod and a grim expression and then opened the door. A large office waited on the other side. In the center a rug, fabricated to mimic a freshly skinned tiger, dominated the floor, and beyond loomed a large desk with a massive chair.

The man in the chair seemed sized to fit this expansive space. When he rose he stood more than six feet tall and was well-muscled, with broad shoulders and a barrel chest that tapered sharply. He wore no coat, vest, or tie, but was dressed in a form-fitting pullover shirt and slacks so tight I could imagine him nicknamed 'Captain Tight-pants'.

Eddie came from behind the desk, reaching out with an equally large hand, and took mine with a too-tight squeeze.

"Why, hello, good to see you."

He slapped me on the back, but the friendly gesture took on an ominous color when his arm went about my shoulder and he pulled me in, directing me to a chair before his desk. My opinion didn't matter. Eddie sat me where he wanted me.

"Pammy," he said in her direction as he circled back to his seat, "you're always bringing me the best customers."

With a flirty tone she said, "I aim to please."

He leered at her, fanning my growing anger, and said, "No one pleases me like you, babe."

He cocked his head to one side, studying her face. "You should have never—"

"That's old business." Her voice held a snap. She nodded toward me. "This is new."

He turned his attention to me and despite his smile and despite his 'aw shucks' manner I sensed a menace coiled under that square face with its slightly bent nose.

"Pammy tells me you have a list of—"

His eyes turned from me to Pamela and widened with surprise. I followed his gaze and Pamela had her pistol out, holding it level and steady.

I jumped up, knocking my chair over, and clumsily pulled my own gun. With the massive desk between us I was already out of Eddie's reach, but I still took a protective step backward.

"Greedy girl," he said, in an almost melancholy voice.

"Shut up, Eddie." She turned to me and nodded to a far door. "Forge is through there."

I hesitated, looking to her and back to Eddie. "Should he be tied—?"

"Forge first. Disconnect it like I showed you, bag it, and then we'll deal with Eddie."

I started toward the door

"That would be a mistake, Pammy. You don't—"

"Say another word and I'll shoot you."

The tone in her voice chilled me and I hesitated, turning back to look.

Smirking yet with a careful tone in his voice Eddie said to me, "She's a real piece of work, our Pammy."

Pamela stretched out her arm, the gun's muzzle steady and level with his chest.

"Get it," she ordered. "He won't cause any trouble."

"No," Eddie agreed. "That's coming all by itself."

I went through the door and found Forge sitting on a desk just as Pamela had described. It presented a display with a few controls on its top, and aside from a power cable only one cord connected it directly to the colonial network. I disconnected the network connection first, switched off the main power, and as I reached for the power cord gunshots rang out.

I dashed into the office; Pamela took a cool step backward as Eddie, up and beside the desk, reached out toward her with one hand, blood spreading across his wide chest. Her gun fired again. A fragment of my mind noted how soft the shot sounded, not what I had expected. Eddie jerked, his face went slack, and then he toppled face-first, bounced off the desk and hit the floor with a dull, wet smack.

Pamela's eyes turned toward to me and she flew into my arms.

"He came at me," she sobbed into my ear. "I had to do it."

I looked down at Eddie on the floor, a pool of blood spreading from the body.

"I didn't want to," she continued as I held her, stroking her like a child.

What the hell do we do now?

"We've got to get out of here," I said. "Before anyone comes looking."

The gunshot was so soft that I doubted anyone outside of the suite heard a thing.

"Is Forge disconnected?"

"Almost."

I released her and started back toward the other room. She grabbed my hand and pulled my attention to her.

"Not yet. We can use it to get rid of Eddie," she said.

"You already did that."

"No, I mean his body. We can't have anyone finding it. Not while we're still trying to escape."

I looked past her to Eddie, face-down and unmoving.

"Forge?"

"Eddie's done it before," she explained. "Forge fabricates some sort of enzyme stuff that just dissolves bodies."

My stomach flipped and threatened to empty itself. She was starting toward the other room when Eddie moaned.

She stopped and we both stared at him. A finger twitched but other than that he didn't move. I stepped one pace closer and studied him. His back moved as he breathed short shallow breaths. Pamela moved around me and knelt next to Eddie, pointing her gun at his head.

"No!"

I rushed over and grabbed the pistol, pulling it out of line. She fought me for a moment and then let me point the gun harmlessly toward a wall. I tried to look her in the eye, but she stared at Eddie with intense, burning hatred.

I said, "We can't just kill him."

"It's only finishing what we started."

I managed to walk her a step or two away from Eddie, carefully avoiding the growing pool of blood.

"Defending yourself is one thing," I explained. "Shooting him in the head, when he's wounded and helpless, is plain murder."

"He's dangerous." She tore her eyes away from Eddie and looked at me. "You have no idea. If you did, if you knew half the things he's done, you'd shoot."

"I hope not." Again I moved her a bit farther away. "He can't hurt us. Nothing has changed. We take Forge, we cover our tracks, and he can't find us."

Her face turned hard and grim and for a moment I expected her to throw a punch at me, but then she sighed and her shoulders dropped.

"He's probably going to die anyway."

She was right. We couldn't risk calling any of his people for help. Maybe they'd find him in time, maybe they wouldn't. Either way I wanted to get out of there without becoming a murderer.

"Help me with Forge," I said and pulled her toward the other room. Pamela had acquiesced but I wouldn't have bet that her anger had run its course. She gave Eddie one last glare and followed me.

Quickly we disconnected Forge and slipped it into a bag. I was hefting it over one shoulder when an alarm sounded. Pamela, moving faster than me, hurried to the desk and snatched up Eddie's slate.

She cursed and yelled, "More customers coming!"

Teetering under Forge's weight, I hurried to her side. The slate announced Phil and Stewart had already cleared new arrivals. A bright red icon flashed as the elevator climbed the building.

"This way."

Pamela led me through several rooms, including Eddie's bedroom, a gaudy, tasteless affair. We emerged from the powered and occupied parts of the floor into dark deserted hallways.

"No way can we get to the other elevator," she said, keeping her voice to a whisper. "So we have to use the stairs. Can you do it?"

I nodded and we were off.

★　　★　　★

We used our slates as lights, and even then only switching them on here and there, frightened about possibly drawing attention. The unfinished hallways were a maze of support studs, exposed piping, and wiring without any signage. We made several wrong turns and then doubled back to search for the stairwell. Once we entered an exterior suite and through the darkened window I saw Nocturnia laid out, the bright buildings appearing like some fabled mirage.

I stopped and pulled out my slate. Covering the face with one hand I activated it, casting a faint glow into the hallway.

"We're never going to find that stairwell." I kept my voice low, though we had yet to see anyone else. "We have to get to that other elevator."

Pamela leaned against a post, a shadow in the gloom.

"That's never going to work. They've found Eddie by now and if they're not searching for us they will be."

The gun in my pocket seemed to pull down on my overcoat with more force than its weight justified. What if they found us? Would there be a gunfight in the dark? I looked at the unfinished wall and exposed cables dangling behind Pamela.

"Can we hook up Forge?" I asked. "Maybe get a map or some kind of help?"

She turned and followed my gaze, then smiled. "Let's find a more secluded spot."

Keeping one slate turned down low and pointed at the floor, we set off again. We found a room where the walls on all sides sheltered us from sight, and quickly slipped inside. I set Forge down, my shoulder aching from the bag's strap, and Pamela pulled out the device.

I watched closely as she connected a network cable.

"Is there power out here?" I asked.

"Forge has an internal supply, but God knows how long it's good for."

"Forge reporting ready." The almost-natural voice sounded loud in the shadowy room and Pamela hurriedly lowered the volume.

"Establish a connection," she ordered.

"A fully operative interface requires independent power and 4,357 seconds to establish," Forge replied.

"All we need is a map," I whispered.

"We don't need to fake anything right now, Forge. Just establish a standard connection."

"Security directives forbid direct connections that are not fully operative."

Pamela's voice turned hard and unforgiving. "Forge, we need that connection."

"Security directives forbid direct connections that are not fully operative."

She turned to me. "This is no good."

I started to answer when the soft sound of footsteps echoed through the hallway. I moved to the door and waved for Pamela to switch off her slate. I turned off my own and then pulled the door open an inch.

Light reflected off a wall at a junction in the hallway and voices joined the footsteps. The light grew brighter and the footsteps louder. Stewart and Phil turned the corner. Phil carried a light and a pistol, while Stewart had only a gun. They stopped at the intersection, flashing their light down the corridor. I threw myself back from the door, certain they'd seen me. Our room was dark save for the very faint light coming from Forge's main display.

Moving an ear to the barely open door, I listened. Their voices were low and indistinct, making it impossible for me to understand anything. The footsteps grew louder and the flashlight's beam jumped about in wild arcs.

"Nothing down here," Stewart said.

"They had this planned. They're long gone."

The footsteps stopped and now their voices sounded clear and strong. In the dim light from Forge's main display Pamela's face looked lean, mean, and feral. She crouched next to the device, one hand gripping her pistol.

"They didn't take the elevator," Stewart argued.

"If she took Forge, you think she couldn't hack the elevators?"

I listened as they turned around and their footsteps receded. I waited several moments, blood rushing in my ears and my heart pounding in my chest. Finally I moved over to Pamela.

"It sounds like they left."

Her gun hand didn't relax as she continued gripping the pistol tight. I put a hand on hers and gently lowered the pistol.

"It's okay," I said. "They've left."

I looked down at Forge. "They think you've hacked the elevators."

"I did, but only the back one." She put the pistol away. "He didn't say he had more customers, the idiot!"

"I take it we can't get to that elevator?"

She shook her head, her black hair nearly invisible in the faint light. "We can't go back into Eddie's apartment. Not now."

"So we still need to find those stairs. And you've never taken them?"

"Ten flights? Hardly."

We fell silent and the seconds passed without any more signs of searching. Pamela was reaching for Forge's controls when an idea blossomed. I touched her hand, keeping Forge powered a bit longer.

"Maybe Forge doesn't need a connection to help us. See if it has a building map stored locally."

She checked and a few moments later we had a full map in our slates. We de-powered Forge and packed it back into the bag.

"Next time we pull a heist let's get that map first," I said as I shouldered the bag. Despite the attempt at humor my stomach remained in a tight cramp and my heart was beating fast and strong.

Pamela took the lead and we left the room. This time finding the stairs presented no trouble; in fact we had passed that unmarked door at least twice. With the door closed behind us, we both switched our slates to full illumination and began a downstairs march.

Ten flights of stairs carrying at least 25 pounds quickly tired me. We slowed as my gait became unstable and I used the railing, afraid of tumbling. Neither of us spoke. I don't think our silence was from fear of discovery. The terrible memory of murder made me mute. In every shadow I saw Eddie with his ruined chest covered in blood.

I had never seen anyone die, and certainly not murdered. When the

Administration found him what would they do? I assumed that with Forge's help Eddie had vanished from the colonial databases, becoming an invisible man. I imagined panic would run through Security. Not only had an invisible man existed but their utter ignorance of his existence could only terrify the government. Trouble was coming for everyone. For Pamela and me only Forge provided safety.

My calves screamed with pain. I was leaning heavily on the rail, barely able to walk, when we reached the ground floor. Pamela held one finger up and I stayed quiet while she opened the door. The night air, still carrying a hint of the far-off bay, blew in, cooling me with an almost sensual delight. She nodded, then left, and I hobbled after her.

Outside stars filled the sky except where Companion's massive bulk presented its dim glowing sphere. We switched off our slates and moved along the street guided only by Companion's light. Pamela knew where she wanted to go and we hurried along until we had crossed an intersection and followed a ramp down into another decommissioned loading area. A small door was unlocked and we entered.

Inside several lights burned bright and my eyes watered in the sudden brilliance. Pamela stopped short and I nearly ran into her.

"Shit!"

She turned and looked around the loading bay, but I couldn't see what she was searching for.

"What is it?"

"Eddie's car."

She stalked over to one spot and threw up her hands in frustration. "He keeps one right here, for emergencies."

Looking down at the spot where the car was supposed to be, she fell silent and squatted down. She touched the hard surface and brought up a bloody finger.

"They've taken him." She looked at me hard. "If he were dead they wouldn't have done that."

"Well, we're not going to become murderers, Pammy."

She stood, pulling herself up to her full height. "Don't ever call me that."

"Sorry," I muttered, ashamed at throwing Eddie and his abuse into her face. "Let's figure a way out of this."

She nodded and came back close to me.

"We can't take the streets," she said, sitting on the ground. I set down the bag and joined her. My legs trembled and quaked in relief. Pain, like a thousand slender daggers, probed my muscles. I breathed heavily, scared, tired, and confused.

Pamela turned my attention to the business at hand.

"There are no drone patrols around this building but, thanks to Forge, Security thinks there are. If we go more than a few blocks we'd be in danger of getting spotted."

I nodded but said nothing. We couldn't stay here. Maybe in the morning Pamela wouldn't be reported missing, but I would be, and in Nocturnia few people went missing. Unless I showed up there'd be trouble.

She moved close to me and snuggled under my arm.

"I'm sorry for snapping," she said. "This is too much for me."

We sat illuminated by the one light, the bag with Forge just behind me, Pamela in my arms, feeling trapped. If only we had some place to hide for a couple of hours with power and network connections. My apartment had both but it was too far away. Eddie's place was just a block away but I doubted we'd get a friendly reception. The rest of the district, unfinished and unpopulated, presented us with places to hide, but if we breached a building that would only bring Security down on our heads.

"Maybe we could sneak back into Eddie's tower and hide out on another floor, then connect Forge and when it's fully operative secure transportation?"

Pamela shook her head. "The only floor with working power is Eddie's."

"It makes sense."

Of course Eddie wouldn't have powered up the entire building. Covering that much usage would have just made Forge's task that much harder, not to mention with so much of the building unfinished there would be a lot of physical work involved just wiring the power. A thought tickled at the back of my mind. Something about the wiring, but I couldn't make it appear.

I stood up. The short rest had helped but I quickly sat back down, my legs protesting the exertion. Wiring, the answer was in the wiring, I knew it. The solution popped into my head and with it adrenaline that banished my fatigue.

"Eddie can cover tracks in the network, but to get his little headquarters set up he had to physically get the power connected, from the main trunk line."

She nodded, following along.

"He couldn't have done it with Security watching, so that means the main lines running his building have had their monitors hacked. If we can get down there, Forge would have everything it needs, time, power, and network access."

We hugged and kissed longer than was advisable, then I scooped up the bag and we headed back toward the street. Staying close to the shadows, we moved down the block, back toward Eddie's tower. Pain ran through my calves, but hope and excitement pushed me onward.

"How many people does Eddie have in there?" I kept my voice to a whisper.

"Not a lot. Most of the people working for him live in the city center."

The building and driveway ramp to the loading area looked dark. We stood there, our backs against the neighboring tower, working up our courage to go back into Eddie's den. Time was not on our side. We had the building map from Forge and I had already located the main trunk access in the basement, but how long would it take to get there and how long to find the right place to plug in and connect? I didn't know any of the answers and this night wouldn't last. Finally I took her hand in mine and we dashed across the street.

Pamela used her slate to light our way as we hurried down the ramp. All the lights were out. We found the door and pushed it open. Evidently in their hurry to get Eddie to a doctor they hadn't bothered to lock up.

Once we were inside I consulted the map and headed toward a basement stairwell. If the access there was locked I could only hope that between the two of us we might be able to break it down. The building seemed silent and dead as we hurried along the hallways and I couldn't help but wonder – just where had they taken Eddie? If he showed up at a hospital that would also blow open the entire 'invisible man' issue, but I imagined given the choice between dying and being exposed, Eddie wanted to live.

I was surprised that the basement door was unsecured. No matter the reason it was a godsend to us that night. It didn't take long to find the main trunk hatch, but it did take the both of us to lift it. Once we did a ladder descended into a tunnel filled with cables and piping. I went first and Pamela lowered the bag to me before she followed. We wasted another 25 minutes searching for a network access nodule and only then were we able to connect Forge.

★   ★   ★

Few lamps lit the tunnel, leaving us to sit in gloom and shadow as we waited. In the dark, in the silence, my mind replayed the evening's horrific events: Eddie flinching with each bullet, falling to the floor, blood splattering everywhere. He had been an evil man who had forced Pamela into sexual slavery, but still each bullet strike, each fountain of blood provoked sympathy. I tried to tell myself he had brought this down upon himself, and he deserved it, but murder, even in self-defense, came with terrible guilt.

In the shadow and darkness Pamela's face looked long, thin, and gaunt. With her eyes unfocused, she sat absorbed in her thoughts. My guilt increased. I had only watched the shooting, while Pamela now had to live having killed him. I slid over to her and put an arm around her shoulders. She tensed and I almost pulled away, but then she relaxed and nestled against me. We said nothing. There seemed to be no words for the moment, so we waited in silence.

In that deserted tunnel the hour and a half seemed like days but finally Forge signaled its readiness. Pamela started to summon a car, but I put a hand on hers.

"Wait."

Her head snapped in my direction and fierce anger burned in her eyes.

"I've waited down here long enough." Her voice cracked and she shot hard angry stares at me.

"They –" I gestured to the tower above us, "– may have come back. I don't think we should go back up the way we came. Have Forge get us a car, but several blocks away, and make sure we're not seen."

She smiled, but much of her body remained taut, her muscles tense.

"You're right." She brushed her long hair from her face and added, "I'm not very good at this."

"Neither of us is, but together we'll do okay."

She finished making arrangements for a car, obtained a map of the main trunk tunnels, and had Forge unlock a nearby access. Once everything was in place we disconnected Forge, bagged it up, and I slung it over my shoulder. My legs shook and nearly buckled. Pamela slipped under my arm and supported me like a crutch. Following the map, in about 20 minutes we reached the access, a recessed doorway located on a smaller side tunnel.

I tested the door and it opened easily. We stepped out into a drainage channel, climbed a set of steps, and emerged onto a deserted street where a car waited. The door popped open as we approached and with my muscles trembling from exhaustion and stress, I collapsed into the seat. Pamela shoved and helped me across until she could climb in. The door sealed behind her.

She fell heavily into my arms. I held her as tight as my exhaustion allowed, trying to soothe away her fears, but she quivered all the way to the theater. Finally away from the deserted outer district, finally back in familiar surroundings, finally safe, we fell into bed together and, fully clothed, slept.

CHAPTER ELEVEN

I awoke to gunfire. Adrenaline flooded my bloodstream, sending my heartbeat racing as I jerked and fell out of the bed. Slowly my mind cleared and the gunfire resolved into the loud blaring of my morning alarm. I shouted to the network to silence the alarm and with unsteady balance I climbed to my feet.

Standing there in the previous night's clothes, dizzy and with a pounding headache, I remembered the robbery and murder through a fog of unreality, as though it had happened to somebody else. I half expected to find everything, including Pamela, had been an elaborate dream.

As I looked back at the bed, reality cut through my mental fog. Pamela lay spread across the bed sleeping, evidently undisturbed by the alarm. Like me she still wore her clothes from the previous night. Her dress was hiked up toward her waist, exposing a pale luminous leg, and she had thrown her arms across her face, blocking the light from her eyes.

I stripped off my soiled and ruined clothing, shoved the material into the recycler, and made my way to the shower. Two hours had barely touched my exhaustion and even after a cold shower I wanted nothing more than days of deep sleep. Abandoning such fantasies, I dressed for the day and stumbled to the kitchen. I had just begun ordering breakfast from the fabricator when Pamela sidled up behind me and slipped both arms around my waist. She put her head against my back and sighed deeply.

"You need sleep," she said.

"So do you."

"So, let's do it."

"I have to work."

She pulled at my hand, tugging me toward the bedroom, but I stood firm and finished ordering breakfast.

"You have to sleep," she insisted.

"I wish I could."

I turned around and took her in my arms, pulling her in close and tight. My knees threatened to buckle and my calves screamed with pain as I leaned in to her, wanting nothing more than to close my eyes.

"If anyone comes looking for me and sees you...." I paused, tired and thickheaded. "Then last night was for nothing."

Pamela looked up into my face. Her eyes, even bleary with sleep, were still the loveliest I had ever seen. She said nothing, just nodded and let her head fall against my chest. We stood there, supporting each other through our fatigue, until the fabricator finished. I pulled back from her and retrieved breakfast. She moved to the table and sat.

After taking the plate to the table, I used a slice of toast as a small plate for myself, loading it with about half, leaving the rest for Pamela.

"Once we have Forge running we can use it to cover excess food production," I said around the open-faced sandwich of toast and egg.

Pamela began delicately eating.

"It can," she said around bites. "No trouble there."

I nodded and quickly drank half of my coffee, leaving the rest for her. I knew enough to know one of the most common ways 'degenerate cohabitation' was discovered was from mismatched fabrication and occupancy totals. Certain that Pamela wasn't about to make that sort of mistake, I headed out.

No one else had arrived yet but I still left my apartment with caution. I crossed the hallway and entered the office. Though it was Wednesday and no films were scheduled for that night, there remained plenty of work and I expected Brandon soon.

I tried to focus on work, readying snippets and synopses, reviewing reports, writing, editing, and revising proposals, but sleep stalked me and even with a steady supply of coffee, my attention wavered.

"You look like crap," Brandon said.

I blinked and looked up from the interface. He sat at his desk, his coat already off and tie loosened, working. How long had he been there?

"Thanks."

He ignored my sarcasm. "Seriously, did you sleep at all last night?"

"Not much."

I looked over at the lobby monitors. Maria and Patrick crisscrossed the lobby, hard at work. My thoughts fogged and it looked wrong.

"Why not?"

Brandon jerked back my attention.

"Huh?"

He got up and crossed over to my desk. He pulled up a chair and sat close, peering intently into my face.

"Why didn't you sleep, Jason?"

Befuddled, I nearly told him. Unlike others, keeping secrets did not come to me instinctively.

"Nightmares." Well, it wasn't really a lie, just metaphorical.

He nodded but didn't say anything, though his face betrayed a longing to give me a long lecture.

"Coffee's not doing the job," he said as he stood. "We need to get you something more effective."

"Doesn't matter," I mumbled. "No movie tonight. I'll sleep like the dead."

He stopped and gave me a long hard look. "You haven't read your messages?"

Of course I hadn't. I'd been working. I flipped back through the files and folders and found my messages, all unread. Too exhausted to remember exactly what I had done, I scanned them.

"Oh, Christ."

"Don't blaspheme." Where Seiko reprimanded me seriously, Brandon was only half-serious.

"You didn't read them," he continued. "We've got, oh, about three hours or so before Jones gets here."

She wanted to inspect the facility and all the data files. I needed to stall this, find some excuse to put it all off for at least one day, but my numbed brain locked up like a malfunctioning interface.

"I can fabricate some pep," Brandon offered.

I nodded, unable to conceive a counter-argument. Everyone in Nocturnia had an authorized supply of pep, and a lot of people used it. Taming an alien world for most people consumed a lot of hours, but if anyone asked why I needed it I'd have no answer.

He placed the pills in my hand along with another mug of coffee. Surrendering to the inevitable, I took them. Within moments the medication refreshed me, filling me with artificial energy. Later, there would be hell to pay. Brandon and I slaved away through the morning, readying ourselves for Jones, but my thoughts never ventured far from Pamela.

★   ★   ★

Before Jones arrived I hurried over to my apartment while Brandon finalized our reports. I closed the door quickly behind me, locked it, and went straight to the bedroom, but it was empty. I looked in the shower but she wasn't there either. Seeing her in neither the kitchen nor dining room, I began to panic until I found her in the study with Forge set up on my personal desk, power and network cables connected. She wore one of my shirts, and only that. From the look of it she had taken it from the recycler.

"My love," she said, her voice low and sultry.

I crossed to the desk and took her up in my arms. We kissed and embraced, our bodies pressed together. The shirt's thin fabric concealed nothing of her figure as my hands slid around her curves. Our kissing grew passionate and before I lost all control I pulled away.

"No time," I whispered. "Today, things are not going great."

She gave me a puzzled look.

"Jones is coming to 'inspect'. Of course that's just an excuse to harass me and search for something she can hang me with."

"Bitch."

I nodded.

"I know you're going to stay out of sight." I kissed her quick on the forehead. "You're too sharp to pop out and give the game away, but make sure everything up here is as quiet as an empty church."

Pamela laughed and said, "I once knew this preacher, after hours his church was anything but quiet. Don't worry, I'll do something silent, like read."

"That's my girl."

I moved to the kitchen and fabricated a quick lunch, a cover story for visiting my apartment.

"Do you think she'll do anything with the security files?"

It took me a moment to realize Pamela meant Jones.

"She might, but I don't think that's much of a danger." I gave her a smile. "All the really interesting things happened after I shut down for the night and the monitors were off."

She moved over to me as I took the food out of the fabricator.

"After they were *supposedly* shut off – Jason, those could have been activated remotely."

"If she had done that we would already be in front of a judge for moral degeneracy."

"I guess you're right." She didn't sound convinced.

"You don't think so."

"That bitch has been after you long before I came along, right? Maybe she's been activating those monitors already, looking for a club to beat you with, but with everything that's happened lately this might have been her first chance to inspect them."

I slipped a slice of fake potato into my mouth and thought while I munched. Pamela was right and we couldn't ignore the possibility.

"Can Forge verify that?" I asked.

She nodded. "I'm not familiar with the theater's network. That business with the movie files was more about the Admin directories. Can you show me some of them, at least the security ones, and I'll work on it this afternoon."

"Sounds like a plan."

I took out my slate and accessed the security interface and then handed it to her. After a short explanation Pamela understood it enough to direct Forge. I gave her a long, deep parting kiss.

"We're an unbeatable team," I said before hurrying back to the office.

I slipped through the door, my plate of food in one hand, just as Brandon sat upright at his desk.

"That took a while," he said, though his tone was decidedly offhanded.

"I changed my mind three or four times." I moved over to his desk. "How are we looking?"

"Not bad. The sociological uptake reports are good, and both attendance and home viewership are climbing. If Jones wants to argue we're wasting resources the facts are on our side."

As I ate I looked over his shoulder and scanned through the numbers. Naturally, I found nothing amiss. Brandon understood social science with an intuitive grasp I never matched. His eye for artistic style and popular appeal, however, left something to be desired, but that's why we made a perfect team.

"I have a new slate of proposed titles," I said, moving over to my desk.

"Hopefully they're better than that last list. We need to calm down Jones, and socially 'challenging' material is not the way to go."

"Give me some credit for brains."

He said nothing but followed me over and looked up at the office's main display as I threw up the various listings. Finding acceptable fare for exhibition remained a challenging task. The deep digital storage aboard the Ark had preserved more than two centuries of popular mass media. The builders had preferred to err on the side of including something even if they found it objectionable. However, the Administration enforced strict guidelines, as oxymoronic as that sounds, on what constituted acceptable media that did not risk corrupting our citizens' fragile moral character. Later period works were tagged with endless metadata that made selecting and excluding media fairly straightforward, but most of the twentieth-century films possessed only scant descriptions, and except for a few, no critical reviews and essays.

While Jones walled off entire directories based on vague genre definitions, combing through the rest of the archives was still laborious and time-consuming. My listing reflected the last few weeks' work, but I also included projections indicating that I would soon greatly expand the number of approved titles.

Brandon looked over the list without much reaction until he reached the projections.

"There's no way you can meet those numbers."

"I have a new algorithm that'll open up the process."

He shook his head.

"If it doesn't work, Jones will have your head." He pointed to the screen. "Make a promise like that and fail and she'll use that to toss you out."

I smiled. "I won't fail."

With Forge sitting in the next room I knew that I could more than double my productivity while actually doing a hell of a lot less work. Of course I couldn't share my plan with him. There was so much here he really did not want to know. I planned on neutralizing Jones and maybe even eventually replacing her.

"Trust me."

He started to say something, but a chime alerted us to Jones's arrival.

We proceeded to the lobby and arrived just as Jones entered. She wore a red dress, the color of fresh blood, and a matching hat. Taking her time, she made a production of removing her hat and gloves. True to her duplicity, she warmly greeted Maria and Patrick, calling each by name and inquiring about their families, leaving Brandon and me waiting. Once she finished playing the thoughtful and considerate official, she finally turned her attention to us.

"Gentlemen," she said, a touch of ice creeping into her tone. "Shall we get started?"

Jones insisted on a physical inspection of the facilities. Of course with all the automated drone assistance there was little chance that anything would be amiss and yet we moved through every room, every space, until she pronounced herself satisfied. After that we moved to the office and the tedious network inspection.

She drank our coffee and gave us condescending looks as she studied our reports and proposals. She even engaged in work chitchat, but her tone remained cool, aloof, and formal until even Brandon's patience wore thin. When we finished with the expected reports she demanded access to the theater's network and data storage. We couldn't refuse and I trusted that sweet Pamela's work had already secured this front, but Brandon looked concerned.

Jones wasted another two hours searching fruitlessly through the playback records. Over her shoulder, and receiving her wicked evil eye as a reward, I noticed her search concentrated on the night I fell for the trap. Finally, with more than a hint of irritation, she shut down the applications and glowered at us.

"I don't know how you altered the records, Kessler, but everyone here knows you did."

"I have no idea what you're talking about," I said, a strong current of sarcasm coloring my voice. Brandon rolled his eyes but said nothing.

"Bullshit."

She stood and stalked over until she was just inches from me. If she hadn't been so short it might have been intimidating, but instead I giggled.

"Laugh while you can. I know you accessed those files. I also know there's someone else involved in all this."

My giggles stopped.

"There's no way you hacked the colonial network." She sneered and added, "You're too stupid."

"Chairperson," Brandon snapped. "Personal abuse is a violation of the Administration Code of Ethics. You owe—"

"I owe him nothing!"

"Yes, ma'am, you do. Jason's been cleared of any wrongdoing—"

"And you know that's—"

"What I know –" Brandon put real steel into his voice, "– is that he has been cleared, and that verdict has already been entered into the record. I also know we can file a complaint against you for harassment and abuse."

"Do it," she dared. "Because I don't think you will."

She backed off from us and began gathering her things. "I've gotten anonymous reports that Kessler's involved in some rather unsavory and very immoral sexual liaisons. If he's been using Administration facilities, including the quarters we were foolish enough to provide, then he'll be tossed over the wall."

With her bag under her arm, she stepped close to Brandon as she approached the door. "And if he's been using this facility, then it's fairly certain you know about it."

She looked at me. "Security is already searching your monitor files. What do you think they'll find?"

Wearing a smug expression, she left.

Brandon looked at me as I crossed to the office sofa and collapsed. "Well?"

"She won't find anything."

He put his arms akimbo. "Is that because you made it vanish or because there's nothing to find?"

"She won't find anything," I insisted.

Either angry or frustrated, Brandon stormed to his desk and resumed working.

★   ★   ★

We worked through the afternoon. The pep faded from my bloodstream, replaced by exhaustion. Even with my eyelids drooping and sleep calling to me I couldn't ignore Brandon's stern, uncompromising silence.

"Brandon."

I rose and went over to him. "Listen, I don't want to leave it this way."

"You really haven't thought it through, have you?"

I shook my sleep-deprived head. "I'm not following you."

"Jones said she'd gotten an anonymous tip."

The light lit up, though in my state I expected nothing more than a flickering candle over my head. "And there's no way you did that."

"I like my job."

He stood up. Thanks to my slouching and desire to go horizontal, he loomed. A silent beat passed between us and then again I understood.

"I'm sorry," I said. "I shouldn't have accused you."

"I wouldn't do that." He placed a hand on my shoulder. The extra weight almost sent me to the floor. "But someone is doing it, and they mean you no good."

He gathered up his slate and started out. He stopped at the doorway, looked at me, then he adjusted his tie and set his hat atop his head.

"I trust you when you promise that Jones will find nothing. After that bit with the directory it's clear you've got someone in your back pocket, but Jason, be careful. People like that only look out for themselves."

He left the door open and vanished down the stairs. Unsteadily I stumbled to my apartment.

I stepped through the door to an empty living room. I closed the door behind me and collapsed against it, letting its comforting rigidity hold me upright. After a few moments Pamela poked her head out of the bedroom down the short hallway. I nodded and she rushed to me. She grabbed me by the shoulder and held me upright.

"Jason, are you okay?"

I nodded, too tired for speech.

"What's wrong?" Panic edged her voice.

"Tired," I mumbled. "I need sleep."

"My poor man."

She threw one arm under mine as she half carried and half led me back to the bedroom. I fell face-first into the bed and slept.

★   ★   ★

I awoke hungry, thirsty, and with a modicum of energy. I leveraged myself upright and changed from my rumpled suit into something more casual. Feeling modestly human, I searched for Pamela.

As I approached the study I heard her voice very softly commanding Forge. I couldn't untangle her complex and detailed orders before I arrived.

"The dead walk," she said as I entered.

"Not feeling anywhere nearly as dead."

I asked the time and the network advised me it was just nearing 10 in the evening, not as late as I had feared. I stepped over to her. She was now fully clothed in an off-white dress but with scandalously bare shoulders and a plunging neckline. Taking her in my arms, I kissed her deeply and she enthusiastically participated. We continued for several moments until my stomach growled loud enough to shatter our mood.

"I didn't know the Ark brought lion embryos," she said.

She pulled away and turned her attention back to Forge.

"If I don't get fed soon I'll be eating you."

She smiled, her black hair falling and half concealing her face. "Promises."

I moved next to her and studied Forge's main display filled with files, folders, and directories. I waved my fingers questioningly toward the device.

"While you slept I worked," she said, adding, "Typical man."

I didn't rise to her baiting and let her continue.

"Eddie Nguyen used this for everything, but I only know maybe a tenth of what he was up to. I'm too scared to delete at random, so one by one I've been working out his scams and businesses."

I laughed under my breath when she mentioned his full name. She looked at me with incomprehension.

"You haven't watched as many movies as I have."

I quickly explained how back on Old Earth names were tied very closely to ethnic heritage and that our Eddie was about as far-flung from the ancestry of that surname as one could be and still be from the same planet. The mention of Eddie did spark another curiosity in me.

"We should see if Eddie's turned up."

"Dead, hopefully."

I didn't join her in the sentiment, but I didn't contradict her either.

"Forge, can you search all the databases, public and secure, to see if Eddie's been reported at any hospital or doctor's office."

"That task would take 354 seconds for public databases, including all private postings and communications. To intercept colonial security communication no deeper than a 'classified' level will require 3,798 seconds. For all classifications of secret or above the time factors increase to—"

"Classified will do," I said. "Alert me when you're ready."

"You are not authorized to initiate tasks."

I looked over at Pamela.

She held up a hand and ordered, "Forge, you are to give Jason Kessler identical access privileges to my own, confirm."

"Confirmed."

I repeated the order and this time Forge began working.

"Now," I said, taking her by the hand, "we eat."

We ate in the dining room. I ordered the lights lowered for a soft romantic atmosphere. Pamela told me that Forge had already been at work on my fabricator's reporting, covering all our excess production of food and clothing.

"Where did Eddie get that thing?" I asked.

"I always assumed he made it."

In the soft lighting her skin shimmered like pearl and her dark hair nearly vanished into the shadows, highlighting her lovely face.

"Really? Was he an engineer?"

"Before he was a criminal?" She shrugged. "I don't know what he was. He never talked about his past, even though he loved talking about himself."

"He just didn't strike me as someone, well, smart enough to build Forge. And how do you build it without the Admin knowing you built it?"

"I don't care." She reached across to my hand and took it in her own. Warm, soft, and firm, her touch soothed me.

"Forge brought me to you. That's all that matters." She squeezed tight. "Even when I get a place, you'll always be mine."

A place. Of course Pamela couldn't stay here, not even under normal circumstances, but with Jones butting in and looking for degeneracy, living with me would be idiotic. I explained to her about Jones and the anonymous tips.

"I already have Forge working on the security files," she said. "We'll make sure that bitch finds nothing."

An idea popped into my head.

"Maybe Forge can even tell us who the snitch is."

Pamela smiled and said, "If there is a snitch. Jones might have lied to panic you into giving yourself away." She leaned over and kissed me. "But we're too smart for her."

After dinner we returned to the study.

*   *   *

Forge continued working in the study and I put the question to it, "Forge, who created you?"

"That information is beyond your access classification."

I looked to Pamela and she tried, but Forge shut her out as well.

"There are still a lot of applications that Eddie created," she suggested. "Maybe I'll unlock it once I've gotten them cleared out."

I shrugged. Finding out who made it didn't strike me as terribly important. All the danger lay behind us.

"Results on network search for Eddie Nguyen," Forge announced. "No reports."

"What do you think that means?" Pamela asked.

"I know it means he didn't make it to a hospital or doctor. Without Forge there's no way to hide that sort of treatment."

She cracked a sly smile. "He's dead."

"It's a good bet."

"I don't feel sorry," she confessed. "I know that makes me a bad person, but I don't."

I came around the desk and took her in my arms. "No, you're not a bad person. After what you've been through no one can blame you."

We worked sifting through Eddie's files. Drugs, unregistered residences, prostitution, sexual orgies, there didn't seem to be a moral crime that he didn't manage without Forge. Pamela was right about his paranoia. I found a lot of applications devoted to keeping an eye on the security forces and their communications. There was even a program for tracking every car's course, with alarms for any movement toward his home.

And one other transportation-related alarm.

"What's this?"

Pamela stepped over next to me.

"I don't know."

I looked again but the map coordinates didn't make any sense. I threw them into a mapping application and studied them on the room's main display. The map showed a spot 500 kilometers – Forge didn't seem to be set up at all to use miles but performed everything in scientific measurements – north of the city, well beyond even the farthest work crews.

"What did you find?" she asked, slipping her hand into mine.

"He was concerned." I looked back at the program and its authority to override whatever else he had directed Forge to perform. "*Really* concerned about anyone traveling to or from that spot." I turned my attention to her. "What's there?"

"I don't know."

"The man of mystery," I said softly.

"Not to me." Pamela moved over and slid into my arms. "There's nothing more for us to do tonight. Not here."

I took the hint and we retired to the bedroom, where she reminded me why I had risked so much.

★   ★   ★

Much later I slipped out of the bed, leaving Pamela sleeping, and returned to the study. Forge sat on my desk, its display a constant scroll of tasks underway. I toyed with the idea of trying to probe further, but decided to leave it alone and I opened my desk's personal interface.

Highlighted in red, a message from Seiko waited for me. I could imagine what she wanted – more useless and fruitless dates, chaperoned into deadly dull conformity. I ignored it and went back to bed.

CHAPTER TWELVE

Pamela stayed in my apartment the next two days while Forge arranged her new residency and identity. We couldn't just drop her down in the middle of a well-established tower with floor after floor of nosey neighbors. No, we needed a newly opened but mostly empty tower. Fortunately, the Admin's policies ensured a rapidly growing population and provided numerous options.

The more thoroughly we needed to penetrate the networks the longer Forge required. Altering fabricator records was a simple task and altering fund transfers, apparently Eddie's principal concern, was slightly less simple, but whole histories that were capable of withstanding an inspection from Security took days. I asked if Forge could create money – after all it's just entries in the colony's financial databases – but the level of security on those networks meant that counterfeiting required months.

Seiko left more messages, but I pushed them aside, promising myself I'd fix everything with her once we firmly established Pamela's new life. Brandon and I worked cordially those two days, but he suspected something. I didn't see the need to enlighten him.

On Saturday morning not even the arrival of hordes of unruly noisy children dampened my soaring spirits. Maria and Patrick acted as herders, keeping the brats in line, while I made a few last-minute changes to the program.

The office door opened and Pamela slid swiftly inside, closing the door quickly but quietly.

"You shouldn't leave the apartment," I said as she moved next to me. Her fresh, clean scent filled the air, and I very nearly felt the heat of her skin.

"I miss you."

She reached around my waist and pulled me close. I kissed her, holding her tight. She explored my waist with one hand and then went lower.

"Not now," I said, though that bit of protest consumed a great deal of my willpower.

"But I leave tonight," she pleaded.

"You're not going to be that far away."

"It's going to be too far."

She turned me to face her and pressed her ample breasts against my chest as she undid my trousers.

"They don't need you down there. Not the kiddies."

She slid to her knees and destroyed the last of my resistance.

*   ★   ★

Pamela and I dressed. She slipped the dress up and over her creamy shoulders and then stepped over to where I sat and leaned over, peering at my monitor while Maria played housemother to the brood downstairs.

"She's a very pretty girl."

"Yeah," I agreed, finally getting my shoes on and turning my attention to my vest. "Patrick dreams of things she's never going to agree to."

Pamela shrugged and stood straight. "Oh, you never can tell."

She gave me a quizzical look and said, "You ever think about her?"

I stopped, one arm bent as I put on the vest. "She's a teenager."

I hurried with the vest, stood, and slipped on my jacket.

"That's never stopped some men." She moved over and started taking care of my tie. "Or even most men."

I adjusted the jacket, noticed an approving look in her eyes, and kissed her quick on the lips.

"I like women, not girls."

She smiled and slid into my arms. "Score another one for Forge."

"What's Forge got to do with this?"

"He said you weren't like most men."

She wrapped her arms around my neck and we kissed longer. Only the rapidly approaching end of the animation shorts prevented further exercise. We broke and a thought percolated in my mind.

"Speaking of Forge, any word on Eddie?"

She shook her head, her expression dark and apprehensive.

"I don't like it," she said. "There should be something."

"Unless he's dead."

I extricated myself from her embrace and checked the time left for programming. It wasn't much.

"Don't you think someone would have found his body? Don't you think there'd be some report, something?"

I gave her my best reassuring smile. "I'm not surprised. Even if his people were idiots and just tossed him into Founders' Bay, it seems unlikely anyone would stumble across it. No one fishes and the beach is mostly empty."

"But it's not like the fish would eat it," she said. "If the native animals are inedible to us, then we're inedible to them, right?"

"They can still try." I tried to sound confident, but I truly didn't know the answer. The planet's bacteria broke down our corpses as readily as it did native animals, so eventually his body would vanish, but without scavengers how long would that take? I hoped that Eddie's people weren't idiots.

The alarm sounded and I did a final check of my appearance. I moved to Pamela and took her by the shoulders.

"No news is good news," I said. "It means he didn't find a doctor. He really is dead."

She tried to smile. "I'd feel better if I had dissolved that bastard."

I kissed her on the forehead. "We've got no worries, my love. Everything is behind us now."

★   ★   ★

Even with Maria and Patrick helping and a seemingly endless line of cars it took more than two hours to discharge all the children back into the colony.

At long last, though far too soon, evening arrived. In my apartment I helped Pamela disconnect Forge's power and network connections. Naturally, we had no need to pack anything. Once we got her to her new home Forge would hack her fabricator. I packed Forge into a specially printed case, then closed and locked it.

"I hate going," she confessed as I carried Forge downstairs, following close behind. Her sweet clean scent washed over me as we descended the stairs to the lobby.

"I hate you leaving."

I pushed through concessions and held the counter's door open for her. We stood in the lobby and memories flooded my mind. The first time I spotted her, standing out in the crowd like a giant among little people, our lovemaking on the sofa and floor, the hard laminate inconsequential to our passion. I knew she wasn't going to be very far away and yet this felt like an ending.

We said nothing as we went outside, the cool night air blowing stiff from the bay, the sharp tang of salt filling my nose. A car rolled up, popped open its door, and waited. Pamela started down the steps and I followed, handing Forge to her after she settled into her seat.

"I want to go with you."

"Neighbors." Her voice cracked. "I'll visit."

She looked up at the theater behind me. "Your place will always be special and it's more private."

She kissed me, fast and without passion, but tasting of tears, then the door closed and the car sped away. I watched until it vanished into the shuttered districts, leaving me alone.

As I turned and went back inside it seemed to me that Companion's reddish light gave everything a hellish tint.

That night I didn't watch anything. After two days with her company my apartment loomed large and cavernous. I wandered around the theater, missing her, and even the knowledge that I'd soon see her again failed to improve my mood. When I finally went to bed I didn't sleep, but tossed and turned, filled with loneliness.

★   ★   ★

The alarm roused me early. I showered, breakfasted, and dressed alone. Picking out a freshly fabricated suit for church, I acted by rote memory. When I finished I took my slate and tried to call Pamela, but she didn't answer. With her preference for sleeping in I thought nothing of it and left an affectionate message. After making sure I looked ready for church, I summoned a car.

I walked to the street where the morning light dazzled my eyes and the distant thrum of Nocturnia filled the air. The car door closed, sealing me in a pleasant silence. I didn't watch the landscape as I sped through the city, my thoughts fixed entirely on Pamela.

As I crossed the park to the church the sea breeze carried the smell of salt, freshly cut grass, and decay. People mingled on the lawn and children chased each other while mothers watched with wary eyes. I spotted my family, Seiko standing with them. They stood a distance from the building, eschewing their favorite spot by the doors for the seclusion of a stand of trees. As I approached no one smiled. Their expressions darkened and Seiko moved out to intercept me.

"I know you don't believe, but really? Coming to *church*? Even from you, that's a lot."

The anger in her voice stopped me short. She stood there, a little more than an arm's length away, glaring, waiting for my answer. My hands fluttered uselessly in front of me as I tried to understand this sudden fury.

"Don't play stupid. I know all about it, all about her."

"Seiko, there's nothing going on."

Her small eyes narrowed and her voice dropped in volume and an octave.

"So you're not fucking Pamela?"

I tried not to react, but the guilt must have shown. Seiko stepped forward and slugged me. Not slapped like you see in the films, but a closed-fist roundhouse that rocked my head and sent my hat flying.

"You bastard."

I opened my mouth to speak, but no words came, my mind blank with shock.

"I knew you were 'unconventional' but I thought you were smarter than that."

"It's not true." Even as I said it I knew the lie was useless. Her anger and my guilt pushed us onto a predestined path.

Tears flowed down her cheeks. "I thought you loved me more than that."

"I do—"

A slap stopped me.

"You've got no right to say that. You've got no right to treat me like this. You've got no right to that whore."

She turned and stormed off, away from me, away from my family, away from my life. I wanted to chase after her, to erase this morning, but I just stood and watched her leave. My family, scowling as though I had murdered a nursery of babies, headed toward the church.

I turned away and searched for my hat, the blazing sunlight painful through my watery eyes. Several yards away I found the fedora caught on a low branch. After stretching on tiptoes I grabbed it and heard Jones smirking behind me.

"You're not having a good morning, are you?"

Her smile provoked my fury, but I resisted anything monumentally stupid.

"It's personal."

I stomped past, at first heading on automatic toward the church, but then realized I did not want to go there and stopped.

"Is it?" Jones taunted, watching me waver indecisively.

"Yes! It has not a goddamned thing to do with you!"

With an overly dramatic movement, like a poor actor playing a brilliant lawyer, she pulled out her slate.

"Moral degeneracy is enough cause to remove you from the committee." She made a show of studying the screen. "But it appears you're more than a sexual hedonist."

"What the fuck are you talking about?"

"Did you really think you could hide that sort of activity? Well, you always were stupid. Security is finally doing a proper investigation and this time you won't scurry away."

She left wearing a smug victorious smile.

I yanked out my slate as I hurried down to the street. Secrecy didn't matter shit now. I had to get to Pamela and I had to have Forge. As I waited for the car to arrive I called her but again she didn't answer. I left a frantic message and ended the call as the car rolled up. I climbed inside and the vehicle sped off for her apartment.

The blocks whizzed past and I tried to calm myself. Seiko's tears tore at my heart, Jones's smug arrogance fanned my anger, and the thought of Security terrified me. Right then, riding in the automated car, was the first time I truly wished Pamela had never walked into my life. I loved her, I wanted her – but with her, troubles piled up high and fast.

The city center fell behind me as the car wound its way toward Pamela's tower. The streets became less populated and other cars became infrequent. Too late I realized I should have set my destination a few blocks away from her home. It wouldn't matter. Forge could just erase this trip.

Her tower was still half-closed, the upper floors covered by protective shutters, and the loading ramp was desolate and empty. As soon as I climbed out the car sped off on another call.

People mingled and loitered in the main lobby, families that were so new to the building that their slates displayed maps. I ignored them and went straight to the elevators. Forge had set Pamela up on the highest populated floor but the trip took just a few seconds.

The doors opened on a modest lobby. I stepped out and took a few moments to orient myself. Four hallways radiated out from this bank of elevators. In two of them lights burned bright and welcoming, but a thin plastic wall sealed off the other hallways, not yet ready for occupancy. I was starting toward Pamela's apartment when the elevator behind me sounded an arrival.

Perhaps it was because of all the things that had gone wrong that day, perhaps it was because this was supposed to be a sparsely populated floor, but whatever the reason, I glanced back at the arriving elevator. The doors began opening and through the narrow gap I spotted Eddie.

CHAPTER THIRTEEN

Eddie, with his head turned down studying his slate, hadn't seen me. I dashed to the plastic barrier. With a shove it slid aside and I rushed through and pushed it back in place. Holding my breath, terrified to make a sound, I heard him step out of the elevator. He paused in the lobby and then his footsteps faded down a hallway.

I pulled out my slate, turned the volume all the way off, and called Pamela. There was no answer, only that damned message. I wanted to rush after Eddie, to save her, but he was more than a head taller and much broader. Unarmed, he'd win any fight, easily. Maybe he was armed. My muscles clenched and my head swam. I called again but she still didn't answer.

His voice bellowed from down the hallway, "Open up! I know you're here!"

I breathed in short rapid bursts and my hands shook as I held the barrier in place.

"Bitch!"

I jumped. That barrel-chested yell had sounded so close.

"I'll get it back, and you're going to regret crossing me, you, and that little runt!"

He pounded on the door and shouted some more. I don't believe in a God, but at that moment I gave him thanks that she wasn't home.

Suddenly Eddie stomped up the hallways, the footsteps sharp and loud in the freshly opened lobby. An elevator arrived and alarmed people shouted. Eddie maintained continuous cursing until the closing elevator doors silenced him.

I fell against the barrier, panting in great heavy gouts, and waited for my strength to come back. When the lobby fell silent, I slipped out and headed home.

★   ★   ★

I put several blocks between Pamela's tower and me before I summoned a car. A few blocks would never throw Security off my tail and frankly I wasn't thinking at my best. Several minutes later my heart still raced, pounding so hard that my chest hurt. I waited for the car, my hands shaking, constantly swiveling my head, looking for Eddie. The car arrived and when I climbed inside, the little enclosed vehicle provided a sense of safety.

Eddie tormented my thoughts. Besides him being alive, I wondered how he had found Pamela. Did he know the truth about me? Right there in the car I nearly panicked, envisioning him, with murder on his mind, waiting at the theater. I pulled out my slate and diverted the car to Founders' Park.

It changed direction, but the new destination did not settle my frayed nerves. I pictured Eddie waiting near, or even inside the theater, a pistol in his hand. My chest muscles twitched as I imagined bullets shattering my sternum, tearing through my lungs and heart. With Forge we had considered him powerless, which in hindsight was a foolish and maybe fatal screwup.

Without Forge?

Pamela said Forge couldn't duplicate itself and now I wondered if Forge couldn't or *wouldn't*? However Eddie had come by Forge it was possible that he had another. Maybe that was how he found her. If so then he had to know about me. He had to know everything.

The car stopped and I climbed out. Without everyone at the service the park was mostly empty. The car sped off and I wandered the park's paths. I briefly thought about going to the Administration, throwing myself on their mercy, but I couldn't do that. Pamela and I had tried to kill Eddie, and just for that we'd be exiled out into the wild. Out there we'd face a terrible and painful death by starvation.

My meanderings had brought me to a bluff overlooking the park's center. Several yards under me the full-scale Ark replica sat gleaming in the bright sunlight. We were the last remnant of humanity, the only seed that found fertile ground, and look at us – just as murderous and vicious as anyone from Old Earth.

In the distance church bells rang out. I didn't want to face anyone, particularly Seiko or Brandon. I pulled out my slate and accessed the theater's network and security monitors. No one appeared anywhere, but if Eddie had another Forge then no network was trustworthy. Unable to formulate any other plan, I summoned a car and headed home.

When I reached the theater my stomach was a twisted knot of pain and my hands shook. Walking up the steps, I dropped my slate. It took me two tries to access the network and unlock the door. As I stepped across the threshold my senses seemed enhanced. The air was still, every shadow held a deep darkness, and the faraway city sounds conspired to cover hiding assassins.

I reached the center of the lobby and Eddie hadn't attacked. Alone and in silence I climbed the stairs. As I did I fumbled with my slate, futilely calling Pamela. I left another frantic message and stepped into my office.

Brandon wasn't there. He was undoubtedly at Sunday brunch with my family, being more welcome than myself. I sat at the desk and fired up my interface. The network responded but granted only limited access as urgent messages flashed in red. Jones hadn't bluffed. Already Security had frozen a number of my accesses and informed me of their investigation. Until they finished the theater was closed. I slammed my fist into the interface.

Frustrated, angry, and frightened, I jumped to my feet, yelling at the top of my voice. I grabbed my chair and hurled it across the room. It bounced off the wall and crashed to the floor. My anger still not spent, I rushed to the office window and repeatedly slammed both fists against it.

Eventually pain pierced my rage and I stopped, collapsing against the window. Through tear-filled eyes I looked down at the lobby, both wanting Pamela more than ever and regretting ever seeing her. I slid down the angled window until I was sitting on the floor, my back to the wall, and I cried.

When the sobs and anger were spent, exhaustion overtook me and I stumbled to my apartment. I stripped off my suit, dropping articles on the floor like a breadcrumb trail, and collapsed into my bed.

★ ★ ★

Few things are more terrifying than having intruders surprise you in your sleep. The door to my bedroom opened, and I fluttered my eyes as two people rushed inside. I tried to jump to my feet, but tangled in linens I stumbled and they easily seized me by the arms. Both wore nondescript gray suits and ominous masks covering their noses and mouths. One was a woman, but her smaller stature did nothing to lessen her tight grip on my bicep.

Each taking an arm, they pulled me out of the bed. When my legs cleared the sheet I kicked out, but missed.

"Settle down," one said, his voice muffled by the mask.

I struggled more, trying to tear free.

"He's a Feral," the woman said with a bored explanatory tone.

They dragged me toward the door and when we got there I kicked up both feet to the walls on either side, and shoved hard. All three of us tumbled backward to the floor.

I wrenched my arms out of their hands and tried to hurry to my feet. The woman, lithe and fast, swept my legs out from under me, and I tumbled forward, planting myself face-first onto the floor. The man jumped on my back, pinning me, while his partner pulled a cylinder from her pocket.

"Told you," she said to him.

She sprayed a mist into my face. An overwhelming scent of lavender filled my nose and my muscles relaxed, leaving me limp and helpless. They regained their feet, and again with each taking me by an arm, hefted me to their shoulders. My head rolled helplessly around on my neck and one took a gentle hold.

"Careful," he said. "We don't want you to pull a muscle."

"You needed to tell him that before he went all Feral," she said as they dragged me out of the bedroom.

With my muscles limp, they half carried and half dragged me down the stairs into the theater lobby. Another man waited there. He was tall, also wearing a fairly uninteresting gray suit, with white hair and dark eyes. Something about the three of them made me think they were siblings.

The new man frowned as they carried me across the lobby, my feet sliding uselessly behind me.

"Was that truly necessary?"

They both answered yes and the guy added, "He was in danger of doing himself a bit of harm, Doctor."

"I suppose it was to be expected."

"In fact," the other quipped. "I did warn you."

"Arrogance," the doctor warned.

"Sorry."

The pair sat me gently on the sofa and then vanished back behind concessions into the stairwell. The doctor sat next to me and gave a small mysterious smile.

"Let's have a look and make sure that you haven't been injured."

He examined me, never making a noise, but prodding with gentle, expert fingers. As I sat there, my head rolled back on the sofa, it struck me that all three had the same complexion. It was quite a tan, but they were no particular ethnicity I recognized.

He stood and said, "You're going to have some bruises. I expect that's a rather minor inconvenience given your predilections."

I tried to talk, but my mouth just hung loose with spittle spilling from a corner.

"Hm." He shrugged. After a moment's consideration he reached into a breast pocket and pulled out an aerosol applicator.

"We're not going to have a meaningful conversation if you're like that, are we?"

He leaned in close and looked me sternly in the eye. "Then again, I remain fairly safe if you're incapacitated. That produces a bit of a conundrum."

I managed to move my lips, but produced no sound, only more spit, drooling onto my bare chest.

"I dislike binding a person against their will."

Did he bind people with their consent?

"However, for the safety of both you and me, there is simply no rational alternative."

With strong deft motions he flipped me onto my stomach and tied my hands behind my back. The plastic restraints didn't bite into my wrists, but nor were they loose. Then he sat me upright, taking care not to twist my arms, and sprayed another mist into my face. This one smelled of unwashed feet, but after a few seconds my muscles quivered, trembled, and then were normal.

He had pulled a chair across from me and sat, as though we were friends having a chat.

"Feeling better?"

"I can move."

"So, let's be quick and let's be rational. Where is Vulcan's Forge?"

"I don't know what you're talking about."

"All people lie, but not all people lie well. You do not. Where is Vulcan's Forge?"

I had a feeling that this guy wasn't going to call down his goons and beat me like Eddie would have, but on some deep ineffable level, that frightened me more.

"Who are you?" I asked, not willing to give up anything.

"Dr. Clinton Hardgrave. There, does that make it possible for you to help me and help yourself?"

"What makes you think I need help?"

I wanted to stall for time, though in the middle of the night and with the theater shuttered there was no chance of anyone just dropping by.

"People such as you are always in trouble. You cause it and that attracts even more. Your associate is already...."

He paused, not like a dramatic villain's pause, but a person encountering something utterly repellant and revolting.

"Murderously angry with you, but I imagine that's an expected reaction."

I stammered, confused by his sudden assertions.

"Eddie came to us after your murder attempt failed. Naturally we couldn't let him die, and I had hoped, rather foolishly I admit, that he had seen reason and would return to us. Alas, that is not his intention and faced with his brutality we had no option but to release him."

Hardgrave leaned in close, his voice modulated in perfect concern.

"So to survive you need my help and I need Vulcan's Forge. Where is it?"

"I don't know."

He studied me closely and a long silence fell between us. Footsteps echoed from the stairwell as the pair returned.

"It's not here, Doctor."

Hardgrave stood, his expression more of sorrow and disappointment.

"Too bad. If Eddie has it you are almost certainly going to be murdered."

Again he stumbled over the word like churchgoing people did over profanity. He jerked his head toward the door and the others moved there, but Hardgrave still towered above me.

"Is it really worth it?" He squatted down and peered at me from eye level. "All this violence and treachery for what, money? There are causes worth dying for, but I've never understood dying for material gain."

Lost and confused, I said, "I truly don't know what you're talking about. I mean yes, I know about Forge, but the rest of this—"

"Where is Vulcan's Forge?" He cut me off with a sharp insistent tone.

I wasn't about to have this man and his nameless thugs descending on Pamela. "I don't know."

He shook his head. "I thought that for a moment, you might have been reasonable."

With a fast draw he produced an applicator and sprayed me. It was the lavender, and again I lay helplessly limp. He turned me over, unbound me, and then sat me back in a comfortable and supported position.

"If you decide to make a reasonable decision, and very likely save your life, you can reach me here."

He laid a memory tab on the sofa's arm.

"A criminal such as yourself isn't about to turn to the authorities, and if Eddie Nguyen has Forge, then we are your only hope."

He stood, still wearing the disappointed father's expression.

"All that capability and what did you do with it? Badly forge commercial transactions. If we found you, so will colonial security."

He turned and they walked out.

CHAPTER FOURTEEN

Hardgrave left me looking at a clock and I sat there drooling onto my chest for over an hour until the drug wore off. In a spasm of tremors I thrashed on the sofa before my muscles answered my commands.

With pains stabbing every inch of me, I stood and pumped my legs and arms trying to regain sensation. I didn't waste much time before hurrying to my apartment and my slate. Hardgrave's brother and sister might have searched for Forge, but they did it without causing a mess. For criminals all three struck me as uncommonly polite.

I called Pamela, but this time instead of a useless message I received a network alert announcing that there was no such person. I double-checked her contact information, but the network again insisted that she had never existed.

A cold chill shot down my back. Something had happened, something very bad. Eddie? Hardgrave? The thought of either man holding her prisoner set my blood boiling. Not worrying about the consequences, I quickly dressed and summoned a car. I was still pulling on my jacket and heading down the theater's steps when the car arrived.

I climbed into it, setting my destination. The car sped along nearly deserted streets and the ride tested my patience. I ran from the loading ramp into the lobby and to an elevator. As it climbed the tower my heart raced with fear that turned to terror with memories of Eddie's previous enraged visit overpowering my thoughts. My knees quivered and sweat coated my palms.

The elevator doors opened and I moved carefully down the hallway to Pamela's door. With an easy push it slid open. I stepped into the dark room, my slate throwing a wide diffuse beam of light as I searched the empty apartment.

Every room, every cupboard, every closet was empty. Nothing looked damaged or overturned, so there hadn't been a fight, but no Pamela. Eddie slamming his massive fists on my front door would make me move too. She must have dumped her compromised identity and when she was safe she'd contact me. I started to leave when a light on the fabricator caught my eye.

The printer still had power and it didn't take very long to call up its records. There were the usual sorts of things, dresses and personal items, but also in the inventory was a duplicate Forge. She had printed a duplicate, but one in a ruined and destroyed state.

★　★　★

Dawn tinted the sky pink and red as I climbed the steps, unlocked the door, and went inside, wondering about Hardgrave's comments. I went to the office.

I accessed the colonial network, inspecting all my accounts, and at first everything looked all right, but then I noticed a little extra money. Digging deeper, I tried to uncover exactly when and where these funds had appeared. They led me down a rabbit hole of accounts with clumsy and ham-handed attempts at concealing their connections to me. These accounts were fat with money, far more than I had ever seen or accessed, even when I oversaw the theater's construction. A spiderweb of transactions from all over Nocturnia fed into 'my' fake accounts.

Realization dawned like an exploding bomb. Eddie, either with Forge or a second one Pamela didn't know about, had created these, setting me up for Security. I looked again at the amounts and whistled softly. If he could afford to throw this much away to make sure the Administration burned me instead of him I could only imagine what sort of totals his operation pulled in. No doubt he'd claw some of it back once I was convicted.

I didn't have much time. Security's investigation would turn this up as soon as someone looked. I needed Pamela, I needed Forge, and I needed them now. I looked back at those faked and damning accounts. Eddie's trap was foolproof and I was the fool. Calling Pamela would only be a futile waste of time. She had ditched that identity, but I couldn't wait for her to turn up. I had to find her, or find Forge.

I wasted hours tearing my hair out. I knew nothing except the location of Eddie's tower and nothing would drag me in there. No matter how I approached it, I came up empty. Pamela, Eddie, Forge, and Hardgrave: I needed to know how all the elements came together but like a badly edited film it refused to make sense. Hours burned by and carafe after carafe of coffee did nothing to spark my brilliance. It seemed utterly ridiculous to have survived everything like that terrifying night in Eddie's tower, and yet lose all to Jones and Security.

An idea fluttered at the edges of my thoughts. I sat at my desk and tried to relax, though the massive amounts of caffeine surging through my bloodstream fought me. At Eddie's tower he watched the movement of every person that came to him, and not just those, but also some from elsewhere.

I grabbed my slate and flipped through its history. Yes! It was still in there. I stared at the map. I saw the desolate spot hundreds of miles north in the island's rocky and high mountains, the focus of Eddie's ultimate paranoia. I had no idea what lay there, but desperation and time left me with no options.

★   ★   ★

I called Wolfgang, and defying my luck of late, he answered.

"Jason! What the hell is going on?"

He didn't sound angry, but the worry and concern in his voice carried volumes.

"There's far too much to tell."

He ran his fingers through his buzz-cropped red hair. "You can't leave me in the dark. There's rumors flying that this isn't just Jones, but that Security is looking to put you over the wall."

I sighed. I didn't want to confirm that for once the rumors were more right than wrong, but I needed him.

"That's not very far off."

He fell back in his seat, stunned. "I can't believe it. I mean, I know what sort of trouble you got into as a teenager, but that's not the sort of thing they exile people over."

He leaned forward into the camera. It always astounded me the way people assumed cameras transmitted personal space with their images.

"What the hell did you do?"

"I didn't do anything! At least I haven't done what anyone thinks.

There are some very bad people, people who can hack the entire colonial network—"

He confidently shook his head. "Can't be done."

"The hell it can't! I've seen it!"

"Jason, the network was established by the Founders. It's not something people are going to hack. There's simply no way a human intellect can compete with the designs laid out by a fully functional artificial one."

"Are you going to argue with me or are you going to listen? I tell you they can do this and they are doing it."

He paused and then asked, "You're serious about this?"

"Yes, I've seen it. This guy's able to rewrite any database, forge any entry he needs, and now he's setting me up."

His expression grew serious. "That's really bad news. How the hell did you get mixed up in that?"

"A woman."

I tried not to get angry at his smirk.

"That's always been your problem, hasn't it?"

"Well, now it's a little bigger than that." I took in a deep breath. "I need your help."

"What can I do?"

"I need a flyer."

Wolf sat back, the request surprising him. "A flyer? How is that—?"

"You have to trust me on this. Also I need satellite imagery."

I tapped at my slate and sent him the location that terrified Eddie.

"A flyer's not like a car," Wolf complained. "We don't have hundreds, just—"

I snapped. "Wolf! I stuck my neck out for you a couple of weeks ago. You begged for me to cross Jones and I did it."

"No need to throw that in my face."

"Well, I need that flyer, I need that imagery, and you're—"

"I didn't say no. It's just not that easy."

He paused, thinking, and then said, "But I can do it. It'll take a few hours. Do you want it in the morning?"

"I don't have the time. I'll take it out tonight."

"All right, I'll see you then."

*　　*　　*

The sun dropped toward the horizon, vanishing behind the westward mountains as I arrived at the landing field. I passed hangers, maintenance buildings, and simple offices. The Founders had established a reasonable space capability. Too many critical resources were only obtainable from space, but in terms of commitment from the Governing Council, space ranked low. The Founders had mapped the planet, located and moved into orbit a few valuable asteroids with enough material to satisfy a couple of centuries of unrestricted growth. With those resources already at hand Admin wanted to ignore space, which left true believers like Wolf fighting to keep their ships flying.

The car drove to the more populated area of the field. Here flyers, each boasting four large ducted fans and their own micro-fusion plant, lined the tarmac. As my car approached, Wolf waved from the far end of the line. I stepped out and a wall of noise battered my ears as another flyer landed.

"I've got something set up in the old flight office," he shouted over the roar and led me back to an older building, really nothing more than a shed.

We stepped inside and I closed the door behind us, diminishing the roar somewhat. Wolf waited by a wall display, his slate in his hand.

"It's kind of noisy in here."

"When the Founders built this office the field was three kilometers away."

I shrugged and ignored the noise.

Like all space types, Wolf used a scientific measurement system while the rest of the colony followed our ancestors' preferences. Truly nothing symbolized the insanity of our cultural 'preservation' better than that.

"Here's the spot you wanted."

He pointed to the display. Low mountains, jagged broken boulders, and a whole lot of native plants filled the screen. I stepped closer and studied the image of wild, native land and nothing more. No buildings, no roads, nothing, and yet this spot held Eddie's attention.

"There's nothing there," Wolf said, stating the obvious.

"Yeah, that's how it looks."

"Still want the flyer?"

I hesitated. What could I possibly gain by going out there? I almost told him no, but I lacked options and even if there was nothing there at least I would be doing something. Something had to be there, something hidden, something that terrified Eddie.

"Yes."

"Okay." He did something with his slate and added, "I got you one, but do me a favor and try not to crash it."

"I thought they flew themselves?"

"Joke."

"Right now, Wolf, I don't have a sense of humor."

We went back outside where operations had stopped for the day, leaving the field quiet. He led me to the closest vehicle, pulled open the cockpit door, and I climbed into the seat.

"It's like a car," he said. "You can just punch in a destination, latitude, and longitude, and it'll take you there. They have to be keyed for access and this one is set up for you."

"Is there a record?"

"Of course, I listed it as film research. It'll be on your head to explain that."

He slammed the door closed and backed off. I identified myself to the flyer's onboard network and once I set the destination it leapt into the air.

The field fell quickly away as I shot high into the night sky. Nocturnia's dazzling buildings shrank and quickly vanished behind low mountains until only light reflecting off low clouds indicated the city's presence. Even that vanished once I broke through the cloud layer and soon I flew over a gray unbroken expanse with the Milky Way sweeping across the sky above me.

I let the automatics fly uninterrupted for 30 minutes and then I inputted new commands. Wolf meant well, but after the last two weeks I decided on caution as my new watchword. I changed my destination. Instead of landing directly at Eddie's coordinates, I selected a spot two miles south. It would be easier to stay hidden on foot. The next thing I changed was my altitude. Aborting the planned high-altitude flight with a direct descent, I instructed the autopilot to drop under a few hundred feet and follow the contours of the landscape. With a small range of mountains to shield me I hoped I might arrive without anyone being any the wiser.

Satisfied, I leaned the seat back and tried to rest.

CHAPTER FIFTEEN

Despite the constant thrum of motors I managed a few hours of sleep. The alarm roused me as the flyer dropped altitude for the final run. Companion rose high in the sky, its red and orange clouds reflecting a disturbing light across the landscape. I rummaged through the flyer's supplies and produced a few meal bars, which I ate as the ground approached.

Just 150 feet above the ground the flyer leveled off and followed the terrain. Under me strange alien foliage passed in a dark, ocher-tinted blur. I was quite a distance beyond our terraformed colony and I had slept while crossing the wide patch of sterilized ground that marked Nocturnia's current reach. Out here no one came and no one had any business. Ahead mountains rose, thrusting their jagged peaks before Companion's massive bulk. I searched the passing ground for animals, but I saw none. Long before the Firsters had emerged from their artificial wombs the Founders had eliminated all the apex predators and left hunting drones to keep everything in an ecological balance until it too could be sterilized for terraforming.

Another alarm sounded and I strapped in for landing. The flyer's radar displayed the topographical terrain and I adjusted the final landing site, selecting a place up the side of the mountain, but still shielded from direct sight by the ridgeline. With only a slight jostle the flyer landed in a small clearing and then it quickly shut down the ducted fans. I sat there for a moment, staring out of the canopy as blood roared in my ears and my heart beat far too fast.

I was tired of everything going wrong so I locked the flyer to my identification. There was no one out here, and Eddie's paranoia was probably nothing except his own twisted fears, but I decided that no one was going to strand me. Once I finished securing the flyer, I climbed out into the brush.

Nocturnia's natural smells assaulted me. Instead of pine, grass, and sea spray, the mountain forest smelled of burned paper, fresh sweat, and copper. The air even carried a hint of taste and I couldn't shake the sensation that I had just eaten chicken and pickles.

I hiked north, following the contour of the hills for an easier path. My slate still accessed the navigational satellites and I had little chance of becoming lost, but the colonial data network lay out of reach.

On the map the distance from my landing site to the coordinates measured a mere two miles, less than an hour's stroll. Actually walking those particular two miles was an experience vastly different than strolling in Founders' Park. No path led directly to my destination. While I knew that the terrain was listed as hills and low mountains, experiencing it taught me that I remained a city man.

I followed animal trails through dense alien foliage. The paths snaked back and forth and several times I diverted around gullies and canyons that suddenly yawned before me. Three and a half hours later I crested a ridge, left the brush and stood above the tree line. I turned around and looked back for my flyer, but the rolling hills and thick woods hid it.

The summit provided a spectacular view of the valley matching Eddie's coordinates. Dim red light from Companion illuminated the depression, showing me trees and brush, and on the far side the land climbed into high jagged mountains. Studying the scene, I found only wilderness and brush. I sat on a rock outcrop, letting the gentle night breeze sweep away my sweat.

Nothing. The entire trip had been a waste of time and in just a few short hours Security would move in and destroy what was left of my life. The empty valley taunted me with its placid, useless presence.

I snatched up a rock and threw it as hard and as far into the damned valley as I could. It soared out into the night and in the dim light I quickly lost sight of it. I waited for the thud of its impact but the night remained silent, with only the slight rustling of leaves as a breeze blew across the mountain. My frustration unabated, I picked up another rock and this one I hurled downward, trying to squarely hit a tree that offended me by merely being there.

The stone flew straight but suddenly changed direction, heading up as though it had bounced off the air. My breath caught in my chest and I stood very still, listening, but again there was no sound or impact.

I peered down the slope into the valley, but nothing looked amiss. There were trees, strange alien ones, each one with twin trunks and a tangle of branches and foliage. Moving with care, I started down the hillside, picking out each footstep with caution, certain that just ahead waited some ghastly trick. After a few dozen yards the sky darkened as I stepped into shadow. I stopped and looked up.

Thick gauze shielded the sky and I stood in its shade. Here, where it was fixed to the slope, it wasn't very far off the ground, but as the land fell away it covered and concealed acres. I reached up and touched it, running my fingertips along its smooth fabric. Carefully retracing my steps, I backed up the hill a couple of yards and emerged into the light of an undimmed Companion. Now that I knew what to look for the massive tarp stood out.

It stretched across the entire valley, projecting a convincing image of an untouched locale. I knelt and hesitated, my fear all too real. This was no obscure outpost that someone slipped out from Nocturnia unnoticed. This was massive, and something this massive didn't spring out of a small criminal conspiracy. I could return and report it, but if I went back now no one would believe me. It was simply too fantastic.

My knees shook but I stood and slowly stepped down the hill under the tarp.

★   ★   ★

Boulders sporadically pierced the ground and I moved from one to the next. The slope leveled and ahead light reflected off the tarp's underside.

I stopped and listened. The murmur of voices, movement, and machinery wafted on the wind, not quite the sounds of a city, it was too subdued for that, but it was more than a campsite. Taking care to stay hidden, I continued forward. The light grew brighter and the noises louder until I found myself perched on the edge of a bluff.

The ground dropped sharply away, cliff-like, and I peered into a natural bowl. A small settlement filled the bottom, with buildings and narrow streets far too small for vehicles, where pedestrians walked under soft white lighting. I couldn't say exactly why, but the scene looked wrong. Something was off. I pulled out my slate and recorded everything.

As I captured still and video images of the strange settlement I noticed the center of the town held a string of lights. Bright and harsh, they encircled a vast pit. At first I thought it might be a natural sinkhole or some other formation, but I spotted people winding their way down into it by pathways carved into the wall.

Satisfied I had seen enough and praying I could use it to bargain my way out of trouble, I stood and started back toward the flyer. I had taken just a few steps when I spotted people ahead blocking my way out.

Half a dozen people moved down the slope and each carried a light in one hand and a pistol in the other. I dashed behind a boulder and held my breath. I prayed, I begged, hoping that this was just a coincidence and that they hadn't followed me. I lowered myself to the ground, lying flat in the dirt, and slowly peeked from my hiding spot.

They were closer and I managed a better look. It was four men and two women, all wearing similar one-piece off-white suits, and they clearly weren't concerned with hiding. It took a moment for me to notice their complexion. Just as with Hardgrave and his goons, each of these had skin that looked a little darker than a golden tan.

"The Feral definitely came this way," one of the women said.

"Don't use that term. It's insulting and derogatory."

"I meant it that way."

An argument started but the man nearest the center of the line suddenly spoke up.

"I have his tracks." He pointed toward my area. "He went in that direction."

The line moved forward but slower and more alert.

The center man called out, "We know you're here! It's no use hiding. Come on out. No one will harm you."

Eddie feared them and I wasn't about to doubt his instincts for self-preservation. The line grew closer; they swept the area with their lights, tracking with their pistols. Soon they'd have me cornered against the bluff. I picked the end anchored by one of the two women and readied to dash.

"You are safe!" the leader shouted. "If you do something irrational people may be injured. Please, let's reason this out!"

Still behind the boulder, I pulled myself up into a squat. I listened to the sound of their feet on the ground, the crunch of each step. Suddenly a light played across the boulder, throwing my shadow on the ground as the beam centered on me.

"There he is!"

Simultaneous with the woman's shout I leapt up and dashed forward. I sprinted but they chased, forcing me along the bluff's edge. One of the men, arms and legs pumping, ran to intercept. I dodged but he turned quickly, blocking my way. I swung at his head, trying to knock him aside.

In the movies action heroes swing once and nameless baddies spin and fall conveniently out of frame but that was not what happened. He ducked in and tried to tackle me, but my swinging fist still connected, hitting him in the shoulder. We both stumbled and instead of striking me square on, he glanced off my side and we toppled to the ground.

I tried to hustle to my feet as he scrambled through the dirt while his partners closed in. He hit me when I was only halfway to my feet and drove me backward with his shoulder digging into my stomach. I pounded on his back and then lost my footing, falling to my ass. What happened next had nothing to do with skill, strength, or prowess. I twisted and rolled to one side while shoving him in the other direction – toward the bluff.

Off-balance, he tumbled onto the dirt and rolled off. He screamed but that stopped when he hit the embankment.

I scrambled to my feet as his partners ran for the bluff and I dashed across the open ground, heading for the wood. Behind me, as he fell, I heard him hit repeatedly. I only hoped that his friends would be more interested in saving him than catching me.

I was wrong.

"Feral!"

I couldn't tell if she yelled it as my name or a curse – or both. A pistol fired but the sound was so soft that my panting almost covered it. Something whistled close past me but missed. I dodged left and tried for a nearby boulder. There were more pistol shots – she wasn't shooting alone. Before I reached the boulder several stinging bites flared along my side.

My legs collapsed and I fell face-first into the dirt, plowing a good deal of it into my mouth. I gagged, but something hampered my reflex and I started choking. I lay there with dirt filling my mouth, unable to breathe. Several of them ran up to me.

"He's choking."

"He's a Feral," a woman's voice snapped. "It would be no loss."

Even as hands turned me over, someone punched me in my stomach. The leader reprimanded his wayward follower.

"You've been here too long," the leader added.

Someone rammed their fist into my solar plexus and a great burst of breath and dirt blew out. With almost sensual pleasure I took in great gasps of air. They slapped something like a wet cloth across the back of my neck and I blacked out.

CHAPTER SIXTEEN

I awoke on a bed, my clothes and slate gone, wearing only a simple gown. A slight fogginess floated in my head, but I sat up anyway.

"Move carefully," a woman with this same curious tan complexion suggested as she came to my side. "Most of the adverse events should dissipate quickly, but a lingering vertigo is possible."

Wavering slightly as I sat upright, I nodded in agreement and that set the room spinning. She steadied me with one hand, and then examined me with an even, sure competence. The dizziness passed.

"Where am I?"

She gave an apologetic smile. "That is not for me to say."

"Who are you?"

"Personally? You can call me Shirley."

Too many of those forbidden films got the best of me.

"Surely, you can't be serious."

"Why wouldn't I be?"

"Never mind."

Shirley finished her examination and stood. "There is no lasting damage. You're very lucky. You might have died from asphyxiation."

Memories of the chase and fight arrived. Guilt swamped me.

"Did he die?"

She gave me a quizzical look.

"The man who went over the bluff?"

"No."

I relaxed. My troubles were far from over but at least I had dodged killing someone.

"He's quite badly hurt." Her eyes were cold and I had the impression she treated me with the compassion one might show an injured animal. "You very nearly killed him."

"That wasn't my intention."

"Well, that is unlikely to matter to a murdered man, is it?"

"It was an accident. I didn't throw him over that edge on purpose."

"A child could have reasoned out the danger." She snorted. "Then again a child would have done as they were told and avoided the fight."

I stood up, my anger rising with me.

"Listen, Shirley, I don't know who you people are or what you want, and I'm not about to trust you with my life."

"Nearly killing him wasn't your intention." She turned and headed for the door. "But it is the consequence of your choices."

She opened the door and I thought about charging out, but a couple of beefy men, again with the same pigmentation, stood ready. I watched as she stepped out, locking the door behind her.

Left alone, I searched my room. For captors they had a rather generous spirit. The room contained every comfort I might possibly need. The food fabricator appeared to be well-programmed with a wide range of options. The same for the utility printer, which was even loaded with the latest fashions, and I wasted no time running off a suit and shoes. In unreasonable optimism I even printed a hat for traveling. I explored fabricating something that I might use as a club, but there my hosts' generosity ended. A network interface gave me access to entertainment options that included libraries of embargoed material. However, I didn't have access to the colonial network, or anything beyond entertainment or signaling my jailers.

Whoever these people were they didn't play by the same rules as the Administration. That did not make them friends. Despite their apparent distaste for violence, they frightened Eddie. The hours passed slowly enough and while the forbidden films of the libraries should have been a powerful distraction, my troubles ruined their entertainment value.

These 'Tans' were kind enough to let the network interface display the time so I wasn't utterly disoriented by my isolation. Sometime in the early evening I received a non-medical visitor – two, actually.

They came in, their skin tone continuing that odd sensation of familial relation, but otherwise they appeared quite different. She was tall, nearly six feet with golden-blond hair, perhaps in her late twenties, and with high stern cheekbones and a sharp long nose. He stood a few inches shorter, with dark brown hair and a rounder, friendlier face. Without their masks it took me a moment to recognize them from the theater as Hardgrave's goons.

"May we talk with you?" she asked.

"Do I have a choice?"

He smiled a big open and warm grin. "Of course you do. Do you want us to leave?"

"No, *I* want to leave."

He looked truly apologetic but her expression remained hard and aloof.

"We can't allow that," she said.

I sat on my bed. "That sounds like a threat."

He started to speak but she got there first.

"You aren't being mistreated."

"I'm a prisoner, I'd call *that* mistreatment."

She sighed and again asked, "May we speak with you at length?"

I waved toward a pair of chairs. "Go ahead. I've got nothing else to do."

With slight but deliberate bows in my direction, they moved the chairs across from me and sat.

She started the interrogation.

"Mr. Kessler, how did you learn of this facility?"

"Who are you?"

She looked as though I was a misbehaving kid.

The guy tried a friendlier tack.

"Jason, we don't mean you any harm, but we can't be certain that you feel the same way."

"The last time we met I ended up drugged and tied. Now you want me to be chatty but you're not even willing to tell me your names."

They looked at each other and a moment of understanding seemed to pass between them as they came to some silent agreement.

"We've been impolite," she said. "My name is Nataya and this is Terrance."

"And you already know who I am, so I really doubt you'd think I'm much of a threat to anyone."

Terrance answered, "I wish we could be sure of that, Jason. I really do. This entire affair is very – distasteful. However, people can often be quite surprising with hidden talents for violence. Don't you agree?"

I nodded but said nothing. Nataya returned to the interrogation.

"Tell us how you knew about this facility."

"You tell me why you have Eddie Nguyen so scared."

At Eddie's name their faces betrayed a moment of shock, maybe even fear. Who was scared of whom?

"We can't answer that," Terrance said.

"And I can't answer any of your questions."

Nataya started to say something, but I refused her the chance. "I mean it. I'm not answering anything until I know what's going on here."

I crossed my arms and stared at them, ignoring their questions until they finally left.

*   *   *

Nataya and Terrance didn't return for the rest of the day and I wasted Tuesday afternoon fretting. They knew who I was, they knew who Eddie was, but they seemed ignorant about recent events. Maybe they'd built Forge but God knows how and why.

The Tans had gone to a lot of effort building this base. The sheer logistics staggered my imagination. The Governing Council watched inventories and individual fabricators so closely that as a teenager when I had printed a single condom they knew it. How the hell had these people slipped out the materials for a small settlement? I couldn't estimate the number of people hiding out here in the bush. If most of the buildings were barracks it could be hundreds, or there might only be a few dozen. I needed to know more and they weren't going to tell me.

By the late afternoon I'd returned to the interface and scanned through the entertainment options again. They wouldn't tell me who they were, but they left clues. Mass media is a reflection of the people who consume it.

No one on Nocturnia made any new media. We were too busy making the colony and colonists. We did consume it though, and what we consumed, and were allowed, told you a lot about our messed-up society, our obsessions over family life, a God-fearing population, and everyone's roles. Anything even slightly subversive to the Admin's perfect order was banned.

The Tans' selections revealed a very different set of concerns. They accessed a lot more of the Ark's archives, though their libraries were far from complete.

Where the Admin banned anything that even suggested sex was for anything other than procreation, the Tans' library burst their directories with every sexual, romantic, and sensual title I could remember. More than just that, I opened a few files of titles I didn't know and sexually pornographic images greeted me.

I stood and stretched. The hours working the interface had played havoc with my spine. Pacing back and forth in the cell, I tried to work out how they had kept themselves hidden. Granted their skin tone was different, but if you passed one on the street you wouldn't give them a second look. It was only when they gathered in groups that their uniformity stood out. With only a few hundred or fewer scattered among Nocturnia's four million they blended in, but that didn't answer the big question. *Who the hell were they?*

That uniformity suggested genetic manipulation, a simple enough effect to produce but a thoroughly banned procedure. The Administration embargoed everything about genetic manipulation except what we needed for health and reproduction.

True to our mission, we preserved the ethnic populations from the United States in their recorded ratios. Changing ethnicity was a crime against colonial objectives. Before Old Earth's ruin that had not been the case and by the time of its destruction some people had abandoned their native ethnicity. The Tans, however, were something different. They displayed no single racial look. Someone was producing these unusual raceless people right under the Admin's nose.

I sat down and searched more of the entertainment files. No doubt these Tans were a hell of lot more sexually accepting than anyone else. They even considered same-sex intercourse normal and not a sinful aberration. For a moment I wondered if Pamela was one of them. Her sexual appetite and adventurism matched but her pale skin contrasted too greatly with theirs.

Slowly I noticed the taboo in their mass media – violence. They allowed very little of the rough and nasty sort of film I had discovered during the later twentieth century's exploitative genre. Nocturnia's issues were with sex and theirs were with violence.

So far they had treated me fairly, but I also hadn't given them what they wanted. I wouldn't want to bet my life on their goodwill after I surrendered all my leverage.

I shut down the interface and noticed it neared midnight. My stomach growled from my inattention and I fabricated a quick meal. As I ate,

I tried to fit the pieces together, but the puzzle refused to take shape. Even if these Tans were as nonviolent as they acted, how had they gotten involved with someone like Eddie?

I threw the refuse into the recycler and stripped for sleep. Climbing into bed, I envisioned Pamela. Her long black hair, her dazzling smile, her seductive eyes, all reminded me I wasn't the only one with a lot to lose. We had to find a way out of this mess, and a way to escape Eddie, the Tans, and the damned Administration.

CHAPTER SEVENTEEN

I slept fitfully, tossing and turning throughout the night and pestered by dreams of blood and fire. I rose early, ate a small breakfast and returned to examining the available media files. In addition to their aversion to violence and an amazingly open sexual attitude, the Tans also tilted toward collective action. Again and again the themes reflected the power of people working together for goals greater than themselves.

Everything pointed to a secret subculture plotting something big. No one needed anything like Forge for petty reasons. Eddie was no Tan. Did he steal the damned thing? How did he even discover them?

I really liked my secret subculture conspiracy theory, but it couldn't be true. A few hundred to a few thousand people aren't a culture, they're a club. Even if someone covertly raised babies from gene stock, without parents just like the Firsters, there would simply be too few to be a culture – they'd be a clique.

Mid-morning brought a visitor and he didn't surprise me.

"Good morning," Hardgrave said as he stepped into my cell. "I hope you are well."

"As well as can be."

He gave me a perfunctory apologetic smile and pointed to a seat, waiting on my permission.

"Go ahead, but this false politeness is irritating."

He sat, leaned back in the chair and settled in comfortably. "Mr. Kessler, there is nothing false about our treatment. If anyone has been rude, or harsh, or has harmed you in any way, tell me now."

"You mean aside from making me a prisoner?"

"Truly, what result did you expect from your skulking about?"

"I didn't even know you were here. I certainly didn't fly all this way to throw myself into a cell."

"You know nothing about Forge, and you know nothing about

this place or us. Mr. Kessler, for a criminal with vast ambitions, you show a surprising ignorance. It is literally beyond belief."

I stood from my chair and paced back and forth in front of him. Hardgrave didn't twitch. If he feared me he hid it well.

"Fine! I lied about Forge. Obviously I knew about it, but I didn't know you were here. I have no idea who you are."

"Your partner is fond of secrecy, isn't he?"

I stopped pacing and bent over, getting close to his face. "He's not my goddamned partner!"

"If you insist."

I threw up my hands and stomped to the far side of the room.

"Why are you here?" he asked.

I fell into the chair and crossed my arms. "Don't you know everything?"

"I never claimed such a thing." He leaned forward, resting both elbows on his knees. "When they signaled me about you I assumed that you had come to bargain, perhaps offering Forge for protection from your –" he sat up straight at my reaction, "– Mr. Nguyen. We searched your flyer but you didn't bring Vulcan's Forge with you."

"No I didn't."

"Either out of criminal paranoia – thieves are always fearful of theft – or foolishness."

"Insults are so very persuasive."

"The truth cannot be an insult. Facts are what they are."

"I didn't come here to bargain, so you had better mark it down to foolishness."

"So why did you come to us?"

"I told you! I didn't know you were here. All I knew—"

I shut up, before my anger started me spilling. Hardgrave waited but I stayed silent. We sat there, eyeing each other, waiting for someone to talk as the minutes passed. An idea presented itself to me.

"You know that the Administration is going to come looking for me. When they do they are going to find you." I continued in a flat factual voice, something I suspected would work well on Hardgrave and his ilk. "It's already been two days, but if I fly back now—"

"You'd face very serious charges."

He smiled much like my brother did whenever he caught one of his brood in a fib.

"You filed no flight plan and as we speak Security has declared that you've gone 'over the wall' trying to escape a series of rather complex criminal conspiracies."

"They'll find the flyer. That's—"

"The beacon is disabled." He stood. "We are still working past the interface locks, Mr. Kessler. Rest assured we will break them, but no one is looking for you."

He moved to the door, but paused before stepping out. "Except, of course, Mr. Nguyen."

The door locked behind him and I slammed my fist into the wall. I had nothing to work with and now the Admin thought I was one of those nutcases that go native, fantasizing that they can live off the land. The Tans could kill me and no one, not a single person, would know or care.

I remembered reading every few months about some poor idiot going 'over the wall'. How they started calling it that when the city didn't have a wall I had no clue, but it always meant the same thing: someone's gone out of their head.

It was a pretty serious subject for the Administration. Every human life counted and when someone removed themselves from the breeding population it was not just themselves they affected but all those generations now denied their existence. Of course, anyone taking a deep look at my life wouldn't be surprised if they announced I had taken to the hills, but criminal charges on top struck me as overkill.

Sitting in my cell, hundreds of miles from the city, I suddenly wondered just how many of those wall jumpers had truly been insane and how many Hardgrave and company had helped to disappear. Time was running out and no matter how sincere his assurances, I didn't trust Hardgrave or anyone, except Pamela.

*　　*　　*

Evening rolled around and my situation remained unchanged. Locked in this cell I couldn't help Pamela or myself. The only way out seemed to be playing along, at least long enough to get free and work out this tangled game. Once I knew who everyone was and what they wanted, then maybe, just maybe, I could escape with my life and skin intact. I activated the interface and sent a message that I was willing to talk.

When the door opened Hardgrave, Terrance, and Nataya stepped inside. It didn't go unnoticed by me that those two were armed with their little dart guns.

"Are you prepared to be reasonable?" Hardgrave asked as he pulled a chair over.

"Sure, this is getting me nowhere."

He pointed to the chair. "Sit. Time is not a resource we can waste."

"I'm not in the mood to be ordered around."

"Moods are for romance and fiction, not adults conducting serious business." He shrugged. "However if my brusqueness struck you as impolite, I apologize. You and your partners have proved far more talented at creating chaos and trouble than predicted."

I took the seat while the trio stood, looming over me.

"First off, you're still wrong about Eddie. He's no partner of mine. Never has been."

Hardgrave held out a hand and Terrance dropped a slate into it. As Hardgrave studied it, I looked close but didn't recognize the model. He turned it around so the display faced me.

"As you can see we know all about you and Mr. Nguyen. The sharing of financial spoils from your joint criminal empire and, now that you've attempted to murder him, the dissolving of your partnership."

I shook my head.

"You're still wrong on just about every point. I never knew Eddie before I knew Pamela and I certainly never did any of this with him." I handed the slate back to Hardgrave. "You know about Forge, hell's bells, you probably made the damned thing. You can't trust any record in the network."

"Who created this counterfeit, then?"

"Eddie. He's pissed at Pamela and me. That's his way of seeing to it that the Administration does his dirty work for him."

Hardgrave nodded and for a few moments said nothing.

"Who is Pamela?"

I snorted at him. "You really know nothing. I'm not telling you anything about her. I don't want those two drilling her with darts."

"Is this her?"

He again turned the display toward me. A still image from the theater captured Pamela as she crossed behind the concessions. It looked like she was heading toward my apartment. The image lacked any sort of time stamp and I had no idea how long ago they had taken it, but I did notice it hadn't come from any of the security cameras.

"Don't bother lying," Hardgrave suggested. "You're not very talented in that art."

"Fine, but I'm not talking about her. These two —" I gestured toward Nataya and Terrance, "— are likely to use her as target practice."

"We don't go looking for prisoners. You came here, remember?"

"Yeah, that was a colossal screwup."

"Where's Vulcan's Forge now?"

"Who are you?"

"This is not a negotiation. Our concerns are not yours."

I started to back talk him, but Hardgrave didn't give me a chance, barreling right over me.

"But, if you help us, while we can't answer your questions, we can resolve your problems."

"That has a frightening note of finality."

"Mr. Kessler, I can allow some latitude in your unreasonable suspicions but you are truly abusing your privileged position. If we were inclined to do you that sort of harm by now you would have had rather unpleasant confirmation of that base nature."

I shook my head. "But you won't tell me who you really are, what you really want, and even how you're going to help me. You're asking a lot on faith."

Terrance spoke up. "Faith is for fools."

Hardgrave gave him a fast, cool stare and turned his attention back to me.

"I have been honest with you, Mr. Kessler. We will not share information about ourselves, for our safety and your own. As for our resolution of your troubles, we need the specifics from you. If a problem is not clearly understood, in all its parameters, then it cannot be reasonably solved."

"So it still comes down to trust."

"Trust is not the same as faith. How have we acted in any manner that is not trustworthy?"

I smirked. "You bugged my theater."

"It's not your theater, but you are correct there. It is also clear we have not turned such information over to the colonial authorities."

"You sent anonymous messages to my fiancée about Pamela."

"We did no such thing." His expression turned to one of an adult baffled by a child's unreasonable worldview. "Truly, we haven't any concerns over your desire to chain yourself to an unreasonable standard of monogamy."

I tried glaring at Hardgrave, hoping for something to break, some sliver of information, but he regarded me with a cool detached expression. I gave in.

"Fine, I'll tell you what I can."

Hardgrave nodded to Nataya and she commenced recording. I sketched for them in broad general terms almost everything that had happened since I met Pamela. How Eddie had kept her as his personal sexual slave in addition to his criminal empire. I emphasized rescuing her from Eddie, and that we had no intention of harming him, but that Eddie had attacked her and she had been forced to defend herself. As I recounted the aftermath with Eddie bleeding out on the floor and how we left him for dead, I noticed under their perfect complexions both Nataya and Terrance looked unwell, aside from a general expression of disgust. Hardgrave appeared unaffected. I didn't tell them the location of Pamela's new apartment and I left out enough so that it sounded as though I had kept hold of Forge. They didn't challenge me about it and my hopes for escape rose.

"So where is Vulcan's Forge now?"

Hardgrave studied me close as he waited for an answer.

"At the theater."

"We've searched it."

My heart raced, but reminding myself that he hadn't known most of this, I was determined to prove my lying skills.

"I hid it. I didn't want the Administration finding it."

Several silent seconds slid past with Hardgrave simply staring into my eyes. He didn't know everything and he didn't read minds. I kept quiet while hoping his doubts and needs would carry the lie. Under other circumstances I might have enjoyed his squirming and his facade of control crumbling, but at the moment all I really wanted was escape.

"Where in the theater?"

"I'm not going to tell you."

"That's hardly co-operative."

"I'll show you."

He gave me an incredulous look. "We don't trust you. Just tell us how to find it and we'll take care of everything."

"No." I stood up. "I'm not going to give it to you until I'm home and safe. Afterward, when you have your magic gizmo, we can talk about fixing everything, but not until I'm home and free."

"You've given us no reason to trust you," Nataya said.

"You'll have to take it on faith."

That earned me a nasty sideways glance from Hardgrave, but he said nothing. He wrestled with my proposition. Undoubtedly he expected an escape attempt, and he'd be right, but I held the one thing that they had to have – Forge. As long as they believed that, I had leverage.

"Fine," Hardgrave agreed. He turned to the other two. "Get him to a ground car. I'll join you."

CHAPTER EIGHTEEN

Terrance and Nataya escorted me out of the cell and through a short maze of hallways. It quickly became evident that whoever the Tans were they had made no real provisions for prisoners. The other rooms of the building were just office, storage, and recreational spaces. My cell had been nothing more than an apartment with the door modified to lock from the outside.

The pair walked behind me, giving me verbal directions as we made our way outside. The small of my back itched in anticipation of a flurry of darts, but nothing happened. As we passed other rooms I spotted more people who with only slight variation had the same skin tone. Those who noticed our passage tended to give us no more attention than any other passing person. No one stared at the freak being marched outside.

We exited into the night. Companion was just rising above the mountains, but the facility's artificial lighting washed out its dull light. The building sat on the edge of the pit I had seen that first night. I had a little better view now and I spotted ramps cut into the side that spiraled down into the shaft. Light stands evenly spaced along the paths provided illumination and one ramp looked large enough for vehicles, but the pit's depth prevented me from seeing the bottom.

"Left," Nataya said, stopping my gawking.

A gentle ramp led down to one of those narrow streets, though it was more alley than street. A few people moved around the other buildings, but either by chance or by design my escorts and I had a path to ourselves.

"That way." Again it was Nataya, but behind me I heard both of their footsteps.

We moved down one of the alleys but after just a few dozen yards the buildings gave way to a flat expanse like a flyer pad and several parked ground cars. I peered overhead. The camouflage screen covered the sky with a gauzelike effect, but Companion and several brighter stars still shone through.

Terrance came around to one side. He had his pistol out and aimed at me, though his jumpiness made the barrel waver. Pamela could show him a thing or two about staying cool. Nataya took off in a jog across the lot to a storage building, leaving us alone.

I'm no fighter, and even if I overpowered him without getting shot by his sleepy-time darts I'd have no way out of the valley. Playing for time, I stepped back, but with my hands raised, and sat on the edge of the lot.

"And they say Ferals can't be taught."

"People keep calling me that. What the hell do you mean?" I wasted time, and tried to put him at ease with this fishing around.

"Forget it," he said. "I shouldn't have said anything."

"I assume it's an insult." He started to object but I continued. "I'll forget and forgive. That's the Christian thing to do."

I stretched my legs out in front of me, sitting with a posture that hopefully assured him I wasn't about to spring up.

"After all, you people have been very decent and charitable to me. Hardgrave's right about that. I got myself into this mess. I guess the only real threat to my life is Eddie."

At Eddie's name he flinched and anger flashed across his face.

"I'm glad you're deciding to be reasonable." Terrance sounded friendly, but the gun still wavered in my direction.

I shrugged. "I don't think I've been that unreasonable. When you get right down to it all I've really wanted is to not get tied down, have the kind of fun the Admin doesn't approve of, and watch my movies. Is that so bad?"

"It's not up to me, but you threw Cornelius over the bluff. He's going to be a couple of weeks recovering."

"That was an accident. I was scared and just trying to get away, Terrance. I've never deliberately hurt anybody."

He started to reply but Nataya's arrival with a ground car cut him off. The door popped open and she stepped out. She looked over at me, sitting flat on my ass, and Terrance a few yards away. Her hand went to her own pistol.

"Did he behave?"

"He did, like a proper Celes— person."

She glared at the almost-spoken word, which seemed like a serious transgression.

"Hardgrave called," she said, moving the conversation along. "He can't come right away. We're to take him back to his craft and fly with him back to the theater."

"What's happened?"

"He didn't say." She spared me a quick unfriendly look. "But it didn't make him happy, whatever it was."

"Let's go." He pointed with his thumb to the waiting car.

Terrance seemed unflustered by the changes, perhaps from confidence in his leader, or perhaps just in themselves. I clambered to my feet, noticing that Nataya never took her eye off me, and moved to the door.

"Sit in the back," she ordered.

I took the seat as ordered and Terrance came up to the car.

"Get in back with him?"

She shook her head. "No, we'll raise the screen."

Unconcerned, Terrance moved to the driver's compartment and she joined him. The door closed and we started toward the valley's rim.

It took me a few seconds to realize that Nataya was manually piloting the car and there were no automatics. That puzzled me until I worked it out. They couldn't use the Planetary Positioning System, not without a valid network handshake. That might give away their little game. They needed Forge to cover their tracks just as Eddie covered his.

That got me thinking about Eddie's network and Forge. With Forge gone and no way to cover his network footprint, it wouldn't be long before things started tripping Security. All those fabricators printing contraband had to be stopped, and even if just a few kept operating it would be like shooting off a flare. One way or another Eddie's enterprise was crashing to the ground. The only question was, who was going to be crushed by the debris.

The car crawled out from under the tarp and we headed south toward my flyer, and hopefully, escape.

★   ★   ★

Without a road into the mountains and forest the ground car crawled. Terrance and Nataya kept a screen raised between the driver's compartment and me. I needed to find a way to give them the slip, but as long as the car was moving I was trapped. It looked like a standard model, meaning the doors locked whenever it moved. I sat forward, listening to their conversation, hoping for a plan.

Terrance fiddled with his pistol. He took the clip out, counted the darts, slid it back into place, and after a few minutes repeated the process.

Finally Nataya lost her patience and snapped, "Will you stop that! It serves no rational purpose!"

"It makes me feel better." Despite his protests he holstered the weapon.

"You know who's waiting there," he complained.

"She's there, but she's not waiting, and certainly not for us."

"She's there, that's good enough for me." His hand went to the pistol, his fingers playing along its surface. "I'm not going to take any chances, not with her. She's going to sleep the moment I see her."

"I'm not arguing," Nataya said. "Just getting all emotional and worked up is going to make you unreliable and that's no good to you, to me, or to our mission."

A beat of silence passed between them, and then she continued.

"And if I see her I'm dropping her first." She gave an exaggerated shiver. "She's a murderer. I don't care if Eddie lived. She tried and that's enough."

Pamela! She was at the theater. I realized that Hardgrave's image of her was from tonight. I had to make sure that she didn't fall into the Tans' clutches.

Then their conversation veered into new territory.

"When this is all over and we've got Forge back," Nataya said, "I was thinking we might celebrate."

"Sounds good, what did you have in mind?"

She gave him a sly smile and without a hint of embarrassment she said, "A good fuck, of course."

"With or without Annabelle?"

"Bring her along. I was going to invite Pavel. He's always wanted to have a fling with you."

Terrance shrugged. "Sure."

"I don't think I've seen you with a guy. Do you need a dose? I've got plenty."

Terrance laughed, carefree and utterly lacking in self-consciousness.

"I'm not a messed-up Feral."

"I didn't think so, but you know even with the Aguru's best efforts we still get a mono from time to time."

"Well, that's not me."

I fell back in my seat. Who the hell were they? Terrance turned to look at me. He laughed and then turned to Nataya.

"I think we shocked him."

"You can't shock a Feral. All you can do is bewilder them."

They both laughed, but continued plotting their celebratory orgy in hushed tones, apparently out of consideration for my Feral sensibilities.

The car wound through gullies and over small crests that had taken me hours to cross. We weren't traveling in a straight line, but time was running out. I needed to find a way to stop the car, and maybe if I got really lucky, grab a pistol. Carefully, making sure I didn't disturb their orgy planning, I checked the doors but as I expected they were locked.

I couldn't attack them. Shouting and demanding they stop wouldn't work. I was a 'Feral', whatever the hell that meant. They regarded me as little more than a housebroken pet.

That sparked an idea, one that disgusted me, making me certain they would find it far more repulsive. I scanned the forest. The night was dark and the canopy cut out most of Companion's reflected light. Neither of my captors appeared to have any sort of visual enhancement gear with them. If I dashed a few dozen yards in the night I might lose them.

I pulled out my penis and began pissing onto the car's floor.

After a fairly brief moment Nataya shouted and Terrance turned to face me.

"What in reason's name are you doing?"

"I have to go."

The car lurched to a stop and the door automatically unlocked. Without bothering to tuck anything away and not giving a damn where my stream went, I threw the door on Terrance's side open and ran. Ignoring their shouts and orders, I sprinted for the deeper forest.

I ran, jogging erratically left and right, as darts whizzed past me with a terrifying soft *whoosh*. As I ducked around a tree, solid impacts sounded loudly in the night as darts slammed into the trunks. I headed downhill, gaining a little extra speed, but the ground slipped under my feet and I almost tumbled. The sounds of shots stopped and I turned at a right angle, heading off in a new direction. After a few yards I slammed to a stop and pressed my back hard against one of the tree's pair of trunks.

I bit into my lip, tasting blood, but breathed through my nose only. Footsteps continued toward my general direction, but slowly, with caution. I took a moment and put everything away, though my trousers were wet and stank.

"This is pointless!"

Terrance didn't sound very far away.

"We have the ground car. You can't possibly escape, Kessler!"

Ah! Nataya was searching for me too, perfect. I had feared she would stay with the car. Her voice came from slightly farther off. I crouched down low and peeked.

Terrance searched down the slope with Nataya maybe 10 yards beyond him They carried lights and played them back and forth, but away from my hiding spot, searching in the wrong direction. Up slope from me white light spilled from the open car.

They continued calling out, pleading for me to be reasonable – how they adored that word – but I stayed quiet. Moving from shadow to shadow, I circled back around and up the hill toward the car. I had no idea how long before they would give up and call for help.

I reached the car, went around to the driver's position, and slid into the seat. God, the compartment stank! I ignored it and with deliberate care I pulled the doors silently closed. I accessed the controls, and a helpful screen alerted me that I had failed to provide proper credentials. I smiled. I tried again, and again the security system refused.

Peeking into the mirror I saw their lights stop and converge, as they conferred. I nearly panicked but turned back to the task at hand. After three more failed attempts the screen informed me I had exceeded the allowed number of attempts and was locked out of all of the controls.

Suppressing a giggle, I slipped out of the car. They were climbing the slope, but still a good 50 yards away. I turned and headed south, following the route I had taken days earlier, leaving them without communication or transport.

★   ★   ★

Retracing your path looks so much easier on a display screen than actually doing it. Of course the Tans had kept my slate, forcing me to wander the alien forest while navigating by remembered landmarks. The rough uneven ground hampered movement and the frequent stops while I guessed the right direction hardly helped my speed. At least I spotted Companion periodically through the thick branches, helping me stay on a southerly course.

It wasn't long before wavering beams of light pierced the night behind me. They also moved south, though not directly toward me. I clambered up the side of a ravine and watched as they moved off to one side. If they stayed with that direction they'd never cross my path. Breathing easier I crossed a small ridgeline and started down the other side. Inspiration blossomed and I skidded to a halt, prompting a small avalanche of pebbles and twigs.

I turned around and moved back to the ridgeline. Terrance's and Nataya's beams still cut through the night, making them visible for miles. They moved steadily southward on their own course. They weren't hoofing it back to their base. I watched for several moments but they never turned or scattered in a search.

They weren't searching for me; they were heading directly to my flyer. I had to give them credit. They hadn't been very competent jailers, kind and polite, yes, but competent, no. However, as pursuers they showed more skill. The flyer was my only hope for real escape. Now that I was lost in the forest they were leading me right where I needed to go. I moved fast to stay ahead of them, letting their lights point the direction. If they reached the flyer ahead of me, or hell, even at the same time, I'd just be recaptured.

My calves screamed with pain as I dealt with uneven ground, slippery footing, and the need for speed. More than once I fell and tumbled down a slope, losing some of my precious lead.

A clearing loomed ahead and Companion reflected off the flyer's curved windscreen. I looked back over my shoulder. Their damn lights were a lot closer but I had no more tricks. I sprinted for the clearing. Head down, arms and legs pumping, I pushed myself past the pain, past the exhaustion.

Behind me they chased, again shouting useless orders to stop. As long as they ran they couldn't shoot. My calves burned, my sides cramped, and my lungs were raw from the chilly air, but I ran. As I entered the clearing, I skidded on wet foliage but didn't fall. Regaining my footing, I pushed myself harder. The flyer was just yards away. It grew closer and a *whoosh* broke the night as darts flew past.

When I threw open the cockpit door several darts slammed into it. I scrambled inside, ignored the preflight checks and started an emergency launch. Terrance outdistanced Nataya and from the flyer's fans a cloud of dirt, leaves, and twigs blew into him. As I lifted, he waved his gun, his shouts drowned out by the straining motors. I flipped a rude gesture in his direction, and then topped it off by blowing him a kiss. The flyer heeled about and sped toward home.

CHAPTER NINETEEN

I flew well-east of the colony, switched off all network interfaces, and steered clear of actively controlled airspace. Luckily for me no one in three generations had hijacked a flyer for evil purposes and Security remained fixed on finding the odd lost pilot and not those trying to remain unfound.

Once the course and programs were set, I moved to the back compartment and inspected the rudimentary fabricator. Flyers are expected to support teams working in the bush, but those teams pack sufficient supplies for their tasks. The flyer's printer could handle very basic emergency jobs, fabricating dressings and simple medical equipment. The clothing options presented to me were limited to a patient's gown or basic work clothing. I ran off a quick set of coveralls and shoved my soiled and smelly clothes into the recycler.

A search revealed that the craft had no food printer, just packaged survival rations of tough chewy bars packed with nutrients but lacking anything close to flavor. Resigning myself, I took several up front and settled into the pilot's seat.

Pamela was at the theater. I wanted to call and warn her, but if I activated the flyer's communications I'd alert the network and everyone else with access, legitimate or not, to my positions. I couldn't even fly directly there without alerting Security, and once they spotted me they'd take control remotely. Right now they thought I had gone over the wall and until I fixed everything it was best to let them continue to think that.

Munching on the tasteless bars, I turned the problems over and over in my mind. They broke down into three major hurdles.

One: I had to erase those forged records in the colonial network. Sure, I had done illegal things and watched a few banned movies, but nothing like what Eddie had set me up for. Without Forge covering his tracks, his criminal empire would pop into view like an invisible man whose potion has run out. I was not going to take his fall. I needed Forge and only Pamela knew where it was. I had to hope that she wouldn't bolt before I got there. Together we could beat this; apart we were dead and perhaps not just metaphorically.

Two: we had to make sure Eddie couldn't keep coming after us. It couldn't be murder. My stomach still threatened to empty itself every time I thought about those gunshots and his blood pooling out onto the floor. Forge couldn't fix this. If Security grabbed him Eddie would surely talk. He needed to be removed so that he didn't threaten me or Pamela and so that Security couldn't get the truth out of him. That sounded an awful lot like killing him, but there had to be another answer. There had to be a way. Maybe his enemies the Tans were an angle?

Three: Hardgrave and the Tans were my biggest unknowns. Someone in Nocturnia knew about them, someone high up had to have helped them set up that clandestine operation, but why? Despite all those hours as their prisoner I still had no concept of what, besides Forge, the Tans ultimately wanted. Maybe giving them Forge would placate them and they'd leave Pamela and me alone, but that was a lot to take on trust and even with their overly civilized manners I did not trust them. If we handed over Forge we'd be helpless if Eddie or Security came after us.

I tried to raise my spirits by reminding myself that even if Eddie had gotten Forge, Pamela had still escaped, and she mattered more than any of the rest. She meant more than Seiko, or even me.

The flyer banked as it swung from a south-west path to a more southerly one. I looked up and in the distance Nocturnia's light reflected off low clouds, giving the city an unreal and ethereal glow. I passed the final hills and crossed high above the surf. I programmed in a few more flight instructions and the flyer followed the beach toward the city.

It landed just over a mile from the outer districts and I stepped out into the hard-packed sand. This time I knew where I was, where I was going, and the ground did not slow me.

★   ★   ★

It didn't take long to reach the trail for Founders' Park. As I ascended the path, the night sea breeze blew in gently from my back, carrying with it the stinging smell of salt and decay. When I topped the small bluff the Ark monument greeted me.

I slowed and stopped next to the monument. The crashing surf was the only sound. I thought about the Founders themselves, those computer intelligences tasked with guiding our journey, clearing and terraforming our initial site, and gestating the Firsters before committing cyber-suicide and leaving the responsibility in our screwed-up hands. In only three generations we had divided ourselves into colonists and whatever Hardgrave and his Tans were. We devolved into bickering, greedy, murdering syndicates. I never wanted the responsibility of unborn generations. I had plenty of brothers and sisters taking up that task, but now for the first time I questioned the entire project's wisdom. Maybe there was a God and that brown dwarf barreling into Old Earth had been his twenty-second century's biblical flood.

Shaking off my melancholy mood, I started walking. The sound and smell of the surf died away as I left the park and navigated Nocturnia's illuminated streets. Here, near the city's center, the towers beamed brightly because every floor was occupied and the evening was not yet late enough to dampen everyone's enthusiasm. Firsters occupied many of the central towers, living bizarre, idiosyncratic lives, but when you're raised by machines instead of a family you're allowed to be odd.

Brandon's family had moved in with his grandmother, to take care of her as she declined through a rather nasty degenerative neurological disease, some terrible mutation in her genetic code induced by the long slow flight through interstellar space. After she had died, Brandon stayed on in her apartment, a decision that tonight brought a little good luck my way by housing him within walking distance of the sea.

The lights of his tower burned as bright as the others. Thirty floors later I stood, dressed in those ridiculous coveralls, and signaled at his door. His wife, Nikita, slid it open, her sandy-brown face set in grim anger.

"You're not coming in."

"Nikita—"

"You didn't listen. I said you're not coming in here."

She stood quite a bit shorter than me and after my captivity I had little patience, but I didn't shove her aside.

"I need to talk to—"

"What you need to do is leave. We don't want your trouble and I'm not going to have your perversion around the girls."

I sputtered.

"Nikita, you know me. You know—"

"I don't know a damned thing, hedonist."

She started sliding the door closed but Brandon's large brown hand appeared on the lip, holding it still. He stepped up behind her, his face sad, but equally grim.

"Why are you here, Jason?"

"I'll tell—" My voice slipped and I pleaded with him. "I'll tell you everything, but I need your help."

Indecision crossed his face while Nikita gave us stares worthy of death.

"They said you went over the wall."

I shook my head. "You know I'd never do that. There are no movies out there."

He cracked a smile, but Nikita snorted her anger and stormed off. Brandon stepped aside and I entered. I caught a glimpse of Nikita herding their two girls back into the master bedroom. She slammed the door closed.

"I've brought you trouble." The sorrow in my voice was genuine.

"More than you know. They're reviewing my position. I think before the quarter's out I'll be in the bush."

"That's not what I wanted."

"What did you want?"

I moved to a sofa and sat. He slid a chair across from me and settled in. I started with the night I saw Pamela in the theater and told him everything, holding back nothing, not sparing my ego. He fetched us drinks when my mouth turned dry, and fairly early on he left me alone for several minutes while he conferenced with Nikita. During those very long minutes my heart raced and my palms grew slick with sweat. I expected Security at any moment, but in the end he came back and I returned to the story.

When I recounted my affair with Pamela, Brandon's fingers tightened around his glass, his dark skin going pale with the tension. He held onto his anger until I reached Jones, her trap, and Forge. Curiosity displaced rage and he leaned forward, asking questions that I had no answers to. His demeanor turned sad and disappointed as I recounted Eddie and Pamela's enslavement. The theft and near killing of Eddie revolted him, but Hardgrave and the Tans left him, like me, befuddled.

I finally finished and looked out the large window toward the bay. The sky remained dark and I realized that in all the terror of the recent days the Long Night had slipped my mind. Somehow it seemed fitting that I'd fix this mess while we lived up to our uninspired name, enduring a thirty-eight-hour night.

He sat silent, then rose and fetched another round of nonalcoholic drinks. Now, even after everything I'd been through, he still clung to Nocturnia's idiotic social customs.

*   *   *

"You got to go to the Governing Council."

Brandon stood and paced back and forth in front of me.

"This thing is simply fantastic. You've got to take the hit, stand up to your punishment."

"That's easy advice to give. You're not the one they're going to toss over the wall." I stayed in my seat, tired and frustrated.

"You don't have a choice, Jason. This is bigger than you and it's bigger than any of us. The Tans, Eddie, Forge, all of that is a threat to Nocturnia, to humanity. For Christ's sake, you can't just think of yourself."

"I have to because no one else will. If there's something I've learned the past three weeks is that no one watches out for you except you."

He stopped his pacing and gave me an unfriendly glare. "You didn't learn that in the last month, that's always been your opinion. You've got a chance to do something right, to do something besides avoid responsibility."

"You do understand that being tossed over the wall is a death sentence, don't you? They can preach all day about leaving it in God's hands and all that but—"

"They aren't going to throw you out. Not with this sort of thing going on."

I ignored his interruption. "Out there there's nothing to eat. If you're not part of this fucked-up colony you're dead, dead, dead!"

He threw his hands up in an overly dramatic demonstration. "They are not going to throw you out. You haven't committed any capital crimes—"

"Attempted murder is a capital crime."

He moved over next to me and took a seat, bringing his dark brown eyes level with mine.

"That wasn't you, that was *her*. Turn evidence and you won't be exiled."

Condemn Pamela to a slow painful death by starvation, for what? For defending herself? For not wanting to be a sex slave? No, that wasn't an option.

"That's if they believe me," I said, avoiding the touchy issue of my love. "They're not going to do that, Brandon. They're not going to believe that there's a magic box out there subverting the network. They're not going to believe that there's a secret society of raceless people living here under their noses."

"You're going to have to make them believe. It's too important."

"Yeah, right."

I stood up and marched around the room, my anger and frustration building. "They're going to be looking for easy answers and easy people to pin it all on. That's Pamela and me. They'll just say I made Hardgrave up."

"There'll be proof," he insisted. "These 'customers' of Eddie's, you said it yourself, their crimes and Forge have to come to light. There's no way to avoid that. That's your evidence!"

"Maybe, maybe that'll happen. Even if it does it might not happen in time. Once Pamela and I are tossed out no one's going to be interested in making anything public and panicking everyone over secret enemies, just to bring back a couple of hedonists."

I stopped and leaned with one hand against the wall. The whiplashing emotions and energy had set my muscles quivering.

"I have to find a way out and the Admin's not going to help me."

A silent moment passed and he considered me with hooded eyes and a wary expression. "Then why come here?"

My anger and impatience exploded. "Because I have to get to the theater! She's there and she needs my help! Hardgrave is closing in and for all I know so is Eddie. I have to get there and you're the only one who can do that!"

He started shaking his head with slow motions reminiscent of an executioner.

"You have to help me! If I call for a car Security will pick it up. That's the end of Pamela and me, and Hardgrave and Eddie will get away with this!"

"Go to the Administration," he insisted, his voice level and calm. "That's the right thing to do."

"That's not an option. Let me use your credentials—"

He snapped his answer hard and fast. "No."

"Brandon—"

"I mean it, Jason." He stood up again and stepped a few paces away, putting distance between us. "I can't let you do that. I've got a family to think about. You would drag me into this murderous mess."

I didn't let him escape that easily.

Moving close, inside his personal space, I said, "If you don't give me help, I'm dead. Do you understand that? I'm not talking metaphorically. Your refusal will literally kill me."

He leaned in even closer, his face just inches from mine, his breath hot and fast across my face.

"Don't fucking try to guilt me. You got yourself into this. You wanted to fuck this woman and you're paying the price – not me, not Nikita, and not my girls."

"Brandon, please…." My voice cracked and a half sob escaped. It wasn't forced. I'm not a talented actor.

"You're not endangering my family."

I collapsed into a chair, my hopes dashed, my mind filled with images of disaster and death. Even if Security didn't arrest Pamela, eventually Eddie or Hardgrave would catch up with her and when that happened she was doomed. She was just a few miles away, in the theater, in my home, and I had no way to cross this damned city and its flying spies.

"I'm sorry," Brandon said, sincere but with enough steel in his tone that begging would be fruitless. "You have to go to the Administration. That's the only option left."

I sat there with long minutes passing in silence and I knew in a few more moments he would throw me out. He was right, but without proof what was the use?

"Okay," I said. "We'll both go to Security, Pamela and me."

Brandon nodded, not quite smiling, but with a trace of satisfaction on his face.

"Let me use your slate."

His satisfaction turned to puzzlement.

"I don't have mine," I explained. "The Tans took it. I'm going to try to call Pamela at the theater—"

"What's she doing there?"

"I don't know. Looking for me, I guess. The Tans showed me with their bug." I sighed, letting my shoulders fall. "I doubt she'll answer, but I have to try anyway. It's safer if we both go in together."

He nodded and pulled out his slate. At least if anyone came snooping in the records they wouldn't think twice about a call to the theater, because it was his workplace too.

As I expected she didn't answer. Hell, she might have left already. Naturally I didn't bother with leaving a message. Brandon patiently waited for me to hand the slate back, while I sat, desperate for another chance, another option.

Knowing it was an utterly futile gambit, I signaled Pamela directly. The line connected! She must have risked Eddie getting onto her trail again just in the hopes I would call. After a few short moments that seemed very long she answered.

"Hello?" she said, momentarily bewildered. I doubted she recognized the ident of the person calling her, then suddenly she smiled and her entire face erupted in joy.

"Jason!"

She started to speak but I cut her off fast. "I can't speak, not long, my love."

When I called her 'my love' Brandon's eyes rolled. I thought, damn him and his refusals.

"Listen, I don't have my slate and Security is searching for me."

"I know." She ran right over me. "Our…friend alerted me. I've been so worried."

Our friend. She didn't want to mention Forge if others might hear and I didn't take the time to tell her Brandon already knew everything.

"I can't signal a car," I explained. "So you'll have to come to me."

She shook her head and her long black hair flew in great sweeping arcs.

"No. That's not safe. I can send a car for you. You tell me where and it'll be there, off the books and Security won't have a clue."

I smiled. "That's my girl."

I quickly gave her an address not far off, then ended the call and handed the slate back to Brandon.

"That didn't sound like turning yourself in," he said.

"We will," I lied. "There's no way I can talk her into that over a call."

I got up and headed for the door. Brandon didn't see me out.

CHAPTER TWENTY

I hoofed quickly from Brandon's tower to the waiting car. Thankfully, I ran into few people on the darkened streets and as I approached the car popped open a door. I climbed inside and the vehicle sealed up, speeding off for the theater.

Pamela had Forge. With Forge, options opened up and our odds of escaping all the traps, plots, and dangers rose considerably. With access to it we could erase all those counterfeit records, destroy whatever Security legitimately had on us, and start unraveling the mysteries around Hardgrave and his Tans.

Thinking about the counterfeit files sparked an unpleasant conclusion that Eddie must have some sort of duplicate Forge or at least something very similar. It made sense and seemed an inescapable answer. It was the only way he could have planted that evidence in the colonial network and it explained how he penetrated our subterfuge and found Pamela's new home. We had been far too complacent assuming that Forge alone made us invulnerable. I wouldn't make that mistake again.

Hardgrave was a different matter. It seemed a safe assumption that the Tans had made Forge and probably Eddie's second one as well. Only with something like Forge could they orchestrate their massive conspiracy, but that didn't explain their zeal in getting it back. Why hadn't they made another? Why all this trouble acting like it was one of a kind when it clearly wasn't?

Keeping the Tans out of our lives was going to be a different kind of problem. Eddie was one man and one man can be stopped. A conspiracy the size of the Tans only stopped when they achieved their goal or believed it unachievable.

Despite the climate-controlled compartment, I broke out in a cold sweat.

One man can be stopped.

The thought bounced around my brain like an echo reverberating through a canyon. Eddie could be killed. It should have frightened me, contemplating such a thing so easily, but the conclusion was inevitable. Pamela had been right all along: as long as Eddie lived we were in danger. That man would never stop searching for us, never stop trying to reclaim Forge, and he'd never let anything get in his way. With nauseating certainty the endgame became clear. I briefly considered summoning Security, but the thought of a lethal exile for me and Pamela killed that temptation. My course was set. In some way it had been set the first night I had seen her.

The car slowed, stopping a short distance from the theater, and the doors opened. I hesitated, fearful that Eddie, or Hardgrave, or Security had overridden the controls, but no one appeared from the shadows. I climbed out and the car immediately sped away. Carefully scanning the area for waiting people, I moved toward the building.

My footfalls sounded loud on the steps as I climbed toward the door. High above me Companion's disc was lit by a brilliant ring as it eclipsed the sun. The pastors called it our protective halo but tonight it struck me more like an insect's view of an examination lamp. The Long Night had more than a day to go and the temperature continued dropping. My breath frosted and the air acquired a stinging bite. At the door I started to reach for my credentials, but stopped. Was Forge monitoring the access that might alert Security? I stood there, unsure how to proceed, when the door suddenly opened and Pamela flung herself into my arms.

*　　*　　*

I hugged her tight. She planted a massive kiss on my lips and for a moment I forgot our troubles, lost in her warm embrace, soft curves, and intense passion. Too soon we broke it off and hurried into the concealment of the theater.

"Darling," she said, dragging me to the lobby sofa, "I've been worried sick. Security is broadcasting your ident all over the colony and you didn't answer when I called and worst, Eddie's—"

"Alive," I finished.

She nodded. Her eyes were wide with terror.

"Forge warned me he was staking out my apartment and I knew I had to get the hell out of there. I ran down the emergency exit carrying only Forge and my slate!"

"I tried calling your slate," I said, "but I got a message that there was no such user."

She nodded, her black hair bobbing across her face.

"Once I knew Eddie was on the loose, I had Forge erase all my records. I don't know how he found me and I was so scared."

Somewhere in the back of my mind a diffuse unease started, but I shoved it aside before I had the time to work through the intuition.

"I saw Eddie," I said.

I quickly recounted going to her apartment and nearly running right into Eddie's overly muscled biceps. She listened with rapt attention, holding my hand tight as a slight fearful tremor shook her own.

"I'm sorry," she said when I finished. "I didn't want to call you until I was certain I had lost him."

She threw herself into my arms, wrapping hers around my shoulders.

"I couldn't bear to lose you, and I know he'd kill you."

I held her for several minutes, stroking her long hair, feeling her chest rise and fall as her breathing slowed. Her panic passed and she sat up.

"I've been trying to find you for days and the only thing the network knew was that you'd taken a flyer. Everyone thinks you've gone over the wall!"

"Baby, you are not going to believe where I've been."

It took a while, but I told her my entire misadventure with the Tans and their secret facility. When I came to my escape by urination she burst out laughing. It proved contagious and very soon we were supporting each other through our seemingly unending laughing jag.

"Sweetie," she said, giggles still erupting in her voice, "I had no idea you could be so dirty."

Once I regained control I finished up with my return to the colony, though I left out Brandon. There was no need to stir up her anger at his refusals and the suggestions that to save my own skin I should betray her. The mood turned serious and all of our earlier laughter died away.

"We're in such danger," she said, her deep blue eyes large and filled with tears.

"We'll survive it."

I stood and moved over to concessions and reached toward the fabricator, but stopped, realizing that Jones would have sealed all access.

"How did you get in here?" I asked as I turned back to Pamela.

"Forge, of course."

"It's here?"

"Up in your study. When you didn't answer I panicked and came here."

"So you've never heard of Hardgrave?"

She shook her head.

"Eddie never mentioned him?"

"Eddie kept a lot of secrets."

"Well, I can tell you it wasn't just Hardgrave. Several of the Tans knew Eddie and they seemed scared."

"He's a scary man."

"But you have no idea who they are, or what they want?"

"Honestly, I've never heard of them until just now." She stood and slid up against me, her breasts warm and firm against my chest. "You escaped, that's all that really matters."

She started nuzzling my neck and landing light kisses. Mustering my willpower, I pushed her back and broke contact.

"It matters," I said. "Hardgrave and company want Forge back—"

"Back?"

"Come on, you don't think Eddie made that thing? He must have stolen it from them."

"That makes sense."

"And Hardgrave isn't going to stop until he gets it, so we have to figure out not only how to deal with Eddie but we have to deal with all the Tans too."

"Not right now, we don't. From what you told me, they're pretty easy pushovers. They're not anything to be afraid of. Eddie, that's a different matter. You know what he's capable of."

I nodded. "Yes, and I know we're going to have to deal with him."

"Not deal with." Her voice took on a hard cold sound. "We pussyfooted around last time and now things are worse. This is no time for half measures, Jason. We're going to kill him."

I hesitated, despite my earlier homicidal thoughts. Speaking of it, agreeing to it, somehow made those earlier transgressive conjectures real, moving them from fantasies to plots. She stared while I said nothing. Life exists as a series of irrevocable decision points and Pamela pushed me from one to another.

"You're right," I said.

She refused any ambiguity. "Right about what?"

"Killing Eddie, we have to do it."

Like stepping into darkness and not finding solid ground underfoot, my stomach dropped and events seemed to take on their own implacable momentum.

"I know you love me," she whispered. "But he isn't leaving us a choice."

She looked up at me; our eyes locked.

"We'll always be together."

We kissed, but not deeply, not passionately. Never again would we be passionate.

Pamela went to her bag and I brought up Hardgrave again.

"We'll still have to work out a plan to get the Tans off our back, and maybe somehow put the Administration onto their scheme, whatever it is."

She turned around, a pistol in each hand. Tonight the hard plastic shells looked cold and impersonal.

"His and hers," she said, pressing a gun into my hands. Mine had a small inscribed *J* on the grip, while hers sported a *P*. She smiled, thin-lipped and grim.

"Now we're ready for Eddie."

*　*　*

As I turned the pistol over in my hands, the plastic was cool to the touch and had a faint whiff from the fabricator. I checked the chamber as she had showed me so many days earlier, making sure it was empty. Even without a ready round it frightened me.

"You can't back out," she said.

"I know."

Saying it made it real. I envisioned bullets tearing into Eddie, blood spraying in great fountains, agony contorting his face, and his final twitches as he died. My heart raced, sweat coated my palms, but in the deep recesses of my mind, or perhaps even my soul if I had such a thing, it pleased me.

It was more than self-defense. It was more than his abuse of Pamela. On a deep and primordial sense killing him thrilled me beyond simply protecting my woman. I was claiming her as mine, denying her to him and all others. For the first time I really lived. Only two things define life, sex and death: soon there would be both.

Mental pictures danced in my vision of Eddie sprawled in the lobby dead, triggering a doubt, but only about execution and not commitment.

"How are we going to dispose of the body?"

She gave me a wan little smile. "Eddie's done it lots of times, so this is justice. Forge has produced an enzyme, one specifically tailored for human flesh and bone. It'll dissolve him and then we'll wash him into the drains."

"The drains are monitored."

She laughed, a trace of cruelty edging into her tone. I shuddered to think of the abuse that justified her hatred.

"Like that's a problem for Forge," she said.

I moved behind concessions toward the stairs.

"Where are you going?"

"To my apartment." I pulled at the crude and itchy jumpsuit. "This thing is awful and I'm going to get something decent to wear."

"No!"

I stopped, the door half-open, the stairs waiting beyond, and looked back at Pamela.

"That's perfect," she said. "It's going to be messy and you'll want that on."

"I can run off a better set upstairs. The fabricator on the flyer was shit. Anyway, I need to check to see if Security has found that flyer."

I turned and headed up the flight, Pamela coming close behind me. I stopped halfway up and turned toward her.

"Don't leave me alone," she pleaded. "It's been awful."

I took her into my arms and whispered, "Never."

Together we entered my apartment. I went to the bedroom and stripped off the smelly sweat-stained coveralls while the fabricator printed something that actually fit. I considered a fast shower, but decided we'd have time for that later. Dressed and feeling optimistic, I went to the study.

Pamela waited there, sitting next to Forge, manipulating its interface.

She smiled and blew me a kiss. I moved over to her and claimed the kiss in person.

"Forge says the flyer is undiscovered. I told it to reroute security drones so it won't be found. That gives us a day."

"Just a day?"

She shrugged.

"Eddie always said that if you messed with the drones too much it showed. Even with the records perfect, people noticed patterns and so he was really careful about that."

I nodded and sat next to her.

"Forge," I asked. "Can you locate Eddie?"

"No."

Pamela looked at me, her expression unreadable. "I don't know how he does that."

"He has another." I pointed to Forge. "There are at least two Forges."

"I don't think so. I never—"

"He has to have another."

I explained about the network files intertwining me with Eddie and his criminal empire and how that had led Hardgrave to me.

"It has to be Eddie," I finished, "setting me up so that Security will eliminate me."

She was silent for several long seconds and then nodded.

"You're right," she sighed. "I can't believe I never even knew about it."

"He's paranoid and he didn't trust anyone, not even you."

"Do you trust me?"

"Of course."

We kissed, but a distance inserted itself between us, an ineffable emotional gulf. Sexual desire drained away, leaving me confused and empty. Pamela pulled back, her nearly violet eyes staring deep into mine.

"What's wrong?"

I stood up, frustrated and mentally off-balance.

"I don't know."

She peered at me, concern clear on her face.

"I guess this has me wound up, confused. It's not what I really wanted from life, plotting murder."

"It's not what I wanted either, but it has to be done." She got a faraway look in her eyes. "You'll feel better later, my love. When this is all behind us and everything is just as it should be."

I nodded, but said nothing. I wandered out of the study, vaguely aware that she followed. I left my apartment and walked to my office, not really with a purpose or destination, just needing movement. On my desk, connected to the theater's main power and network, sat another Forge.

Unlike the pristine and polished box in my study, this one was a ruined wreck. I stepped slowly toward my desk, as though the thing might leap off and bite me. Pamela stayed close behind, her footsteps light and her breath silent.

"What's that?" I asked.

"A decoy."

Peering inside, I saw charred and melted circuitry. I turned around and faced her. "A decoy for who?"

"The Administration, of course."

I said nothing, waiting for her to continue.

"Honey, you were gone and I had no idea where. I didn't know what had happened or if Eddie—" She choked up, but quickly composed herself and continued. "When Eddie's 'clients' start getting caught they'll talk and some know about Forge. With you missing, I knew I'd have to hide from Security as well as Eddie. If they thought that they had Forge I hoped that they'd search for me a little less hard."

It made sense, but still that unease resurfaced. Something was out of place. Before I could ask her further, Forge sounded an alarm.

*　　*　　*

"Eddie!" Pamela shouted and bolted for the stairs. I followed quickly. She pulled her pistol out of her purse and I fumbled to get mine out of my overall pocket. Taking the steps two and three at a time, she beat me to the lobby.

"It's Eddie," she repeated between heavy breaths.

I nodded, my hands shaking, my knees quivering as the moment of truth hurtled onto the scene.

"Unlock the door," she said.

"Why?"

"We want him in here!" She emphasized her point with the gun's barrel, stabbing it toward the floor. "Forge or no Forge, we can't shoot him on the street!"

I nodded and hurried to the door, disabling the security. Pamela stood in the middle of the lobby, facing the door.

"You stand over there."

She pointed to a corner behind the entrance and out of its line of sight. She took up position in the lobby, in full view of the door.

"I'll be right here when he comes through," she said. I hesitated and started to protest her being exposed.

"He's not going to shoot me right off." She paused and took a deep breath. "I don't think he would – and then we'll have him in a cross fire."

"Why don't we both hide back here?"

"He'll be cautious," she explained. "If he sees me that'll pull his attention, at least for a moment, away from anywhere else."

Again her voice broke and she stifled a half sob.

"I'll stand here," I said. "You go to the corner."

"No." Her voice lacked conviction.

"It makes sense. You shot him. He'll probably shoot first and ask questions later if he sees you."

I gave her a hard shove, pushing her toward the hiding spot. She smiled and hurried over. Adrenaline flooded my bloodstream and precise thinking seemed like something from a dream. Time slowed and every sound rang out and amplified in my ears. My sweat stung my nose and my stomach quivered and cramped.

The door opened. Pamela raised her gun, the barrel level and steady, pointed frighteningly in my direction. I wanted to move out of this cross fire, but it was already too late. Nataya stepped through with Terrance following. They spotted me and hesitated. Pamela stood unseen behind them. Both had pistols in their hands. Time slowed and Pamela turned her gun in their direction.

"No!" I shouted.

Nataya looked over her shoulder at Pamela and kept her weapon low. Pamela held her fire and I started breathing again.

"Guns on the floor," I ordered.

Nataya gave Terrance a look so fierce that I doubted her pacifism. They hesitated, looking to each other, to me, and then at Pamela, holding her gun preternaturally still. Slowly, they knelt and placed theirs on the floor.

"Kick them to me."

Nataya turned her nasty look toward me, but complied. Terrance, terror in his face, tried, but his kick only glanced off the gun and it skittered away and angled toward the wall. I worked fast, trying to maintain control of the situation before they spooked Pamela into doing something lethally rash.

"Over to the sofa."

They moved across the lobby and I circled around, keeping them in my sight, my gun ready, never allowing either of the Tans within a leg's length.

They started to sit. I shook my head.

"Sit with your feet bent under you and your hands underneath your shins."

It took them a few moments to work out what I meant. When they had complied they were in a posture that restricted their ability to move quickly. Pamela came over and stood next to me.

"There was a problem with that plan of yours," I whispered. "I was in the line of fire."

"It was on the spur of the moment, sweetie. Anyway I'd never shoot you by accident."

She looked at the Tans.

"These are your Tans?" She kept her voice soft, just for the two of us.

"Yup," I answered, loud enough for Nataya and Terrance to hear. "They're from that secret facility. Aren't you?"

"Irrational Feral," Nataya snarled.

Pamela didn't keep her voice soft. "What does she mean by that?"

"I have no clue."

She put the question to the Tans, but neither answered.

"Secretive, aren't they?" she said to me.

"Yeah, and if these two are here that means Hardgrave knows where I am. Damn it."

Pamela crossed over to them and I shifted to an angle so she didn't cross in front of my line of fire.

"What do you mean by 'Feral'?"

Nataya sneered for a reply while Terrance maintained an uneasy silence.

"I just had an idea," I said as a plan formed in my head. I turned toward Nataya. "All you people care about is Forge, right?"

"'All' is rather comprehensive, but yes, we need it back."

I looked up at Pamela. "We give them Eddie's duplicate."

Nataya started to speak, but Pamela slammed her hard with a pistol to the crown of her skull. In movies that always results in a neat and sudden unconsciousness, but reality was messier. Nataya screamed and her scalp tore. Blood gushed, flowing freely over her face. Terrance started to move and Pamela hit him too.

"Stop!" I shouted, moving over to her.

Pamela stepped back from the sofa, keeping us out of our captives' reach.

"These assholes do not have your best interest in mind," she snapped. "They're going to talk and talk and talk until you're confused and that's when they'll take the upper hand."

"It's not going to be like that."

"You're not going to piss your way out of this one." She waved her pistol in their direction. "This is no time for games or half measures."

"We're not going to kill them."

"One or three, it doesn't make much difference once you get started."

Nataya, her face covered in blood like a red mask, looked up and said, "I told you." But I couldn't tell if she directed that to me or Terrance.

Pamela turned to the sofa, the gun level in her hand, her expression cool and calculating. "Say something else, bitch."

Terrance's eyes flew open wide with shock as Eddie's voice rang out behind us.

"Can I say something, Pammy?"

CHAPTER TWENTY-ONE

The gun in Eddie's hand looked enormous, its massive muzzle a circular chasm of death. Pamela started a fast turn but Eddie pointed the pistol toward her.

"Drop it, Pammy."

She gave me a forlorn look as I stood frozen. Eddie covered all of us. With a snort of disgust she threw her weapon to the floor. It bounced hard and flipped through the air, but Eddie's eyes never tracked it, as he watched us intently. He paid Pamela particular attention. He smiled at me, a charismatic, mirthless, and utterly frightening expression.

"You too, shit for brains."

I dropped my pistol, the hard plastic echoing loudly off the lobby floor.

"Okay," Eddie said, gesturing with his gun, "you and Pammy get over there and keep your hands where I can see them."

I went over to Pamela and we walked to the corner. Eddie stepped away from his spot not far from the theater's entrance and took up a seat on a stool near concessions. He left our weapons on the floor, evidently preferring to watch us. He sat there on the stool, lounging to one side in a phony casual manner, smiling an unfriendly grin.

"Isn't this just special, all my 'friends' in one nice spot."

"Eddie—" Terrance started.

"Now, now," Eddie said. "I have the floor and the gavel...." He waggled his gun. "So we'll be rational about all this, right? Follow the rules, right?"

"Yes, let's be reasonable," Terrance agreed, too naive to understand Eddie's sarcasm. Nataya rolled her eyes, but said nothing.

"Of course if you're here then Hardgrave is too."

Neither of them said anything.

He turned to me. "What about it, shithead? Is Hardgrave here?"

I stammered and my mouth was suddenly dry, my throat tight and raw, and my attention focused entirely on his gun.

"Your boyfriend's pretty dumb, Pammy."

Pamela's voice hadn't abandoned her. "Fuck off."

He laughed, a deep resonating sound from his barrel chest.

"No, sweetie, that's your job." He turned back to me. "Kessler! Do you even know who Hardgrave is?"

Still unable to speak, I nodded.

"Well, now we're getting somewhere. Nataya, where's Hardgrave?"

Her eyes burned with more hatred and contempt than I had seen in any of her compatriots.

"Stop playing with us."

Terrance, panic edging into his voice, said, "Don't listen to her, Eddie. We can make a deal. We can come to an accommodation."

"Of course we can." His voice oozed. "But first, is Hardgrave here?"

"No," Terrance blurted as Nataya turned her contemptuous gaze on him. "He's not, but he knows where we are."

"See?" Eddie said to Nataya. "That wasn't so bad, was it?"

She said nothing.

"Eddie," I croaked.

"Shut up!"

Eddie sat in a moment of silence and then looked over his assembled prisoners.

"I know why you're here," he said to Pamela. "And I know why he's here." He pointed at me and then turned to the Tans. "But you two, this I don't quite get."

Neither said anything.

"We're going to have answers," he insisted.

Still the two Tans stayed quiet, Terrance frightened and Nataya looking ready to kill.

"You're after Forge, that's a given." Eddie nodded at his own wisdom and powers of deduction. "You two never had deep covers, and that meant you were stuck back at the beachhead."

"Eddie," Terrance said. "Listen, this whole criminal enterprise of yours is coming down and Nocturnian security is going to be after you. We can help."

Nataya was in no mood to negotiate. "Shut up!"

"No," Terrance said. "There's a rational path forward. A compromise that is beneficial to everyone involved. That has to be true, even for Ferals."

He turned his attention back to Eddie.

"Look, we need Vulcan's Forge, you know that, and you need to escape. Help us reclaim it and we can help you."

His voice took on an unhelpful pleading quality. Eddie heard but I think everyone, except Terrance, understood he did not listen.

"You know we can get you out of here. You know that!" Terrance's voice cracked.

"Yes I do," Eddie agreed. "And now I also know you haven't gotten it back and that Hardgrave's not here."

The gunshot shattered the air, hammering painfully at my ears. Terrance looked surprised, shocked, and then sick before toppling to the floor. Nataya leapt up but Eddie shot her. She reached her feet, trying to charge, but he fired twice more. Her chest exploded in a geyser of blood and the back of her head erupted in a spray. She fell to the floor just a couple of feet away from Eddie, the back wall splattered with her blood, bone, and brains.

"Well," Eddie said as satisfied as if he had finished a pleasant meal. "That's one problem eliminated. Now on to you two."

I barely heard him through the painfully loud ringing in my ears. Pamela looked at him with undisguised loathing.

"Why don't you two sit down?"

He pointed us toward the sofa. The sofa where Terrance lay dead and Nataya's blood stained the wall. Pamela sat and I pulled Terrance to one side and laid him on the floor. He stirred with blood bubbling out of his mouth. I jumped back.

Eddie shot him again. Blood splattered on my chest and face. With a sinister smile, Eddie gestured back to the sofa and, ignoring the gore, I sat.

"Pammy? Where's Forge?"

"Screw you."

"Later, we have business right now."

"You're just going to kill us!" I blurted, angry and scared.

"No, I'm not."

I was certain he lied, but neither of us called him on it.

"Truly," he insisted. "I'm in this for the money and killing you isn't going to make me anything."

He pointed to Pamela.

"You're going back, whore, and you're going to make good on all my losses and my pain and suffering."

With one hand he rubbed his gunshot wound, but then turned his attention to me.

"And you, shit for brains, owe me for all that money you stole from my accounts and –" he paused to leer, "– unpaid services. You're going to make good, and when we're square after that you're going to sell fuck-flicks. That's a market I missed."

"Unpaid services? I never."

"Pammy, did you lie to your man?"

I turned to her, but she ignored me and spoke to Eddie. "Fine, let's get this over with."

"He'll kill us!"

"No."

Her voice held a calm unnerving certainty. It also sounded less throaty, higher pitched than normal.

"If there's one thing you can bank on with Eddie, it's money." She looked over to him. "He won't kill us while there's profit in the air."

He nodded an agreement and asked again, "Where's Forge?"

"Upstairs," she said, defeat in her voice. "In his office."

"It's connected to the network," I offered, backing her up.

"I can go get it," Pamela said, starting to rise from the sofa.

Eddie shook his head. "Not today, Pammy. You're not getting out of my sight." He looked over at me. "Either of you."

He gestured us to stand and stepped clear of our reach.

"Which way?"

"Behind concessions." I pointed toward the door.

He looked apprehensive and didn't immediately say anything. I wondered if he was trying to make up his mind. Then he broke the silence.

"Okay, you go first, Kessler, then Pammy, and I'll be right behind you."

I turned and made my way past concessions, the spot between my shoulder blades itching as I anticipated a gunshot. Looking behind me I saw Pamela following close and a little farther behind her was Eddie, his gun ready.

"No wasting time," he ordered.

Pamela gave me a faint smile and then I turned and slid open the door, exposing the stairwell.

"Don't get any cute ideas," Eddie said as I started ascending the steps. "You bolt and Pammy's getting one right in the back of the head."

We moved up the stairs. Pamela brushed her fingers across mine, a simple gesture of affection and support. I wished I knew her plan. I feared Eddie's temper once he realized we were offering him a decoy, and a destroyed one at that.

I stepped onto the landing. On my left was the door to my apartment and on the right my office. I looked back at Pamela and Eddie. She rolled her eyes toward my office. Eddie's mood held no patience.

"Get moving."

I paused at the office door; Pamela stood next to me and slipped a hand in mine.

"Are we going through first and then you?" she asked in that strangely higher pitched voice.

"You are," he answered. "And as soon as you're through you're getting out of the way. If there's anyone else in there I'll shoot right through you both."

I nodded and turned around, that irresistible itch now a piercing phantom pain, and opened the door.

I slid the door and stepped inside. Pamela followed close behind. We took another step and Eddie, maintaining his distance, came into the office.

"Fuck!"

He barreled into the room, knocking us aside, rushing to the destroyed decoy. Pamela and I, immediately reaching the same conclusion, bolted for the door. Behind us Eddie roared. I escaped first and as soon as she cleared the threshold I shoved the door closed. Pamela ran, vanishing down the stairs.

"Lock the office door!" I shouted to the network, but the locks did not engage. I repeated the order as Eddie slammed hard into the door. It shuddered under his impact and I put my shoulder to it, pushing with my legs to keep it from sliding open. I shouted the order again but still nothing.

Eddie, though stronger, couldn't get leverage and for the moment we strained in a standoff. The door jumped with each impact, biting into my shoulder. The pummeling stopped and for a moment I breathed easier, then he started shooting.

Bullets tore through the thin plastic, whipping past my face and gouging out divots on the far wall. I jumped and Eddie hit the door. It started sliding open and I rushed back, throwing my weight, pressing it against the frame, trying to keep it from sliding open. He shoved, slowly forcing it open. Bracing the door against his broad chest, with one hand he pulled the gun around to my side and raised it. I dove away, running for the stairs as gunshots exploded loud in the landing's confined space and bullets tore into the walls.

Pamela raced up the stairs, leaping over steps with a gun in her hands, as I charged down. She pointed the pistol up the stairs. Damn her habit of ignoring me in the line of fire! I dove to the steps as she fired. Under the softer explosion of her shots rounds cracked and passed above my head. I rolled on the steps, my back and shoulders flaring in pain. I stopped my tumble before colliding into her.

"You couldn't keep him locked up for two seconds?"

Her accusation stung but I had no time for my ego. I crawled to my feet as she stepped backward down the steps, her gaze intent on the landing above. Eddie's hand appeared around the doorjamb and he shot blindly into the stairwell. Pamela pressed herself flat against the wall and I dropped flat on the steps. Filling the stairwell with her gun's reports, Pamela returned equally blind fire.

"We can't stay here," I shouted. "There's no room!"

She nodded and I sprinted down the stairs as she covered the landing, but from the top no more shots rang out. I clambered to my feet and rushed to the bottom while Pamela leapt. She landed badly and fell forward, dropping her pistol. I cleared the bottom landing and bolted through the door. She scrambled to her feet and slid the door shut. I retrieved both guns and tossed one to her. After a moment's hesitation I also scooped up the Tans' dart guns. I slipped the pistol and one dart gun into a pocket, keeping one dart gun in my hand.

"We're not capturing him," she snapped.

"Unlike you, I care if I shoot the wrong person."

"Whatever. Even if you do tag him with that, I'm still killing him."

Her anger and ruthlessness seemed alien to the sensual, seductive woman I knew and I couldn't shake the sensation that I was meeting the real Pamela.

We stood there, each of us angled on opposite sides of the door, waiting, and nothing happened. No shots, no shouts, nothing. With one hand I reached into my pocket and caressed the pistol, doubting my decision. Pamela looked at me and gave me a faint smile.

"You're right," she said, her voice again husky, her demeanor conciliatory. "I hate and fear him so much it makes me stupid." She nodded to me. "Can you slide me one of those dart guns? I promise to be better."

I knelt down and slid it across the floor. She scooped it up and quickly pocketed the pistol I had given her. We waited. Long moments passed without a sound as my terror grew.

"Is there another way out of there?" she whispered.

"Yes, of course. There are emergency exits for both the office and the apart—"

I never finished, realization dawning with terrible clarity. Forge was in the apartment! If he found it and slipped out the emergency exit we'd be at his mercy. We'd never hide or escape and he'd select the time, place, and manner of our murder. Pamela's face told me she had already reached the same conclusion.

I went to the stairwell door, Pamela following off to one side. My hands shook and I wanted to throw up as I slid the door open. Kneeling, I peeked around the doorjamb – nothing. The upper landing door was closed.

Hating every moment and every movement, I slipped into the stairwell and started climbing. Pamela didn't follow. I stopped and looked back to her.

"What if he escapes while we're going up this way?" she whispered.

"We have to risk it."

She shook her head. "No, which side is the emergency exit on for the apartment?"

"North." I pointed.

"I'll go that way."

She vanished from the doorway, leaving me alone.

I crept up the stairs, trying to make my footsteps as silent as possible. When I reached the upper landing I paused and strained my ears, listening to silence. I heard nothing but my own too-fast breathing. Stepping to one side, I slid the landing's door open. I peered around, but the landing was empty. The office door was open. There were jagged holes where the bullets had punched through and the gunpowder's sharp smell hung in the air. The apartment door was closed and unmarred, but stray rounds had punched through the wall next to it.

I hurried to the wall and started to lie flat against it, but then inspiration struck. I squatted down, bringing my eyes level with the bullet holes. Light streamed through from the apartment and inside a shadow moved about. Getting down on all fours, I crawled to the wall and put my eye to the lowest bullet hole.

Eddie crossed through the front room of my apartment, checking doors and carrying Forge under one arm. I flexed my fingers on the dart pistol while I watched him search, maybe for the emergency exit. He turned and started toward the short hallway leading to the bedroom. My knees complained as I hurriedly stood and went to the door. I couldn't let him get to the bedroom and the back way out.

Drawing in several quick deep breaths, I flung the door aside and dashed in, quickly dodging to my left. Eddie spun at the first sound, his free hand coming up with that monstrously large gun. I shot several darts at him, missing wildly. The room reverberated with his gun's explosions and the wall behind me cracked with impacts. I fell behind a couch and more rounds tore through it, raining plastic shards onto me.

When he stopped shooting, the sudden silence emphasized my ears' painful ringing. I belly-crawled to the far side of the couch and peered around it. Eddie was nowhere. With the pistol ready, I climbed to my knees and looked. He was along the far wall, trying to circle the couch. I fired several quick shots and he dropped behind a chair. In all the films I've watched heroes shoot accurately, but reality rendered my marksmanship very poor. I pushed the end of the couch, swinging it in a wide arc, maintaining cover as I tried to get to the far side of the room.

Eddie stood and began shooting. Bullets passed close by, again tearing up the couch, and a plastic splinter tore my cheek. His pistol again fell silent. I popped up but before I could aim he threw the big chair forward, sending it skittering across the room. I dodged to one side, firing again as Eddie dropped his gun and charged. He snatched up a cushion, holding it in front of him as a makeshift shield. Several darts hit it squarely. I lowered my aim, trying for his legs, but the gun clicked empty.

I tried to run for the bedroom but he caught me in mid-turn and drove his shoulder into my side, ramming me against the wall. The air in my lungs exploded out in a single gust and I struggled for breath. With the pistol still in my hand I beat down on his back and neck, but he ignored my feeble blows, driving a fist into my stomach. Agony radiated through my belly and chest and I nearly dropped the pistol. Dazed and uncoordinated, I was an easy target. With one hand Eddie grabbed my head and slammed it into the wall. Lights exploded behind my eyes and the world dimmed. I dropped the useless gun and tried with both hands to pry him off me, but he ignored my grapples and again used the wall as an anvil for my head. The lights flared less brightly and the dimming darkened.

I dropped my hands from his shoulders and Eddie gripped my throat. One of my hands brushed a coverall pocket and the hard lethal shape of the pistol. With darkness creeping in from the edges of my vision I fumbled to get the gun out of my pocket. Absurdly, I noticed the inscribed *P* on the grip as I struggled with it. Eddie released my throat, going for my hand as I pulled the trigger.

The bullet tore into his stomach and he flinched, stumbling backward. I squeezed the trigger again. Blood gushed from his chest. I shot again. His eyes opened wide with shock and terror. His hand came up, palm out, supplicating. I fired again. He fell to his knees and then tumbled sideways to the floor just as Pamela burst in from the hallway. She came to me, gently took the pistol from my hand and walked over to Eddie. He breathed heavily with blood bubbling on his lips.

She knelt down, staying out of his feeble reach, put the muzzle to his face, giving him a good look at it. Then, after he knew the terror, she shot him. Flesh and bone exploded, splattering her with blood. She shot him twice more, then spit into the ruin of his face.

CHAPTER TWENTY-TWO

My knees quivered and collapsed. I fell backward against the wall and slid to the floor, my head pounding with pain. My ears were beyond pain, moving into a frightening numbness. I sat there, my ass flat on the floor, my legs splayed out, lacking the strength or the will to move. Pamela looked at me, her face a cold, calculating mask. She came close and with a harsh tone cut through my emotional fog.

"We have to get rid of him."

My mind refused all functions and everything felt unreal, like a poorly remembered plot.

"Jason!" She slapped my face. "We have to dispose of Eddie."

I looked at her, the stinging of my cheek an utterly inconsequential sensation.

"We did," I muttered. "We took care of him."

"He's dead but we can't have that corpse here!"

"Oh." I'm not sure if I agreed or if I simply wanted her to leave me alone.

"I've got the enzymes," she said, her voice taking on husky pleading tones. "But I can't get him into the shower. You have to help me, Jason. Sweetie, I can't do this alone."

Yeah, wash it all down the drain. That sounded good, and somehow familiar. She took my hands and pulled me to my feet.

With plenty of pushing and pulling we dragged Eddie's corpse along the floor, leaving a wide wet slick of blood. The shower had a lip and pulling him up high enough to roll him into the tublike bottom proved difficult. Eventually he tumbled into the stall and Pamela stripped his clothes. As she wrenched the fabric free from his corpse she shoved them in my hands.

"Recycler," she ordered, pushing the last bit of torn bloody cloth into my bloody hands.

★   ★   ★

I held the clothes, blood staining my fingers and falling to the floor in large red drops. The smell invaded my nose, and my stomach revolted. I left the shower and hurried to the recycler, shoving the cloth into it. I started the cycle, and then rushed to the bathroom, happy the architect had separated bowel movements from showering. I needed privacy and time to deal with being a murderer. With scalding-hot water and vast amounts of soap I washed Eddie's blood off my hands. Under the scalding stream my skin burned and the pain pierced my befuddled mind, grounding me in the here and now.

I walked slowly back to the shower stall. Pamela was gone but Eddie lay in the tub like discarded garbage, naked and violated by our bullets. He was contorted in a posture only the dead assume. Blood flowed down the drain, vanishing into Nocturnia's waste and reclamation systems.

"It's almost all over."

I leapt at her voice as she stepped around me. She carried a large sealed jug, easily two gallons or more. She smiled. I think it was meant to comfort me, but the expression, coming so close after so much horror, intensified my unease.

"This is pretty stinky," she said, holding up the jug.

I nodded, but stayed.

She shrugged and broke the disposable container's cap. A sharp pungent odor exploded into the confined area. My eyes watered and I fought back a coughing spasm. Pamela held the jug out and let the thick oily fluid gurgle into the stall.

It touched the body and instantly flesh bubbled and fumed, making the stench stronger and viler. Through blurry, watery vision, I watched Eddie's corpse settle and begin to collapse as the flesh liquefied. Pamela moved the spout around, covering him with the stuff. Thick fumes shrouded him in a heavy fog and a soft but persistent hissing filled the room.

Coughing and gagging, she turned and shoved the empty jug into my hands.

"Recycler."

I nodded and hurriedly disposed of the jug. After I pressed the start button I wondered about the colonial logs. No doubt this stuff, the bloody rags, and whatever was sluicing down the drains would attract Security's attention. We needed to get Forge hooked back up again, and fast.

I passed Pamela washing her hands and face and went to the front room. Navigating the overturned furniture, I reclaimed Forge and, from force of habit, took it across the landing to my office. After setting it down on my desk, I reconnected power and data.

"Forge, are you operational?"

"All authorized operations are available."

"Good. Access waste and reclamation management and alter all logs for this location to erase any evidence or indication of violent crime or unusual disposal."

"Specified application already programmed and initiated."

The display indicated the processes started.

"Forge, you fabricated the stuff Pamela used to dissolve Eddie's body?"

"I produced the enzymatic reagent."

"We need more, enough for two more bodies."

My stomach flipped as I visualized stripping Terrance and Nataya naked, turning them into an ugly red sludge and then washing them down the drain like diarrhea. Forge had given me the production time, but I had missed it.

"Repeat."

"That quantity will require 19,386 seconds for production."

Damn, more than five hours!

"We're not done," Pamela called out from the office door. "Just a little bit more, my love."

I followed her down to the lobby and the bodies that waited there.

"I don't suppose there's a shower down here?"

"No, but there's a restroom, of course."

She looked at Terrance and Nataya and then shook her head.

"That won't do. The drains will be too small." She gave me an unpleasant look. "We'd have to cut them up and do it in pieces."

I raised my hands, warding off the image. "I can't do that."

"I know," she agreed. "So we have to get them upstairs." Looking at the bodies, she asked, "The bigger or the easier one first?"

I hated the idea of stripping brave Nataya, to humiliate her in death, and wanted to put that off for as long as possible.

"Terrance."

I slipped my arms under his armpits and wrestled with the corpse while Pamela took the feet. In starts and stops, leaving a bloody stain on the floor and steps, we managed to get him to the shower stall. Before we put him in, we stripped off his clothes. Since he was lighter than Eddie, it was easier getting him over the lip and into the stall. There hardly seemed any rush. We still had to wait hours before Forge produced enough of the reagent to dissolve what was left of Terrance and Nataya.

"Come on," she said, leaving the room. "There's still one more."

I trailed Pamela slowly as I slotted puzzle pieces in place.

Forge couldn't do anything with the colonial network quickly. That fact bubbled to the top of my mind amid a terrifying series of speculations.

When Pamela had vanished, all her records did as well. She had said it was because she had spotted Eddie but Forge couldn't have erased her records that fast, not without leaving a trail that even thumb-fingered Security could follow.

She had the records ready to be erased and set up ahead of time, waiting for her to give the order to Forge. Without telling me a word, leaving me lost as Security closed in, following those faked transactions.

That prompted even less welcome thoughts.

Eddie hadn't created those records to frame me; that sadist preferred physical, hands-on revenge. He had been adamant about getting Forge. There was no backup. He hadn't created those records, and neither had Hardgrave.

We reached the lobby and crossed to Nataya's body. Her face was still contorted in anger and contempt from her desperate, futile charge. The bullet hole from Eddie's perfect aim was centered in her high wide forehead but the back of her head gaped with a massive hole. Again Pamela took the legs while I gripped the body under the arms. We went to the stairs and I walked backward up them.

Pamela had known nothing about Hardgrave; I was certain about that. After Dr. Hardgrave had patched up Eddie he must have realized that Forge had been stolen and saw an opportunity to get it back. The Tans then spotted Pamela's forged records and came straight at me, thinking I was Eddie's business partner.

"Hurry up," she complained. "This bitch is heavier than she looks."

"Sorry, I'm unsteady. My head's still really hurting from Eddie."

"I'm sorry, my love. I didn't mean to snap."

I watched movies for a living and yet it was only at that moment I realized I was looking right at a superb actress. Faking fatigue – it didn't take much – I stumbled, slowing our ascent.

She had produced enough reagent to destroy a body and when Terrance and Nataya arrived she had been certain it was Eddie. More wheels turned into place. If Eddie was killed and dissolved, even if people knew about him and Forge, no one would ever find him. With a fake destroyed Forge conveniently in my office Security would declare that the threat was over. That would leave Pamela with the real Forge, covering her tracks and vanishing among Nocturnia's four million people.

It was a perfect escape that worked only as long as I was not in the picture and not spilling what I knew. Either she planned for both of us to scamper into the crowd or just herself. If she planned to kill me why hadn't she done it already? I looked down into Nataya's face and realized the Tans had never been any part of her plot. Was I alive only because she needed help getting rid of the bodies? Or maybe this was all too much for me and I was paranoid, seeing threats where there was only love.

We reached the landing and I backed slowly into my apartment, warily watching Pamela. Which was it? How could I know? Once we reached the shower stall I dropped my end, and Nataya's head hit the tiled floor with a sickening squelch. I hurried out, squeezing past Pamela.

"We're not done!"

"I know, but I'm going to throw up."

I hurried to the bathroom. I darted down the hallway, dodged inside and faked retching. As I did so I pulled out my pistol with the small *J* inscribed on the grip.

His and hers she had said, but in the confusion I had gotten hers and she mine. Now we had our proper guns back. I had the unused gun that no one had fired – the gun that I had accidentally pointed in her direction when she had laid our trap at the door.

I pointed it at the exterior wall, hoping, praying, I was wrong. I squeezed the trigger.

Nothing.

I checked and rechecked, ejecting rounds and trying again with a fresh cartridge.

Nothing.

My gun didn't work, only hers.

★   ★   ★

Abandoning the useless pistol in the bathroom, I walked back to the shower. Pamela squatted, tearing Nataya's clothes off. The shower poured a heavy rain into the stall, washing away the blood. She turned and looked at me with undisguised annoyance.

"Help me get her into the stall."

"I don't understand." My voice was weak and cracked.

"We have to wash the bodies away."

"That's not what I mean." I watched her hands, paying particular attention to the pocket hanging heavy with a pistol. "Was everything an act?"

She turned toward me, still holding on to Nataya's corpse.

"What are you talking about?"

"Am I just a fall guy?"

Her expression turned cruel and cold.

"You needed someone to take the blame."

"No." But now her act didn't play as well.

"You always intended to murder him. He didn't do a damned thing the night we stole Forge and tonight you *knew* he was coming."

"No honey, it's not like that at all—"

"It isn't? You just happen to have a couple of gallons of corpse-be-gone ready when Eddie surprised us?"

She hesitated and I barreled on, tears in my eyes and my throat tight.

"But you thought he was at the door when it was Terrance and Nataya. Why? Is it because you left clues, leading him to a trap?"

"Baby, you're upset. I am too. This isn't what it looks like. In the morning—"

"Did Forge lead you to me? Did it tell you what to wear? What to say? Did it teach you how to manipulate me or is that really you?"

"I told you Forge led me here, to you, my love—"

"Don't say it."

"What do you want?"

I shrugged. "The truth, but you've never given me that. You're one of Eddie's prostitutes, and all this is your escape." I let the accusation hang in the air without a questioning tone.

She dropped Nataya's half-nude body. It fell across the lip of the shower stall, the head hitting the side with another nasty squelch. Pamela turned, squaring off with me. Her posture changed, becoming defiant and angry.

"I *was* a prostitute. As you can see I've quit."

She tried to smile, but the facade failed to convince.

"I wanted someone who loved me, not someone just using my body."

As she spoke, her eyes, those lovely dark blue, nearly violet eyes, held no compassion, no warmth, no love, and she reached into her pocket. I didn't give her the chance to pull out the pistol, charging directly into her.

We tumbled over Nataya's corpse and fell into the stall. Pamela's head slammed against the wall, but it did not lessen her ferocity. She drove a knee into my stomach, striking hard but with only a glancing blow. As we fell my hand slid along the slick wet wall, across the controls, shutting the drain.

She slipped the gun out of her pocket.

Lying atop Terrance's bloody body, my nose and throat burning from the noxious fumes, but at least the shower had washed away enough of the reagent that my skin didn't start melting. I grabbed her wrist and we struggled for control of the pistol. Her free hand raked my face. I screamed and blood spilled. I held her wrist with both hands. I twisted it hard, but the water made my grip slip and she held on to the gun.

We rolled and scrambled for leverage in the stall. Water poured across us and my knees and legs slipped across the slick and bloody bottom. Again, she clawed at my face. With one hand I grabbed her other wrist and fell onto her, chest-to-chest, face-to-face. All illusions of love vanished. Adrenaline poured into my bloodstream as the realization that this was a fight to the death penetrated my mind. My heart raced, pounding so fiercely it hurt.

Pamela head-butted me hard, the blow knocking me dizzy. I barely kept my grip on her wrists as the world spun around me. She snapped at me with her teeth, biting at my nose and tearing flesh. Pain flashed through my face.

I tried driving her head back into the floor, but Terrance's body kept her high enough to foil my attempts and all I managed was freeing my torn nose from her teeth. We slipped sideways and the showerhead rained water down on us.

Her wet wrist slipped out of my hand and she snapped the gun to my face. I batted at her arm just as she fired a deafening gunshot. Flame burned the side of my head and I screamed. Disoriented, I recoiled, and she freed both of her hands. I opened my eyes as the barrel pointed to my face. The pistol clicked.

Empty.

Terror powered my reflexes and I slammed my fist into her face. We slipped off Terrance's corpse and into the growing pool of water. With a knee she slammed me in the testicles, but fear and anger propelled me past the pain. I hit her again and this blow was more solid. Blood exploded from her nose. My knuckles cracked and my fingers screamed with agony.

We thrashed in the water, wounded, afraid, and angry. Getting both hands on my throat, she tried to throttle me but I slammed my arms into the insides of her elbows to break her grip. She kicked, getting a moment's purchase from the corpse, and slid up the tub until her head hit the wall.

I put my weight on her, my knees compressing her chest, pinning her to the stall's floor. She flailed, but her arms were at the wrong angles and I avoided her grasp. With both hands, one already swelling and afire with pain, I grabbed her by the hair, her long beautiful hair, and drove her head backward into the floor.

The water rushed in, submerging her. I cried out in pain, emotional and physical, as I held her there. She thrashed, her nails clawing at my arms, tearing the coveralls and my skin underneath. My weight crushed her chest, pinning her under the surface. Her hair turned slick and I twisted it into thick cords in my hands, wrapping the strands around my wrists like a rope, never letting up, never stopping.

She fought desperately as her breath ran out. Tears blurred my vision, turning her face into an indistinct smudge. Her muscles trembled and convulsed and I ignored the blood dripping from my face and running down my arms. I blinked away my tears and through the water for a moment, for the last moment, our eyes locked.

She cycled through the same emotions as Eddie had: fear, shock, pleading, but I held tight, keeping her face submerged. She thrashed but escaping bubbles obscured her face. With great spasms from her hips and spine she tried to throw me off. Suddenly her violence stopped. She shuddered and was still. Her eyes, wide and alive with terror, became unfocused and died.

Sobbing so hard my chest hurt and my throat burned, I pressed down, pushing my weight through my shoulders. When the pain in my fingers became unbearable I fell backward, landing heavily against Terrance. I didn't care, and with the water spraying across my face I doubted I would ever care.

She remained still under the water. She was not playing possum. Pamela was dead. I cried for a long time, long enough for the water to reach the lip and spill out onto the floor, running red with blood.

CHAPTER TWENTY-THREE

Eventually I shut off the water and mustered the will to climb out of the shower, leaving the corpses behind, and stumbled to the office.

Forge sat on the desk, the lights from its display throwing off faint glows of red and green. Soaking wet, I dropped into my chair and stared at the cursed device.

I wanted to smash it, break it into bits until it resembled Pamela's decoy, but I held back my fury. Collecting my thoughts, I leaned toward it.

"Forge, how much longer to create enough additional reagent to—" My voice cracked and I choked on a sob. "Enough reagent to dispose of Pamela's corpse as well?"

"671 seconds."

"Start production."

"You are not authorized for that process."

I shot to my feet, sending the chair hurtling back into the office wall.

"I fucking authorized it already, just increase the amount, damn it!"

Forge's voice remained steady, without any trace of emotion.

"You were never authorized for that process. You inquired as to production times without attempting to engage actual production."

If Forge had been a person I would have called it passive-aggressive because it followed this with a verbatim replay of our earlier conversation.

"Forge, who made you?"

"You are not authorized for that information."

"Who are the Tans?"

"Specify, the colloquial term is not known."

I quickly explained what I meant and Forge just as quickly informed me that information was also restricted. I wasted 15 or 20 minutes trying to get answers. Bits and pieces of projects started by Eddie or Pamela I could learn about, but its history, construction, and purpose were forbidden. I gave in to frustration and rage, throwing office equipment about until my chair shattered the window and crashed to the lobby floor.

Exhausted and spent, I collapsed onto the sofa. I didn't cry; I had no more tears. Emotionally I passed through the rage and the fear into a suffocating depression.

The reagent didn't matter. Even if I dissolved the bodies and washed them down the drains enough forensic evidence clung indelibly to the theater. Security would have no trouble proving not one but several murders happened there, and I was guilty of at least one of them. With the decadence, the conspiracies, the violence, and the murders, no amount of bargaining would save me from exile and death.

Forge sat on the desk, implacably obstinate and unwilling to help. Now that my anger had passed I understood there was no way out. No manipulation of the records, no scrubbing of the theater could save me. Soon, all too soon, someone would come looking and that would be the end of me and everything I had ever wanted.

I stood and walked to the lobby window and stared through the shattered glass at the bloodstained and debris-littered floor. Three weeks earlier Pamela had walked through those doors, dressed to seduce, pausing under my window, and I had bit at the bait. She might be dead but her hook was still set firmly in my jaw.

My gaze followed the trail of bloodstains from the sofa to the stair and I remembered something Terrance had said.

"You know we can get you out of here. You know that!"

He had been certain and Eddie agreed that even with a history of drugs, prostitution, and murder the Tans still had an out for him, a way that kept Eddie free.

"I am not authorized to know how to contact Hardgrave, am I, Forge?"

"You are not."

"But you can. You can contact him and set up a secure conference."

"I can."

"Do it."

As Forge connected to Hardgrave I stepped into the office's tiny washroom. The face peering back at me from the mirror was suited only for horror films. Along one side ugly black and red burns marred my skin, my nose was swollen and covered with dried blood, and my eyes possessed a haunted, empty stare. I turned on the water, but just stood there, staring at the unrecognizable man. The pain, fiery hot and cutting all the way to my skull, returned. I wanted to lie down and let it all pass.

Screw Hardgrave. Let him see what I've really been through.

As I stepped into the office the main screen filled with Hardgrave's cool, collected, and tan face.

I hated him.

"Mr. Kessler," he said, condescension and disgust mixing in his voice. "I hadn't expected to hear any more from you."

"No one's getting what they expected."

"The result of irrational and disordered minds."

"I want your help."

"I'm not inclined to give it unless you return Vulcan's Forge."

"I might do that."

His eyes gleamed. He might have played at cool detachment but his greed was as strong as anyone's.

"But I have some conditions."

He shook his head.

"No. We do not bargain with –" I think he almost said 'Ferals', but checked himself, "– criminals, particularly violent ones. I take it you have murdered your business partner?"

My mind flew to Pamela, but then I realized he still meant Eddie.

"Eddie never was my partner. You've been duped."

I snorted, an involuntary expression that sent pain tearing through my nose and blood flowing down my chest. I turned away, tore fabric free from my wet and stained coverall, and cleaned off my nose. When I faced Hardgrave again his smug expression had returned.

"I don't see why you continue to deny—"

"Because it's not fucking true!" I slammed one hand down on the desk, but I had the good sense to make sure it wasn't my busted one. "I was set up. From the very beginning I was set the fuck up to take the blame for everything, and I am not going to do it."

I stormed over to the main screen and continued. "You're not getting Forge back until I get what I want. You will explain not only how you're going to get me to some sort of sanctuary, but you will also tell me who and what the hell you people are."

"That's never going to happen, Kessler."

"It fucking will happen! Terrance said you could make everything okay for Eddie. After everything that man did, after all the crimes he committed, he said you people could fix it. Well, Eddie's dead so you're going to fix it for me."

"Let me speak with Nataya or Terrance."

"Not even Forge can do that."

His expression darkened and his eyes narrowed.

He turned angry when I said, "They're dead. Eddie killed them."

I wanted to hurt him. I wanted to hurt a lot of people.

"Everyone here is dead so you're going to have to deal with me."

He said nothing for several long beats, his skin flushed even through that strange complexion. Then after taking several controlled breaths he spoke.

"Surrender Forge. If Forge verifies your innocence then perhaps we can help, but that's the only offer you're getting, Feral."

The connection broke and I stared at a black screen.

★   ★   ★

Beyond anger and beyond frustration, I simply walked away from the display. Turning my mind to practical matters, I stripped off the torn, wet, and bloodstained coveralls. I nearly walked to the shower, but stopped. I hadn't reached that level of numbness. I threw the soiled garment in the recycler, which was more trace evidence for Security, and fabricated a proper set of clothes. In a pique of vanity I selected a nice suit and dressed myself to the nines, topping it off with a smart black fedora.

Dry, dressed, and looking more presentable, though nothing short of a doctor could do anything about the ugly burns and my wrecked nose, I returned to the office and Forge. Poking around in the commands and processes answered a few more questions. Eddie hadn't been a mental giant and Pamela, while cunning and manipulative, proved to be only marginally smarter. Of course the ultimate irony was that I was fairly certain she rated several points over me.

On her return she had hacked the theater, so anything that went on while she was still present wouldn't be reported to the Administration. Nothing was deleted either. Once she left Forge would retroactively alter the records and before long Security would arrive, finding my corpse and all the evidence of the criminal empire Eddie and I ran. Of course, now Pamela was never going to leave, but eventually someone would come. I had foiled her plan but I had no escape.

Hardgrave's flat refusal made it seem certain he thought I wouldn't destroy Forge, and though I briefly considered it, he was right. The Tans needed Forge and I needed the Tans and their magical box.

I glanced down at the lobby, remembering Pamela as she had walked from one-sheet to one-sheet. The *Samson and Delilah* poster caught my eye. The artist had drawn Samson as a giant of a man, chains shattering under his strength as he snapped columns and demolished the temple, when his death became victory.

No rational solution presented itself, so it was time for an irrational one. I needed to take advantage of Hardgrave's fears about my erratic psychological state. I smiled. Maybe Hardgrave was right about me, because win or lose, live or die, all results looked equally favorable.

Working with Forge and the theater's fabricators it didn't take long to put together everything I needed. I had Forge skip over clandestine printing. I would be long gone by the time Security discovered the fabricator had produced explosives. The monitors and dead man's switches required careful wording, but in the end Forge fabricated them as well. I confirmed that the flyer was still on the beach and undiscovered. That had been Pamela's doing, making sure Security didn't start after me too soon, but now it worked in my favor. After making sure Forge monitored everything, I packed it in a freshly fabricated travel bag. I called for a car and left my office for the final time.

Outside the summoned car waited for me and I paused at its door, looking back at the theater. In the last few hours four people had been murdered. Not all were good people, not all were bad people, and I didn't know what to feel. Visions of Pamela dead and under the water floated to mind, and with tears streaming from my eyes I climbed into the car and left.

★   ★   ★

The flyer lifted from the beach into the skies darkened by Companion's eclipse, and a powerful sense of déjà vu swept through me. Though before

I had left from the flight center with Wolf watching, my destination was the same and its echoes reverberated in my memories.

Nocturnia's lights vanished behind the hills as the flyer sped north. Forge, wrapped in several pounds of freshly fabricated explosives, sat on the seat behind me. Just a few days earlier being so close to a potential explosion would have turned my nerves to jelly, but now it hardly mattered. I didn't bother with a low-profile flight. Let Hardgrave know I was coming; it wouldn't change a damned thing. I'd have my answers, I'd have my escape, or I'd burn everyone.

I activated the flyer's communications, no doubt triggering an alert on some Security console, and signaled Brandon. Instead of sending my call to his message system he surprised me by answering.

"Jason." His tone was distant and noncommittal.

"Brandon, don't go to the theater. Call Security, have them go, but you stay away."

His face softened, taking on a sad 'what have you done?' expression. "What's happened?"

"Trust me." The irony of that plea struck hard, but I pushed on. "If you go you'll have nightmares."

"Jason—"

"They're going to say a lot of things about me. Some of them are going to be true but most will be lies."

"You're not turning yourself in."

"No, it's far too late for that."

"It's never too late to do the right thing, Jason. Don't let *her* talk you into more stupidity."

I suppressed a nervous titter. "She won't, that much is certain."

"She's done it so far. I mean it, that woman's been nothing but bad news for you. Cut her loose and turn yourself in."

"I can't."

"What is it that she's—"

"Pamela's dead."

He stopped mid-sentence and stared at me.

"There's too much to tell, and I'm not ready to relive it, not yet, maybe not ever. Trust me and stay away from the theater."

He silently nodded.

"There's more than just her there. It's—" I hesitated, unable to find the words. "I can't say what it is, but this is all coming to a head. I'm on my way to Hardgrave."

"Why?"

"He has a way out and he's going to give it to me whether he wants to or not. When he does I'll vanish, and if he doesn't I go over the wall. Either way I'll never see you again."

"Jason, come back, turn yourself in. There is always mercy."

He continued pleading and arguing with me, but my attention turned to Forge. I was a murderer, and an accomplice to several more murders.

"It won't work," I said, interrupting his rambling argument. "This is the end, one way or another, and I'm going on my terms."

"You were always a selfish bastard."

I nodded, "Yeah, that's probably true, but...." I hesitated and then plunged on. "I am sorry for the hurt I've caused, tell Seiko I did love her, but I was too stupid and too weak."

"She knows."

"Tell her anyway. Goodbye, Brandon."

CHAPTER TWENTY-FOUR

A sense of tranquility imbued the flight. My emotional chaos transformed into existential nothingness. The sky and ground were equally darkened by the long eclipse and it seemed I flew alone through a void, the sole inhabitant of a barren and desolate universe. The stars not blocked by Companion shone bright and hard in the sky, but their cold light seemed to come from some far dais, where they sat in judgment.

Trusting to the autopilot, I climbed back to the main compartment and raided the first aid supplies. The painkillers did a fair job, dulling the screaming agony of my burned face and ruined nose to a dull and almost dreamlike memory of pain. An application of artificial skin acted as a bandage, though it left my nose with a distorted and bulbous look, as though I were a clown who had forgotten his face paint. It didn't matter; this wasn't going to be won on charm or the Tans' beloved 'reason'.

I returned to the pilot's seat still more than an hour away from the facility. I pieced together almost all of the puzzle, everything except the Tans. Even those anonymous gossip tips to Seiko had been Pamela. No doubt laying groundwork so that the sudden revelation of my 'criminal network' would fit into an already existing narrative of hedonism and degeneracy. The Tans, though, baffled me. They had to have been established by one of the Founders. Maybe there was still a rogue Founder around. Do artificial intelligences fear death? When it came time to switch off and turn the colony over to the Firsters, did one rebel?

It seemed possible, but why build a secret facility? Why so far from the colony? My theory was nothing more than guessing, and even if I were right, how could they create a sanctuary for someone like me or Eddie? I didn't doubt Terrance's promise. He had been bargaining for his life, and Eddie, even though he rejected it, had treated the offer as legitimate. But a Founder willing to harbor murderers? That ran counter to every line of their code. It didn't make sense.

The black void beyond the windscreen hid both truth and threats. My heartbeat raced and the night was suddenly frightening.

I switched on the flyer's searchlights, letting the automated systems sweep across the ground far below. There was nothing to search for, but it dispelled the void and I needed reassurance that the world existed. I considered connecting Forge to the flyer's main power but I didn't. So far, within my 'authorization' it had behaved and performed exactly as instructed, but I had no trust left.

Finally I passed over the low mountains that screened the Tans' concealed valley. As I approached the camouflage screen it parted, revealing the illuminated base underneath. I took the controls and manually hovered above the offered opening.

On the other side of that screen waited salvation or death. My numbness departed, leaving in its place a cold penetrating fear. All my options were bad, but this one had the meager virtue of being under my control. I switched the automatics back on and let the flyer land.

★   ★   ★

The camouflage screen closed above me as the flyer touched down. All around the tarmac's perimeter lights switched on, flooding the field with harsh intense beams. The buildings looked much as they had the day before, and just a few hundred yards away the string of lights followed the path into the massive pit.

I watched as Tans, several dozen, poured out from adjacent buildings, armed with their dart pistols. Keeping their distance, none coming closer than 30 feet, they surrounded me. Hardgrave took up a position directly in front of the flyer, flanked by Tans with pistols at the ready, his face an angry twisted mask.

"You can exit now," he said. A loudspeaker amplified his voice into a booming echo.

I switched on the flyer's external speakers. "Not just yet, you need to understand a few things."

"We are not going to negotiate."

"Listen and then make up your mind." I smiled, though there was no one to see it. "After all, that'd be the *rational* thing to do, don't you think?"

My dig failed to provoke a reaction but he gestured with a hand for me to speak my piece.

"First," I said, "here's the voice of a friend. Say hello to Hardgrave, Forge."

"Dr. Hardgrave, I am here and present in the flyer."

At Forge's voice a shudder swept through the line. Tans turned to each other, chattering in excited voices until Hardgrave silenced them.

"Before you people do something foolish," I continued, "like rushing this flyer, there are a few more things I want you to know, and so that you all understand that I'm not lying, Forge here will speak up if I say anything that's untrue. Isn't that so, Forge?"

"That is what you have instructed."

Hardgrave held up a hand, his voice loud. "You could have instructed Vulcan's Forge to lie on your behalf."

"Then you order it to be truthful, but nothing else, or I destroy it."

Another shocked shudder moved along the Tan line. Whatever this thing was, every Tan, man and woman, wanted it back.

Hardgrave nodded and said, "Forge, on my authority as mission commander, you will represent no falsehood or distortion, confirming everything Jason Kessler speaks as factual with silent acquiescence and stating whenever he speaks a falsehood or distortion."

Mission commander?

"Spoken just as I would have expected from a Tan."

Hardgrave let the backhanded compliment stand and I continued. "I have attached explosives to Vulcan's Forge. I can trigger these explosives manually. They will also explode automatically if there is a sudden change in my vital signs, so you can all put away your sleepy-time darts."

The people looked to Hardgrave and he nodded his consent. Slowly, and with a few Tans showing quite a bit of reluctance, they holstered their weapons.

"There's more. If Forge moves more than 10 feet from me it will explode."

Collectively the Tans stared angrily, but I no longer cared what anyone thought.

"I'm coming out. Unless you want to watch Forge go up in a million useless pieces, you'll keep those guns holstered."

Hardgrave nodded. I slipped Forge into a carry bag and picked up my detonator, a slim cylinder with a simple plunger button under my thumb. Slipping the bag across one shoulder I opened the flyer's door.

My heart raced and my hands trembled as I climbed down from the cockpit. Forge's weight in the bag pulled me off-balance and in my exhausted state I stumbled but kept my footing while the crowd gasped.

I held the hand with the detonator high in the air, making it plain to everyone with eyes. Despite my warnings, some trigger-happy Tan might shoot. If the explosives went off well, at this point I almost didn't care. Almost. I only hoped that their need was strong enough to keep their anger in check. No one shot. Pulling my hand back down, I moved a few paces away from the flyer, toward Hardgrave. Fear and adrenaline gave me strength and I couldn't resist taunting him.

"Are you sure you don't want to negotiate?"

The Tans turned toward him with rebellion in the air. This was more leverage than I had expected. I doubted they would murder him to get it back, but they clearly weren't going to back him up if he endangered Forge.

"What do you want?"

"The truth!" I shouted. "For once and for all I want to know what the fuck is going on and what escape Terrance offered Eddie!"

At Terrance's name the crowd's mood darkened. Hardgrave must have shared the news. I sensed a harsh anger and worried I might have already overplayed a desperate bluff.

I turned and shouted, "I didn't kill him! I didn't kill either of them!"

My words bounced off their hatred, and Hardgrave, while not smirking, stood with a posture reclaiming his haughty smugness. "You don't have any friends here."

Several voices shouted "Feral" at me, but Hardgrave silenced them with a dismissive wave of his hand.

"I don't need friends! I'm going to get what I want, or I'm going to destroy Forge!"

"You'll die."

"That's not a deterrent!"

The crowd took a collective step backward, except Hardgrave, who walked forward until he was within easy, and private, conversational distance.

"I think you will do it," he said with a terribly sad and resigned tone.

"Damn right."

He sighed. "Very well, follow me. After I am done, I hope you will surrender Vulcan's Forge."

"If I get what I want."

He began striding off the tarmac and I stayed close. The crowd surrounded us, but none came within arm's reach. Their faces, all in variations of that smooth golden complexion, watched me with mixtures of hatred, fear, anticipation, and curiosity.

"Mr. Kessler, I can guarantee you a safe, healthy, and long life where Nocturnia's security forces will never find you. You'll have all the comforts you desire."

"I'm not trusting empty promises. Too many people are too good at lying."

When he smiled, it was the sort of expression you might give a child when he failed to understand how the real world worked.

"Yours is a diseased culture, producing only violence and fanaticism. I'm going to offer you something better."

"From the goodness of your heart."

"No, our practical need for Vulcan's Forge. I will do what I must to get that back. Mr. Kessler, humanity's future may be in your hands."

He led us away from the landing field, through narrow alleys, until we reached the lip of that deep pit. A safety rail encircled the pit and lights followed the spiraling paths along the wall to the floor more than 50 or 60 feet below. The walls were sheer, smooth, and perfectly vertical. A flat disc-like expanse of gray metal, easily a hundred feet across, nearly filled the pit's floor. People moved back and forth across the floor, entering and exiting small temporary structures huddled against the wall.

Gripping the trigger, my fingers cramped and sweat filled the space between the cylinder and my palm, but I kept my hold tight. Hardgrave moved to a gate and I hesitated, realizing he meant to enter into the pit.

"There's no need to go down there. You can explain it all to me right here."

"I could, but the truth is so fantastic that'd you'd never accept it. Down there, and with Forge's verification, you'll know that everything I tell you is absolute fact." He stood at the gate, waiting for me to join him, but I still suspected a trap.

"You could try me."

"If you insist, but I doubt you'd be happy with the results." He swung the gate open and stepped through, standing at the head of the descending path.

"You have your detonator, and no one is going to attempt to take it or Forge away from you." He pointed to the pit's floor. "There at the transit pad you will learn who we are, why we are here, and the truth behind some of the lies you've been taught."

"And my escape?"

"Yes, once those things are understood then you'll also understand our genuine offer of sanctuary."

With my knees shaking and the trigger slippery with sweat, I followed him through the gate. As we walked down the path the crater isolated us from the strange sounds and smells of the night. It didn't look quite like a crater. This was not the result of a meteor impact, and the walls were far too smooth for a natural formation. I touched the cool rock, cut without the trace of a jagged edge.

The path maintained an easy grade and was wide enough for vehicles. Despite the bag throwing me off-balance the slope was wide and gentle, presenting little danger of me falling over the edge. The sound of a crowd drew my attention and from the pit's rim dozens or even a hundred faces peered down, following our progress.

I stopped and stared back at the onlookers. The harsh lighting threw dark shadows across everyone, but even so their intent interest unnerved me.

"Mr. Kessler?"

I pulled my attention back to Hardgrave.

"I think the only thing keeping me alive is how much they need this." I jostled Forge's bag and the crowd gasped.

"No. If you were so cruel as to destroy Vulcan's Forge even after learning its importance and the disaster that would befall us, no one here would ever murder you."

"You're too slippery with your words. I know execution isn't murder."

"All intentional killing is murder."

He turned away and started back down the path, leaving me to follow. The faces continued peering over the rim, watching us all the way to the floor.

The path leveled out onto a hard-packed dirt floor free of stones, rocks, and moisture. Hardgrave circled the perimeter of the hole, walking beside the 'transit pad'. It looked to be a single piece of dull gray metal perhaps a yard and a half thick and nearly filling the floor. Other Tans walked on it, crossing back and forth as they entered and left various buildings wedged between the pad and the wall. About a quarter of the way around the pad he stopped at a pedestal.

The pedestal flowed out of the pad as a single continuous piece without joints or seams. On top sat a more recognizable docking interface looking as though it had come fresh from any fabricator.

"Please connect Vulcan's Forge to the interface."

"No."

He grew visibly frustrated, but maintained a calm even tone. "You aren't going to believe the truth if you don't have Forge's verification."

"No. I don't trust you. Forge stays in the bag, disconnected from your systems, until I'm satisfied."

"You won't believe—"

"Then you had better do a damn good job convincing me. If I don't have an 'out' then I have no reason to live."

We stood there locked in silence and then he caved.

"Where do you want to start?" he asked. "The lies that you have—"

"Who the hell are you people?"

"We are the Celestial Renaissance Collective." He paused a moment, smugly letting me drift in the meaningless words.

"Of the thousands of Arks launched by Earth before its destruction, you think Nocturnia alone succeeded in founding a new human population? You have been taught a lie. Hundreds of human colonies have been founded and are now thriving."

"Hundreds?"

"At least. The Firsters knew this. They discovered our interstellar communications network, and reacting with primitive and childish terror, suppressed all knowledge of it."

"Why? That doesn't make any sense at all."

"Have you found that your culture is overflowing with intelligence and good sense?"

"Don't forget I have the detonator."

"I haven't, but everything you've done or claimed to have done you did for your own selfish pleasures, so do not play the offended patriot. We're going to be honest here, so you should at the very least attempt honesty with yourself."

I said nothing, glowering at him.

"Even without a stellar catastrophe it is unlikely humanity would have survived another century or two. Shortsighted, ignorant, and superstitious, humanity's nations were wedded to their primitive economic systems, corrupt governments, and fairy tales. Worse yet, every single culture was willing to murder to defend such delusions. The brown dwarf did not destroy humanity, it saved it."

"You've got a very twisted sense of salvation."

"It is a far more rational understanding than your sin-eater fantasy." He waved away my interruption and continued. "The majority of the Arks launched were, like Nocturnia's, dedicated to preserving diseased cultural heritages. However, a few individuals of uncommon foresight took the opportunity of rebirth and gave humanity a new start, free from the old prejudices, free from the old hatreds, and free to promote a true flowering of humanity's potential. Those precious few Arks formed the Celestial Renaissance. We are dedicated to liberating humanity from the chains of superstitious hatred and suspicion."

I nodded. "Let me guess. People didn't care for your new religion and shut you out, but not before your little cult got this place started. After all, every cult has to have its utopian compound. That's why the Administration is so adamant about shutting down the Deep Space Network. Can't have any more corrupting influences broadcast into the mix, can we?"

"You are close, Mr. Kessler, but it's not as you have guessed. Yes, Nocturnia's administration shut down all deep space reception out of fear. Every signal they found was ours, from nearby Celestial colonies, but we are not dissatisfied Ferals seduced by trickery. We are Celestials!"

He gestured to himself and to the scores of Tan faces peering over the lip.

"We are the new humanity, free from the accident of 'race', embodying an ethos that doesn't subjugate, enslave, belittle, or disparage our brothers and sisters because of meaningless skin hues. Casting aside ignorant Bronze Age myths, we are truly human and truly free. We hope that eventually with our guidance Nocturnia will join us in true enlightenment."

"You were right," I said. "I don't believe you."

I stepped away from him, swiveling my head for anyone approaching, but no one threatened. They came from other colonies? Other worlds? What sort of idiot did Hardgrave think I was?

"Did I not say you would reject the truth, that you would find it too fantastic to accept?"

"I'm not ignorant. I know that no one, not on Old Earth and not here, has ever invented faster-than-light travel. Your story is impossible."

"It is possible and the method lies directly behind you."

"You not only perfected humanity, you also invented –" I glanced at the 'transit pad', "– what, star gates?"

I barely suppressed my snickers.

"We invented neither. The Aguru, our founding computer intelligences, devised our society. No human tainted with centuries of cultural baggage could have possibly performed such a feat. As for the gate network? We don't know who created it, but it spans the local galactic neighborhood, and it *is* how we came here."

My snickering stopped. Either Hardgrave was insane and believed this wild tale or it was true. Far above us the Tans watched in silence. No one laughed, no one jeered, all of them held their breath.

I shook my head, unwilling to accept such a tall tale. Hardgrave gestured to the bag.

"Forge can prove it," he said. "Let us connect it to the transit pad. You will have the proof."

I kept shaking my head at him.

"No. You haven't earned the trust," I said. "You make your magic teleporter work and maybe I'll start to believe you."

Hardgrave's perpetual cool shattered.

"We can't, you ignorant Feral! Your murderous countryman trapped us on this backward world!" He pointed a long index finger at the bag. "That is our only hope of ever returning home to sanity."

A short bark of a laugh escaped from my lips, but the crowd's angry mutter terrified me into silence. Hardgrave's story began taking on a terrible reality.

"Eddie stranded you?"

Hardgrave snorted. "Before stealing Vulcan's Forge, he sabotaged the transit pad. Some of our best minds suspect he might have crashed the entire network. Our entire nation was crippled and humanity's future imperiled all for the sake of greed."

He took several deep breaths, regaining his calm facade.

"We need Vulcan's Forge and now you know just how badly." He raised his voice, making sure everyone watching heard. "Return Forge to us and no harm will come to you. I personally and on behalf of the Aguru guarantee your safety and well-being. We will give you a new home."

"Exile."

"Refuge would be more accurate, but only if you give us Vulcan's Forge."

"You're a fifth column, here to sabotage our culture and turn us into you."

"That is our mission."

"You can't do it without native help and you recruited Eddie and probably others."

"He proved to be far more treacherous than we had anticipated."

"Traitors generally are." I smiled, all the pieces falling into place. "If I give you Forge you go back to trying to subvert Nocturnia, but if I destroy it you're fucked."

"This is not just about the Celestials, this is about humanity. You've seen the records and you know humanity's endless appetite for war and destruction. If this is not stopped, the murder simply continues on an interstellar scale. Give us Vulcan's Forge and not only will you have sanctuary, you will be preserving humanity's future."

"This still is just a story, and one you haven't proven at all."

"I suspect you believe more than you're admitting, but give Forge to me and keep the detonator. You'll see the truth and if you don't, then destroy it."

Exiled traitor or reviled patriot, which did I want to be? As the question tumbled through my thoughts I set down the bag and stepped back, letting Hardgrave claim it. I fidgeted with the detonator as he removed Forge and placed it into the socket on the pedestal.

Anticipation filled the now-silent night. The world held its breath. In the crowd above every face watched intently. It began snowing, and the flakes, light and fluffy, danced as they fell. Several Tans had rushed out and together with Hardgrave they manipulated Forge's interface. My thumb circled the button, ready to destroy their prize.

I looked down at my hand and the plunger switch, but what purpose would that serve? The Tans might not kill me but the Administration would certainly exile me. Why destroy it? So Nocturnia might be saved from itself? Perpetuating this asinine moralistic high-handed culture?

Light appeared on the pad, glowing directly from its gray metal surface. Brightly colored spots and dozens of hues chased each other around the surface like manic children as the crowd let loose a deafening cheer. The moment of decision had arrived.

Even as a refugee I wanted to live.

Hardgrave turned and looked at me, holding his breath as I fondled the detonator's trigger. Then I took it from my hand and disconnected it. I de-powered the dead man's switches and transmitters.

"Vulcan's Forge is yours," I said, my head suddenly light as adrenaline drained away, leaving me drowning in a flood of pain. I stumbled and Hardgrave rushed forward to catch me before I fell onto the transit pad.

"We've got you," he said. He gently set me down next to the pad and footsteps ran toward us.

"Be good to your word," I muttered, slurring my speech. The world spun and turned black. I never saw Nocturnia again.

EPILOGUE

Even after six months, dawn on Garmoniya was a spectacle not to be ignored. The Milky Way stretched across the darkened sky, looking very much as I had always seen it. A dozen or so light-years is inconsequential to its massiveness, but the familiar constellations seemed battered and deformed. Slowly more twinkling lights appeared among the stars and quickly the newcomers outnumbered the well-known stars. Iridescent particles thrown in the planet's atmosphere by massive volcanism reflected the coming day, creating a riot of subtle colors in the pre-dawn darkness. I lay back on my recliner and watched the prismatic sprites appear as the sky grew lighter. First the stars faded into the deep purple sky and then the multihued sprites followed them until I stared at a cloudless azure sky.

In the pre-dawn hours the temperature had been comfortably warm but I resisted the temptation to throw open my light robe. I doubted I would ever master the Celestials' casual nudity. My housemates, mentally defective Celestials deemed too damaged and too dangerous for civilized society, in deference to my 'primitive' upbringing, wore light clothing even here in the privacy of our villa.

Celestials lived in groups much like artificial extended families. Their homes, designed like the houses of ancient Romans, were large square buildings enclosing a central garden. I heard people moving about in their private apartments, voices carrying strong and clear in the early morning air. I rose from the divan and threaded between the fruit trees to my tiny apartment. No Celestial altruism provided my private living quarters, but rather their fear. None would share that much with a violent Feral. Overhead the hum of a drone's lifting fans broke the silence. I tried to ignore it but, even after half a year, having my every step monitored irritated me.

I lived in a hospital, or perhaps a better term might be a sanatorium. It seemed to be the Celestial equivalent of a psychiatric ward. My villa mates and I were all considered either emotionally or socially unstable. For the

Aguru all criminality and antisocial outbursts were nothing more than mental illnesses, treated with compassion, respect, and an utter clinical detachment. Among the Celestials such maladjustments were quite rare, but as a product of a 'wild' culture they automatically classified me as antisocial.

The door recognized me as I approached and it swung inward, admitting me to my own home. I crossed the foyer and went to stand by a floor-to-ceiling bay window. A trace of purple remained in the western sky and the peaks of distant mountains began glowing as the brilliant sunlight fell on them. Celestials didn't build in massive compact cities. Instead they scattered their populations around the planet in dispersed communities. From our villa the landscape appeared natural and unspoiled, an endless expanse of terraformed terrain.

I stood there for quite a while, at least half an hour, too apathetic for any other pursuit. In my private auditorium an almost limitless catalog of films – excepting for my own good those with 'excessively violent' depictions – waited for analysis.

On my private network a slew of reports waited, half written. Very quickly after my arrival the Celestial and their AI Aguru advisors had put me to work studying ancient films and media. I think that they hoped my decidedly non-Celestial heritage might illuminate and expand their understanding of wild cultures, but even those movies no longer held any meaning.

No, all those reports and studies vanished without any meaningful reply. I worked, I produced, but without feedback, so I stopped. Now I did nothing more interesting than watch the dawn, and nurse regrets.

I didn't turn at the sound of my door. No Celestial would breach etiquette by entering uninvited. The Aguru had come to visit me again. The voice behind me carried all the proper inflection for a warm and welcoming tone, but the hair along the back of my neck stood on end.

"You've stopped submitting data for the Nocturnian Project."

"It's pointless." I fixed my gaze on a distant peak where the snow reflected a dazzling bright white light.

"It is useful. Is there something you lack, something to ease your transition?"

With a heavy sigh I turned and faced the puppet. It stood about seven feet tall, its body all white plastic with gold accents. The face was a sort of projection, not quite human, but not quite artificial. How the hell had anyone grown up with these things as their nannies?

"No," I insisted. "There's nothing I need, nothing that you're going to provide."

The thing tilted its head in mimicry of a puzzled expression.

"Your reports are valuable. The insights are unparalleled."

"I doubt anyone cares about my analysis at all."

"You are correct." The Aguru possessed a disturbing honesty. "Your reports are not valuable because of your evaluations. As a product of a diseased and superstitious culture all of your conclusions are flawed and highly suspect. They are, however, valuable because as a product of Nocturnia's wild culture they are the best direct information available for understanding your native culture and how best to eventually cure it."

"I don't care about that. I'm done with them. I just want to live a normal life."

"You have never known a normal life."

I waved my arms, gesturing to the room, the villas, and everything beyond.

"This is not normal! I don't want to be your mental patient. I want to—"

The Aguru cut off my rant with a stern and cold tone.

"What you want is irrelevant. You are a dangerous, asocial misfit and it would be irresponsible to release you unsupervised into society."

"It doesn't have to be here," I pleaded. "You have contact with other Feral—"

"That word is offensive and insulting. Do not use it."

"Fine, other 'wild' cultures. I can go live on one of their worlds. I know you can make that happen."

"We could, but we will not. It is equally irresponsible to subject any culture to your narcissistic and dangerous conditioning. You will stay here, safe from being a danger to others and yourself." There was a moment's pause and I wondered if that indicated that somewhere in the ether of the network the Aguru were conferring. Then the puppet continued, "We will not force your assistance. You have the sanctuary you desired and that you were promised. While it is unlikely you will ever overcome the conditions of your socialization, it is possible, if you apply yourself, to at least be a productive asset to our society."

The puppet turned and left. Angry and frustrated I started to chase after it. The ever-present drone sped in front of me and sprayed my face with that damned lavender mist. Carried by momentum, I tumbled forward and the puppet caught me like a parent saving a child from a nasty fall.

"You are far too violent," the Aguru said. "There is little hope you can be anything except our ward, but we will care for you, always."

ACKNOWLEDGMENTS

It is a well-worn cinematic cliché that writers labor alone, hunched over a typewriter with nothing but their talent and their muse, producing manuscripts that explode fully formed from their foreheads. As with so many film fictions, this bears little resemblance with reality and *Vulcan's Forge* is no exception.

A fully exhaustive list of the persons instrumental in producing this novel would test the patience of the most well-balanced individual but allow me to take a few moments to thank at least a few, while recognizing I do an injustice to all those I have failed to mention by name.

My editor, Don D'Auria, not only provided that critical guidance every writer needs but also shares my love for the classic folk-horror film *The Wicker Man*. Nik Keevil, who produced this lovely cover, and the entire staff of Flame Tree Press, who have done a terrific job in making my book better. I can't thank enough Maryelizabeth Yturralde and the entire staff of *Mysterious Galaxy* for supporting new and emerging local authors.

And finally, my fellow scribes at The Mysterious Galaxy Writers Support Group. I subjected them to early versions of this tale and they never failed to be supportive while providing true gold for any artist: honest feedback.

FLAME TREE PRESS
FICTION WITHOUT FRONTIERS
Award-Winning Authors & Original Voices

Flame Tree Press is the trade fiction imprint of Flame Tree
Publishing, focusing on excellent writing in horror and the
supernatural, crime and mystery, science fiction and fantasy.
Our aim is to explore beyond the boundaries of the everyday,
with tales from both award-winning authors and original voices.

•

You may also enjoy:
American Dreams by Kenneth Bromberg
Second Lives by P.D. Cacek
The Widening Gyre by Michael R. Johnston
The Blood-Dimmed Tide by Michael R. Johnston
Kosmos by Adrian Laing
The Sky Woman by J.D. Moyer
The Guardian by J.D. Moyer
The Goblets Immortal by Beth Overmyer
A Killing Fire by Faye Snowden
The Bad Neighbor by David Tallerman
A Savage Generation by David Tallerman
Ten Thousand Thunders by Brian Trent
Two Lives: Tales of Life, Love & Crime by A Yi

Horror titles available include:
Snowball by Gregory Bastianelli
Thirteen Days by Sunset Beach by Ramsey Campbell
The Influence by Ramsey Campbell
The Haunting of Henderson Close by Catherine Cavendish
The Garden of Bewitchment by Catherine Cavendish
Black Wings by Megan Hart
Will Haunt You by Brian Kirk
We Are Monsters by Brian Kirk
Hearthstone Cottage by Frazer Lee
Those Who Came Before by J.H. Moncrieff
Stoker's Wilde by Steven Hopstaken & Melissa Prusi
Ghost Mine by Hunter Shea
Slash by Hunter Shea
The Mouth of the Dark by Tim Waggoner
They Kill by Tim Waggoner
The Forever House by Tim Waggoner

•

Join our mailing list for free short stories, new release details,
news about our authors and special promotions:

flametreepress.com